NEW PENGUIN SHAKESPEARE

GENERAL EDITOR: T. J. B. SPENCER

ASSOCIATE EDITOR: STANLEY WELLS

WILLIAM SHAKESPEARE

*

HENRY V

EDITED BY
A. R. HUMPHREYS

PENGUIN BOOKS

Penguin Books Ltd, Harmondsworth, Middlesex, England
Penguin Books, 40 West 23rd Street, New York, New York 10010, U.S.A.
Penguin Books Australia Ltd, Ringwood, Victoria, Australia
Penguin Books Canada Ltd, 2801 John Street, Markham, Ontario, Canada L3R 1B4
Penguin Books (N.Z.) Ltd, 182–190 Wairau Road, Auckland 10, New Zealand

—

This edition first published in Penguin Books 1968
Reprinted 1975, 1977, 1979, 1980, 1983

—

This edition copyright © Penguin Books, 1968
Introduction and notes copyright © A. R. Humphreys, 1968
All rights reserved

—

Made and printed in Great Britain by
Hazell Watson & Viney Ltd,
Aylesbury, Bucks
Set in Monotype Ehrhardt

CONTENTS

INTRODUCTION

Henry V is Shakespeare's ninth and last English historical play, apart from *King Lear* and *Cymbeline*, which treat of pseudo-history, and the late *Henry VIII*, in which he collaborated with John Fletcher. In the English historical sequence it is crucially placed. *Richard II* and the *Henry IV* plays look towards it, towards England's unity restored after usurpation and division, and Henry's emergence as true ruler from the ambiguous promise of Prince Hal. Equally, the earlier-written tetralogy of *Henry VI* and *Richard III* had shown the tragic consequences following upon Henry's premature death. So the play of triumph shines like an hour of glory between two periods of storm.

It can be dated with pleasing precision. Its fifth chorus confidently expects that 'the General of our gracious Empress' will shortly return to London, 'Bringing rebellion broachèd on his sword' (V.Chorus.30,32) – that is, that the Earl of Essex, triumphant in Ireland against Tyrone, will soon be greeted in the capital by the rejoicing citizens. Essex had left England in March 1599; he came back in September, having failed in his mission; and the play is therefore coincident with the mood of patriotic expectancy so vivid in the spring but extinguished by the autumn. In Shakespeare's career it marks the masterful flow of his full and confident power, evolved through almost a decade of rich and varied composition.

It was not the first time that Henry's reign had been treated in drama. *Tarlton's Jests* (*c*. 1600), a collection of anecdotes about a famous comedian who died in 1588,

7

mentions 'a play of Henry the Fifth, wherein the judge was to take a box on the ear'. This refers to the apocryphal but cherished legend that Prince Hal assaulted the Lord Chief Justice and was sent to prison. In 1592, Thomas Nashe's comic story, *Pierce Penilesse*, celebrated a scene Nashe had clearly found delightful though it is not exactly paralleled in surviving plays on Henry's reign:

> ... *what a glorious thing it is to have Henry the Fifth represented on the stage leading the French King prisoner, and forcing both him and the Dauphin to swear fealty.*

The diary of Philip Henslowe the theatre manager records thirteen performances of a new play, *harey the v*, between November 1595 and July 1596. And a chaotic, garbled text of an anonymous drama, *The Famous Victories of Henry the Fifth*, entered for publication in the Stationers' Register on 14 May 1594, is extant, though only in an edition of 1598. How these plays related to each other is not clear, nor indeed how *The Famous Victories* relates to *Henry V*; there are resemblances between these two latter which prove that Shakespeare owed the anonymous drama much, though the debt is probably to some earlier, better version rather than to the surviving scrap-heap of mangled incidents and illiterate text.

The popularity of the subject hardly needs explaining. Not only did Henry's reign stand out to later generations by contrast with the preceding troubles of Richard II and Henry IV, and the succeeding disasters of Henry VI, but Henry's almost miraculous conversion from wild youth to ideal king was an article of faith going back to chronicles contemporary with Henry himself. The king reborn from evil to good, and leading a heroic campaign to a famous victory, was irresistibly attractive. Edward Hall's chronicle, *The Union of the Two Noble and Illustre Famelies of*

Lancaster and Yorke (1548), entitles the reign 'The Victorious Acts of King Henry the Fifth', celebrates its hero as king, warrior, justiciary, and shepherd of his people, in an astonishing *catena* of praise, and concludes:

> *He was merciful to offenders, charitable to the needy, in-*
> *different* [impartial] *to all men, faithful to his friends, and*
> *fierce to his enemies, toward God most devout, toward*
> *the world moderate, and to his realm a very father.*

It is not surprising that the renown of 'Henry the Fifth, too famous to live long', 'Henry the Fifth, that made all France to quake', 'Henry the Fifth, | Who made the Dauphin and the French to stoop', sounds like a tolling bell through the calamities of the *Henry VI* trilogy:

> *Glory is like a circle in the water,*
> *Which never ceaseth to enlarge itself*
> *Till by broad spreading it disperse to naught.*
> *With Henry's death the English circle ends;*
> *Dispersèd are the glories it included.*
>
> *1 Henry VI*, I.2.133-7

For Tudor chroniclers and poets Henry's prowess had the quality of myth, like that also of Edward III and the Black Prince, 'Making defeat on the full power of France' (I.2.107): that had been the era when, though for a short while only, England had found her destiny. Henry's reign figures as an Homeric adventure in Samuel Daniel's *Fowre Bookes of the Civile Wars* (1595):

> *O what eternal matter here is found,*
> *Whence new immortal Iliads might proceed.*

Years later, praising Michael Drayton's poems, and in particular his *Battaile of Agincourt* (1627), Ben Jonson likened Drayton's own achievement to Homer's, since he

9

had commemorated England's valour and written verses which

> strike the bravest heat
> *That ever yet did fire the English blood!*
> *Our right in France! if rightly understood.*
> *There, thou art Homer! ...*
> *So shall our English youth urge on, and cry*
> *'An Agincourt! an Agincourt! or die!'*

Henry V has much of epic character, for epic presents, through a story of adventure, a symbolic crisis in a nation's life such as matures it into knowledge of its own being, temperament, and destiny. The manner in which Shakespeare expresses this epic spirit (while at the same time qualifying it and relating it to the unideal truths of human life) makes this one of his most memorable and exciting plays, that which more than any other breathes the spirit of Elizabethan courage and pride and shows him in happy command of his powers. It comes particularly into its own / in times of national peril.   *b*

*

It is, in a way, self-conscious, not in the sense of being embarrassed by its own character (though some critics have taken its chorus-apologetics very solemnly) but in that of standing as a great manifesto or demonstration, proudly doctrinal and exemplary. If it is epic in manner, that is partly because out of the miscellaneous chronicle-events of Henry's reign it makes a clear theme of high adventure, partly because its stress is narrative rather than psychological (the story of the heroic company under its leader), but mostly because England as well as England's King is its principal character. In a general sense, England is the hero of all the histories; Shakespeare writes of his

country's fate. But this is especially so in *Henry V.*
Commenting on the lines in the prologue (3–4) –

> *A kingdom for a stage, princes to act,*
> *And monarchs to behold the swelling scene –*

Dr Johnson rather oddly remarked, 'Shakespeare does not
seem to set distance enough between the performers and
spectators'; and in his final observation he wondered 'why
the intelligence given by the chorus is more necessary
in this play than in many others where it is omitted'. The
answer is that Shakespeare wants to *cancel* the distance
between performers and spectators – this is a play of a
very special sort; and it is through the chorus that this is
attempted, the epic note sounded, and the particular
function exerted (besides that of clarifying the narrative
sequence) of conveying the exhilarated involvement of
Henry's people and Henry's land – and so of Elizabeth's.

Likewise, the Archbishop's parable of the ordered hive,
while not universally admired (one critic thinks Shakespeare must have had 'fun', 'making such a fool of his
Archbishop'), is meant as a genuine celebration of national
harmony; England must be virtually a Chosen Land to
be presented thus. The analogy between hive and kingdom
is admittedly not original; it comes from Pliny and Virgil
through Sir Thomas Elyot's *The Boke named the Governour*
(1531), a treatise by Chelidonius translated as *Of the
Institution and Firste Beginning of Christian Princes* (1571),
Lyly's *Euphues* (1578), and other channels. But Shakespeare treats it in no perfunctory spirit; he gives it a lively
and captivating beauty. Here in *Henry V*, as distinct from
the political rifts of the other histories, the obedient
kingdom is achieved, and the ideal order of Church and
State affirmed not only as doctrine but as reality. When
Henry, 'Being free from vainness and self-glorious pride'

(V.Chorus.20), gives thanks for victory to God, it is England, the beneficiary of God's favour, who joins in *Non Nobis* and *Te Deum* for her salvation. The Chorus apologizes for the theatre's defects less because Shakespeare 'distressfully realized' that his stage could not do what he wanted (the phrase is Granville-Barker's) than because only 'The brightest heaven of invention' and a corresponding imaginative elation in his hearers could match his great theme.

Such is the basic creed and the dominant assumption of the play. As it unfolds, however, it is much more variegated than the above sketch of the epic hero leading a devoted country to triumph would suggest. The nature of kingship, the motives of war, and the qualities of political allegiance are presented with a sense of the tensions that stretch between ideal and reality, and make a political order human. *Henry V* is peculiarly interesting in treating this situation. It stands, brilliantly, for the excitements of heroism and victory, and for the gratification of national pride. At the same time it admits elements which suggest the dark underside of war and policy. Yet in doing so it shows no radical irony, though it provides material which may be used for radically ironical judgements (and Hazlitt, for one, is radically ironical when he criticizes it in *Characters of Shakespeare's Plays*). Within the whole context of the play the ironies seem no more than passing and incidental shadowings to the dominant heroic zest, reminders of human frailties above which the heroism stands sturdily.

Shakespeare's plots may require Romans or kings, Dr Johnson observes in his *Preface to Shakespeare*, 'but he thinks only on men'. The material for this play presented a considerable difficulty – how to make *man* a character whose accepted role it was to be essentially *king*. A being virtually superhuman (and hyperbolically presented so by the Archbishop in the first scene) may well prove a mere mechanism, even if an exhilarating one (as Tamburlaine is). One recalls Sir Leslie Stephen's comment on another ideal hero, the Sir Charles Grandison of Richardson's novel:

> *The greatest man is perhaps one who is so equably developed that he has the strongest faculties in the most perfect equilibrium, and is apt to be somewhat uninteresting to the rest of mankind.*

As a dramatic personality Henry is far from being the fullest of Shakespeare's creations, even if the field of comparison be restricted to the history plays; in situations which are virtually pre-established he behaves in predictable ways, with such mastery that the result is immensely effective, but effective in a manner which falls short of nourishing the imagination deeply. Yet he certainly holds the attention.

*

For his material Shakespeare went to Holinshed's *Chronicles* and *The Famous Victories of Henry the Fifth*. Traces of other works may be found, too; the more important particulars are noted in the commentary. There seem to be recollections of *Edward III* (1596), the anonymous play about Henry's great ancestor, victor of Crécy and Poitiers. Either Elyot's *The Boke named the Governour* or Lyly's *Euphues* suggested some important analogies (see I.2.180–204, and the notes thereon). Henry's night-visit to his camp may derive from Tacitus's *Annals*, translated by Richard Grenewey in 1598; in this, Germanicus, like Henry, disguises himself to test the morale of his troops in danger. Fluellen's devotion to the military art of the Romans is strikingly like the similar devotion expressed by Thomas Digges, in his treatise *Stratioticos* (1579); this is discussed further on page 18. Yet though memories, conscious and subconscious, would certainly come to Shakespeare's mind from books he had read, it seems unlikely that (as some scholars believe) he deliberately sought widely for material in earlier works. In *Richard II* and *Henry IV* he had been influenced by Daniel's poem, *The Civile Wars between the two Houses of Lancaster and Yorke* (1595), but Daniel's treatment of Henry V was perfunctory and offered nothing to the purpose save for a eulogy of the King found equally in Holinshed. Shakespeare, then, seems to have put his play together substantially from two convenient works, one of serious history (Holinshed's *Chronicles*), and the other of popular serio-comic dramatization (*The Famous Victories*).

Holinshed's work must actually have been open before him as he wrote, and it is interesting to observe both where his discipleship was close (and sometimes caused him to take over particulars which in the play create critical difficulties) and where he varied importantly. He followed his source in hundreds of details and expressions, through the main tenor and indeed through much of the phrasing of the historical scenes. In the 'Salic law' harangue the transcription is slavish – this is one of the points where excessive fidelity creates a critical problem, that of interpreting aright the Archbishop's longwindedness. But in general the borrowing is spirited and vivid enough to awaken wonder that Shakespeare could follow common prose so closely and yet produce fine poetry. His mind is everywhere attentive to what he reads, yet almost everywhere freshly creative. Holinshed ends with a panegyric on Henry which gave Shakespeare the lead both for the Archbishop's eulogy at the beginning and the Epilogue's plaudits at the end. A number of features which critics of Henry cite to prove him hypocritical derive, hardly modified at all, from Holinshed, in whose pages they certainly have no disparaging intention. These features include Henry's religious zeal, with the recurrent appeals to God; confident belief in the rightness of his cause, with reiterated assertions of his just title; the conviction that the guilt of bloodshed lies on the French for resisting his claim and not on him for prosecuting it; and the assumption that since he is morally right at all points those opposing him must be morally wrong. Dubious though these traits are to a sceptical eye, Shakespeare takes them over smoothly enough; he remains discreetly reticent over one or two shady manoeuvres, as though he judged (as well he might) that his play would succeed best if Englishmen were not too evidently seen to behave dishonourably. Holinshed, for instance, tells how the Archbishop deliberately schemes to distract Henry from the Church's revenues by instigating him to attack France: Shakespeare, though he starts his play with the threat to the Church, muffles that problem behind the question of Henry's war and, while recognizing the Archbishop's dubious aims (I.1.75–9), treats them more casually than does his source. Holinshed, further, introduces the tennis-balls insult as a separate incident, earlier than the council of war, and itself a main cause of the conflict; Shakespeare prefers *The Famous Victories'* version, that it is subsequent to the council, an aggravation of the quarrel, but only a confirmatory detail after the establishment of Henry's legal claim and his resolve for invasion.

Other interesting modifications of Holinshed are the following. Holinshed presents the French King as lunatic, so that affairs must be directed by the Dauphin: in the play, as in *The Famous Victories*, the French King directs matters throughout, and so (this is not in *The Famous Victories*) the Dauphin can be characterized as a modish gallant. Holinshed records no repentant speeches from Cambridge, Scroop, and Grey; Shakespeare invents these farewell addresses so that even the would-be traitors may acknowledge how the hand of God guards the country's safety. In Holinshed's pages the citizens of Harfleur suffer terribly before they yield, and the town is then sacked and depopulated: in Shakespeare's, the mere threat of horrors ensures their surrender, and mercy is then shown to them all. In the chronicle, Henry himself supervises the execution of a (nameless) soldier for theft: in the play, he approves but does not personally enforce the hanging of his old acquaintance, Bardolph. Holinshed relates in detail the English strategy at Agincourt: Shakespeare ignores it, even the famous prowess of the English bowmen, in favour of heroic oratory which gives the spirit rather than the tactical particulars of the battle. And finally, again like the author of *The Famous Victories* but unlike Holinshed, Shakespeare omits the five years (1415–20) of campaigning between Agincourt and the Treaty of Troyes (as indeed he does everything in Henry's reign which does not relate to Agincourt), and so gives his play a clearer course and greater impetus. His treatment of Holinshed is, therefore, equally striking for close indebtedness and for constructive independence. Summarizing all the above changes one may say that their effect is to clarify Henry's motives, improve the morality of his cause, disengage the Agincourt campaign from the many other concerns of his reign, enhance the force and spirit of the action, and treat the whole in terms of human passion and thought.

As for *The Famous Victories*, crude though it was it clearly afforded Shakespeare guidance. In it the King, dismissing his scapegrace companions (as at the end of *2 Henry IV*), at once consults the Archbishop, who vouches for the justice of his claim though without mentioning the Salic law. The council of war is followed immediately by the tennis-balls scene, after which Henry prepares for speedy invasion; as in *Henry V*, the theme of speed is prominent. There is a clownish leave-taking of husband and wife, which inspired that in *Henry V* (II.3). The French King directs the French campaign, while the Dauphin foolishly thinks Henry 'young and wild-headed' but is warned that he is 'a haughty and high-minded Prince'. The French soldiers (though not, as in *Henry V*, the leaders) dice for prisoners, in pidgin English. The English low comics, garbling French tags, mix farcically in the Agincourt scenes, and Derick the clown captures a French soldier, as Pistol does Monsieur Le Fer. The action passes straight from Agincourt to Troyes, and Henry woos Katherine 'in plain terms', not like 'those countries [that] spend half their time in wooing'. Poor though it is, then, *The Famous Victories* furnished elements not less integral to Shakespeare's play than those from Holinshed, and this brief inspection of his original materials may serve to suggest how shrewd in selection, constructive in assimilation, and intelligent in adjustment his mind was.

*

What no sources seem to have given him, except for the incalculable influence of his reading of books and his observation of men, are the inspirations from which he evolved his account of the death of Falstaff, the comedy of Fluellen and of his fellow captains, the episode of Katherine and Alice (boldly presented entirely in French), and the wonderful night-scene before Agincourt (save that, as aforesaid, the germ of this may have come from Tacitus). These components, varied in manner but all richly humane in quality, are the contribution of Shakespeare's own creative fertility.

Fluellen, above all, is the play's most delightful offering. All four captains, Gower, Macmorris, Jamy, and he, serve Henry well; in them, the constituent peoples of Britain unite behind the King and yet, most entertainingly, preserve their national idiosyncrasies. The play would be much poorer were Henry heading an army merely of likeminded loyalists, the Bedfords, Exeters, Erpinghams, and the rest. Instead, he leads a various host with independent minds, likely at any moment to break out into disputes, yet bound together not only by danger but also by trueheartedness; the quarrelsomeness of the French is of a different nature altogether. So the argument between Fluellen and Macmorris (III.2), with Gower and Jamy intervening, is not just incidental comedy; it proves their fine, vehement spirits and their devotion to the war in hand. Fluellen may owe something to Shakespeare's contemporary, the Welsh soldier Sir Roger Williams, or alternatively to Sir John Smythe, Williams's opponent in a debate on ancient and modern warfare; scholars dispute the matter. His antiquarian pedantry about the Roman disciplines, however, seems to derive from a work on military tactics already mentioned, the *Stratioticos* of Thomas Digges (1579), which perhaps came to Shakespeare's notice when republished in 1590 by his fellow Stratfordian Richard Field, who was to bring out *Venus and Adonis* in 1593. Digges commends 'the ancient Roman discipline for the wars' and 'the most noble government of the Romans (who in military virtue surmounteth all other)'; nowadays, he protests, 'all those Roman orders' are held obsolete, whereas they are more valid than ever they were in the past; it was when Rome's original military discipline was corrupted under the Emperors that her power collapsed – Fluellen's court of appeal, one recalls, is to 'the *pristine* wars of the Romans' (III.2.79). To find the phrases of the ancient obscure book of military science coming so delightfully to life on Fluellen's lips is to sense what Shakespeare's transforming power could do from a few hints. Yet even without this enlivening recognition Fluellen's temper of pedantry, patriotism, generosity, and touchiness unfailingly endears him.

The night-scene before Agincourt, another superb invention, is discussed in the last pages of this Introduction. It works, like that of the four captains, to show that Henry's troops are human beings, not ciphers; at this moment above all Shakespeare remembers the common lot and, to repeat Dr Johnson, 'thinks only on men'.

For Pistol, Nym, Bardolph, the Hostess, and the Boy, *The Famous Victories* gave Shakespeare some sort of cue, though a crude one. The comedy they provide here does not work so richly as that of their counterparts in *Henry IV*. Yet even to think that, like Falstaff, they might have been dropped from the action altogether is to realize how desirable is their ripe ignominy, always human and touching in its nonsense and noise. It is they who feel for Falstaff, and move us as they do so more than anything else in the play; we feel for them, too, as war and disease and disgrace cut them brutally off, one by one, who once warmed themselves gratefully in the solar mirth of Falstaff.

*

It is appropriate to turn to evaluations of the play.

> Small time, but in that small most greatly lived
> This star of England

– so the Epilogue confidently sums up. Yet a drama based on invasion of a foreign land (even if, by definition, justified invasion) may be morally and emotionally unpalatable, and not a few critics find *Henry V* so. There is disagreement about nearly all aspects of the play – about the value of the choruses, the tenor of many major speeches, the motives and morals of prelates and courtiers, Henry's handling of the ambassadors and of the traitorous Scroop, his threats to Harfleur, his debate with his soldiers, his massacre of the French, and his wooing of Katherine. Contention extends to the total interpretation of how the play takes war, honour, kingship, and allegiance. To include it among Shakespeare's problem plays would seem extravagant, yet its apparent simplicity masks a good many problems of assessment, so that one of its shrewdest critics, Mr Derek Traversi, can remark in *Shakespeare from 'Richard II' to 'Henry V'* that it has been 'most generally popular when imperfectly understood'. It is, as he observes, among Shakespeare's simpler plays, without poetic subtlety or symbolical complexity; its plot is clear historical narrative, and its purpose the recognizable one of studying the conditions of kingship. Yet there lurk ambiguities enough for a wide liberty of interpretation.

The play raises fewer questions in the theatre than in the study – impetus carries one over obstacles, whereas deliberation makes them seem larger than they are. It raises interestingly the problem of criticizing a dramatic action, being second only to *Hamlet* in this respect: how much analytical going back and forth over the evidence is admissible when the very nature of dramatic art is to carry the narrative vigorously onwards? Dover Wilson has observed (not the only critic to do so, but the one to make the point most sharply) that *Henry V* is a work 'which men of action have been wont silently to admire, and literary men . . . volubly to condemn', and he believes that he himself learnt more about its hero from Wavell's

Life of Allenby than from all the critics together. He recalls,
too, how in 1914–15 the play suddenly revealed its
enormous power; and in 1945 the film version with Sir
Laurence Olivier again proved how well it could match a
time of mortal danger and of saving courage. At such
moments, and seeing it acted, one yields to the drive of the
action; this is something Shakespeare has made integral
to its effects. A fateful pressure is the dominant theme; to
move fast, to work with energy, is its characteristic:

> *with reasonable swiftness add*
> *More feathers to our wings;*   I.2.307–8
>
> *For England his approaches makes as fierce*
> *As waters to the sucking of a gulf.*   II.4.9–10
>
> *Dispatch us with all speed, lest that our King*
> *Come here himself to question our delay,*
> *For he is footed in this land already.*   II.4.141–3
>
> *Thus with imagined wing our swift scene flies*
> *In motion of no less celerity*
> *Than that of thought.*   III.Chorus.1–3

The play's dynamism as it passes on the stage allows little
time for thought, and the Chorus, as presenter of events,
delivers us over, unreflecting, to those heroic assumptions
which are its creed. And, basically, this is right; the play's
aim is to celebrate heroic actions under a heroic king.

Hazlitt, humanitarian and republican, in his *Characters
of Shakespeare's Plays* held that Shakespeare, while
believing Henry to be the heroic prince and king of good
fellows, had *unwittingly* glorified a self-seeking and brutal
autocrat, licensed by a Machiavellian Archbishop 'to
rob and murder in circles of latitude and longitude abroad',
and had thereby exposed 'the hidden motives that actuate
princes and their advisers'.

Henry [Hazlitt continues], *because he did not know how to govern his own kingdom, determined to make war upon his neighbour's. Because his own title to the crown was doubtful, he laid claim to that of France. Because he did not know how to exercise the enormous power which had just dropped into his hands to any one good purpose, he immediately undertook (a cheap and obvious resource of sovereignty) to do all the mischief he could.*

And more to the same purpose; for Hazlitt the whole baronial Middle Ages amounted to 'accomplished barbarism'. Yet when Hazlitt asks, 'How then do we like him [Henry]?' he answers,

We like him in the play. There he is a very amiable monster, a very splendid pageant.... We take a very romantic, heroic, patriotic, and poetical delight in the boasts and feats of our younger Harry, as they appear on the stage and are confined to lines of ten syllables.

In other words, we enjoy as dramatic adventure what in historical reality was iniquitous. And with this lively formulation of Hazlitt's we approach the problem of interpreting the play: is Shakespeare offering us merely 'romantic, heroic, patriotic, and poetical delight', is he on the other hand exposing the unabashed Machiavellianism of power, or is he glorifying the heroic while still acknowledging the unheroic, thereby making the heroic the more valid, as pure metal and base alloy combine in a tougher and more dependable product?

When *Henry V* is looked at closely, certain features complicate the impression of simple zest and conviction the unreflecting reader is likely to form. If these features are now to be discussed at some length, the reason is not that the play is radically uncertain in its aims; even with its ambiguities it remains powerful and assured. As Dr Johnson remarked in his *Life of Gray*, 'by the common sense of readers uncorrupted with literary prejudices, after all the refinements of subtlety and the dogmatism of learning, must finally be decided all claim to poetical honours'. Common sense long ago decided that the play's subject is unambiguous valour and that its spirit is expressed in Henry's Agincourt speech. It works splendidly – as before observed – at a speed which prevents awkward questions, and it is charged with a rich and compelling emotion. Before Agincourt in particular it achieves a humanity and honesty, as well as a sense of great peril and noble courage, which live in the mind as its valid message. Mr Traversi puts the matter well, in *Shakespeare from 'Richard II' to 'Henry V'*:

'Should we need a word to describe the best positive values of this play, that which distinguishes it from mere patriotic rhetoric on the one side and sardonic pessimism on the other (and both moods are constituent parts of it), it would be ... honesty, which can offer loyalty while maintaining independence of judgement, and which is brought out, as much as the cruelty which balances it, by the sombre circumstances of war which no merely patriotic show of rhetoric or romantic comradeship in death can conceal.'

*

The first problem is that of Henry's claim to the throne of France. This, historically speaking, depended on the fact that his great-great-grandmother Isabella, Edward II's Queen, was the daughter of Philip IV of France and grand-daughter of Philip III, from whom also Princess Katherine descended (by marrying Katherine Henry reinforced his supposed right). But the historical basis of this claim is, for criticism of the play, far less important than the fact that in Shakespeare's time it was held without question to be valid. To hold, as Hazlitt did, that Henry was guilty of aggression against another man's rightful domain is irrelevant to critical judgement. The Archbishop's prominence and Henry's earnest injunctions to him 'justly and religiously' to state the case are meant as proof that the claim is lawful and French resistance to it unlawful, so that by contumacy France provokes an 'impious war' not only against her rightful sovereign but against God, the source of royal authority. The scepticism of later ages makes this assumption hard to credit, as the nationalism of later ages makes it hard to accept that the French are the aggressors for standing their ground. But there is no doubt that the play is based on an honest faith in these assumptions. Should one concede to a work of art tenets which affront one's convictions? If one wholly declines, art can never work its disturbing reorganizations. If one wholly accepts, one quits one's bases of moral evaluation. One needs to give the work its chance, in a willing suspension (if necessary) of disbelief in its premises, and judge whether the result justifies the concession. Certainly *Henry V* takes it as proven that Henry is in the right. The question then is whether this belief is imaginatively brought home, as well as doctrinally reiterated. It is hard to think that, in any deep sense, this is so. The Archbishop's persuasives to war, the nobles' zest for re-enacting ancient prowess, the recurrent genuflections to God – these convince more as gestures in the game of power than as moral validations. What can be said is that Shakespeare does much, by the splendid surface vigour which hustles out of the way the teasing questions beneath, to convince us that the participants themselves, and Henry above all,

believe in their cause, and that while we watch the play
we should do so too. This is the concession which the
vigour of Shakespeare's handling exacts of us, though he
himself in the zest of composition probably never realized
there was a problem at all. Energy here does duty for
insight, eloquence for imagination. One recalls Yeats's
aphorism – 'Out of our quarrel with ourselves we make
poetry; out of our quarrel with others, we make only
rhetoric'. The application to *Henry V* is not precise, yet
there is a sense in which the play, opposing patriotism to
an external enemy, simplifies its attitudes into those suited
to challenge and defiance, and finds its idiom to be rhetoric
– wonderful rhetoric, certainly, but rhetoric in the sense
that words are directed to calculated effects.

*

The second problem is that the play's basic assumptions
seem to be the uncritical patriotism of the chronicles. With
this one cannot in normal times feel as happy as when the
blast of war blows in one's ears, and many who dislike the
play find here their principal ground of objection. In the
first chorus, for example, 'The brightest heaven of invention' is to be ascended so that the warlike Harry shall
'Assume the port of Mars' – the sense is of a bearing
grandly put on; 'famine, sword, and fire' are to crouch
behind him 'for employment'. No irony is hinted, though
this is (if one thinks about it) a disagreeable light in which
to present heroic leadership; nor can the speech be taken
as eye-opening realism, for the Chorus is in a high state of
exhilaration. At once there follows the clerics' statecraft,
received by Henry as honest and intelligent discourse.
How is one to take this? – sceptically? – derisively? –
realistically (this is how things are done in the political
game)? – or, as the play seems to require, in earnest?

Shakespeare, as has already been said, presents things less openly against Canterbury than Holinshed had done or, moreover, than Drayton was to do in his *Battaile of Agincourt*, where the Archbishop works a calculated diversionary intrigue in the interest of the Church:

> *His working soul projecteth many a thing,*
> *Until at length, out of the strength of wit,*
> *He found a war with France must be the way*
> *To dash this bill, else threat'ning their decay.*

Shakespeare does not linger upon this duplicity, just as he leaves unrecalled the Machiavellian advice given to Prince Hal by Henry IV on his death-bed, that, to avert dissension at home, he should (2 *Henry IV*, IV.5.214)

> *busy giddy minds*
> *With foreign quarrels. . . .*

No hint of this appears in the play. Shakespeare, then, means his clerics to argue truly (whatever the motive), as he has meant his prologue to be unambiguous. The trouble is that the 'Salic law' speech falls as far short of proving their *bona fides* as it does of achieving poetic charm. Unrivalled for tedium throughout Shakespeare's works it would, admittedly, be more interesting to subjects of the first Elizabeth than to those of the second, since the accessions of Queen Mary, Queen Elizabeth herself, and the prospective King James depended on the validity of succession in the female line; a similar Salic law argument occurs at the beginning of *Edward III*, when Edward presses his claim to the French throne. Exeter is later to assure us that Henry's right is not based on pettifogging legalism:

> *'Tis no sinister nor no awkward claim*
> *Picked from the worm-holes of long-vanished days,*
> *Nor from the dust of old oblivion raked....* II.4.85-7

But since, by following Holinshed too closely, this is just what Shakespeare made the claim sound like in the Archbishop's mouth, he unintentionally cast into doubt what is not meant to be in doubt at all (and so gave the makers of the film version the chance to turn the whole thing into satire) – the legality of Henry's claim.

Then, from the prosaism of his lecture, the Archbishop breaks out with evident relish into bloodthirstiness, exhorting the King to 'Stand for your own, unwind your bloody flag' (I.2.101), and describing how Edward III smiled to see the Black Prince 'Forage in blood of French nobility'. His language is gross and his mood zestfully brutal as he urges 'blood and sword and fire' upon Henry. The Bishop of Ely is no more felicitous; the King, he asserts, 'Is in the very May-morn of his youth' (the image suggests a generous gaiety and idealism), and so 'Ripe for exploits and mighty enterprises' – what better than war? The lords follow the clerics; Henry's fellow-kings, Exeter proclaims, expect him to rouse himself; his subjects, Westmorland declares, wait to invade France in body as they have already done in spirit. All this comes from Holinshed, but what passes muster on the historical page comes to questionable life in the Shakespearian context. To a modern taste such adjurations are admissible only as satire; one invokes against them Ezra Pound's *Hugh Selwyn Mauberley*:

> *There died a myriad,*
> *And of the best, among them,*
> *For an old bitch gone in the teeth,*
> *For a botched civilisation.*

Yet outlooks and circumstances change; one should not, because of modern experience, judge that the play ridicules war-makers, for its whole tenor is to make the action enormously worth the pain and effort. Shakespeare's first scenes are often significant, and unambiguously so, of his plays' main bearings. Are these scenes of questionable diplomacy pointers to a cynical world, indices of a general hypocrisy, with their arguments so tricky to assess that one critic thinks they 'dazzle us with their brilliance' while another takes them for the chicane with which Henry must learn to deal? Working briskly from his sources, Shakespeare probably thinks the arguments good ones, even if voiced by a worldly prelate, and the encouragements to war patriotic ones, even if uttered by boisterous barons. Henry is certainly not surrounded by paladins of virtue – this is a tough, stirring drama, and it is grounded in the recognizable realities of power – but his counsellors are meant as vigorous and effective statesmen. Having taken the best advice he can get, and being convinced that that advice is correct (as by Shakespeare's lights it was), Henry prepares to fight and (the play unquestioningly holds) is completely justified in doing so.

*

Some features, certainly, ought to be taken as the offshoots of dramatic exuberance rather than as psychologically or morally important; at first sight, and at the speed at which stage action passes, they seem straightforward, at second sight so curious as to imply an ironic intention, and yet on final consideration hardly definable as anything but unironic. When, for example, the Archbishop eulogizes Henry, first one believes what he says about the King's virtues; next one reflects that such fulsomeness must be specious; and yet finally one concludes that, this being the

28

first we hear about Henry, and Shakespeare not usually puzzling his audience with false trails, the eulogy, however extravagant, must be truly meant. Likewise when Henry woos Katherine: one thinks first that he is hearty and honest; next that only a crude nature could be so jocular ('lubberly' is Dr Tillyard's word), and also that he is shrewdly using Katherine to secure his ends; but finally that Shakespeare really means this 'king of good fellows' performance to be genuine love. This fluctuation of possible judgements helps to explain the diversity of opinions about the play. At such points the dramatic intention is best served by taking the material at its face value.

This, however, does not always produce a reasonable answer. It does not do so, for instance, over the massacre of the French prisoners (IV.6.35-8, IV.7.1-10). The massacre was, in fact, a military necessity, and by examining the historical circumstances one can defend it as such. Yet Shakespeare not only neglects Holinshed's description of it as 'a dolorous decree and pitiful proclamation' but allows it to seem an act of almost casual ruthlessness, and moreover glosses it with Fluellen's ludicrous outburst, 'Kill the poys and the luggage?', and with Gower's odd explanation that, because cowards who fled from the battle had done the pillage, Henry has 'most worthily' had the throats cut of brave men who had been captured fighting. In this context, 'O, 'tis a gallant King!' is not the happiest of comments. To treat so dreadful an incident in such a spirit is irresponsible, and the mood of approving gusto in which it is mentioned forbids one to explain it as savage realism. How is one to take Shakespeare's lack of concern? As a demonstration of war's horrors? – but so little is made of it. As insensibility? – but Shakespeare is not usually insensible. As unquestioning endorsement of Henry's leadership? – if so, it is unhappily done. As the carelessness of haste? – probably so; Shakespeare treats the incident as one among many, and passes readily to the Irish bull of Fluellen's Welsh paralogism, that Henry is like Alexander because Alexander when drunk wrongly killed Cleitus, and Henry when sober rightly dismissed Falstaff.

In some respects, indeed, the play is 'popular' in a limiting sense, in endorsing uncritical patriotism with what has been called 'a determined "one-eyedness" ' about England's interests. The French must be frisky and confident, vainglorious and yet reported to 'shake in their fear'; the English must succeed incredibly against odds (few faces remain straight in a modern theatre when, as against the French ten thousand, their losses are announced as twenty-nine); Katherine must be wooed bluffly as befits the hearty English nature. Double-think, common in popular politics, is not unknown; Scotland invading England is a weasel, but England invading France is an eagle. (This seems to be caught from *Edward III*, I.1.94, I.2.90, where England is 'the eagle's nest' and the invading Scots are 'stealing foxes'.) Henry, having decided to invade France even before the Dauphin's insult, then treats that insult as if it occasioned the war, and blames on the Dauphin the 'wasteful vengeance' to follow – Henry, that is, invades France only because he would be legally wrong not to do so, *but* he invades France because he has been insulted and will avenge himself even unto those 'yet ungotten and unborn' (I.2.288). (This particular confusion arises, probably, because Holinshed gives the former motive for invasion, *The Famous Victories* the latter, and Shakespeare works too quickly to reconcile them.) The second chorus, having evoked an army in which

honour's thought
Reigns solely in the breast of every man,

passes without a hint of irony to the motive of plunder:

> *crowns and coronets,*
> *Promised to Harry and his followers.*

When the conspirators appeal for mercy, Henry answers, in effect, that he would have been merciful had they themselves been so, *but* that in any case he could not be merciful since England's safety requires their deaths (II.2.79–80, 174–7). (Here again the confusion results from too indiscriminate a following of Holinshed: no duplicity on Henry's part is implied.)

These are some of the inconsistencies which in the study invite, and have received, sinister interpretations. On the stage they pass unnoticed; the force of the action, like a torrent bearing all before it, sweeps incoherences out of sight. In a sense, they scarcely matter. Why, then, pausing over the text, does one not simply ignore them? The answer relates to the nature of the play. *Henry V* is concerned with moral vindications of national interest and policy, and so undertakes to explain and to justify all that is done in the nation's name. In explanations one expects rational consistency, yet here the patriotic *parti pris* overrides impartial reason. Plays are not, of course, exercises in logic, but it is because *Henry V* argues so much that flaws in the argument may seem significant; it really is felt to matter, more than in the other plays (even the other histories), whether or not acts and their vindications can stand scrutiny. Even so, such inconsistencies in it are signs not (as many critics have supposed) of Henry's politic hypocrisy but of Shakespeare's sharing with his public some of the stock responses to so loaded a subject as the French wars. His imagination was engaged at a brilliantly effective level for dramatic excitement; it was not engaged at the deeper levels of thoughtfulness of which he had already elsewhere shown himself capable.

*

What are the play's attitudes to war? More than any other of Shakespeare's works it takes war as its theme; elsewhere war is incidental even when, as in much of *Henry VI* and *King John*, it forms the staple of the action. Here it offers virtually the whole substance of interest – its causes, the ritual of embassies and ultimata, the mobilizing and the strategy, the discipline, heroism, and horror. War's terrors are recognized, formidably, as in the threats to Harfleur, Williams's recital of wounds and death, and Burgundy's lament over the ruined state of France. Yet the prevailing impression is one which at first warrants the 'romantic, heroic, patriotic, and poetical delight' of Hazlitt's playful phrase; *this* war, if not war in general, seems not only a necessary but an exhilarating exercise of policy. Does this impression survive a closer study?

Shakespeare was not in general an enthusiastic militarist; the previous history plays prove this truth. That here, despite its acknowledged awfulness, war is a matter of celebration is something the chronicles, popular tradition, and the great name of Agincourt rendered all but inevitable. One cannot expect Shakespeare to dodge the accepted data of his story; an anti-war *Henry V* is (or certainly would have been then) quite inconceivable. Since military valour and victory are the theme, and since these are bound here to be treated with approval, Shakespeare could not handle them as he would shortly do in *Troilus and Cressida*; had he, against all likelihood, done such a thing, the resulting play would certainly have been – as the *Troilus and Cressida* Quarto observes of that work – 'never staled with the stage, never clapper-clawed with the palms of the vulgar'.

What then does Shakespeare do? He produces some remarkable multiple effects, which can in one reading be taken as plain patriotic enthusiasm, in another as horrific realism, and in a third as a powerful and valid relationship of these two. This multiplicity of effect may be examined in some of the most famous episodes. In the first place there is the 'Once more unto the breach' oration, widely assumed to express the healthy zest of battle and the joy of martial heroics. So exuberantly compelling is it that, unless one reflects, it seems like a first instalment of the great Agincourt manner: indeed, it finishes in the spirit of Agincourt, with soldier humour ('now attest | That those whom you called fathers did beget you', III.1.22–3), with exhortations and comradeliness ('And you, good yeomen . . .'), with the eager valour of the 'noble lustre' in the eyes, and with the resounding slogan-climax. Nothing, certainly, could be better done. But what precisely is going on? Is one to take any attitude to it other than the impetuous-enthusiastic? To start with, there is the note of desperation; the breach is to be attacked *again*, until English corpses fill the gap (after how many failures?). Then, in a series of extraordinary hyperboles, there emerge like frightful caricatures the beast-violences of action, the histrionic strains of whipped-up ferocity (as when modern soldiers force from constrained throats the insane screams expected at bayonet-drill). The language incites to an appalling *show* ('imitate . . . stiffen . . . disguise . . . lend'), with the frenzy of staring eyeballs and craggy brows. Is the intention really so overtly enthusiastic as it at first seems? Is it, on the other hand, savagely (though covertly) critical of war? Is Shakespeare, as a skilful playwright, making the most of the do-or-die heroics? – certainly this is a famous theatrical moment. Or is he seriously bringing home what, under the heroics, war really means, that (as

33

with Macbeth before the murder of Duncan) one must – against the use of nature – 'bend up | Each corporal agent to this terrible feat'? The speech deserves its fame, not because it prompts a surge of vicarious valour in the unreflecting but because it combines the complex elements outlined above. It is desperate, appalling, and inspiring at once; it makes war awful, but with an awfulness which only victory can compensate for, so that those who hear it shall be swept out of their tremors (except for Nym, Pistol, and the Boy) into a berserk frenzy of assault (though still the town remains untaken – see III.3). Shakespeare is not glorifying war; he is, brilliantly, conveying what war requires from leaders and followers in times of desperate danger.

More ambiguous is the equally famous ultimatum to Harfleur (III.3.1–43). Henry's oath as he asserts his will to win –

> *as I am a soldier,*
> *A name that in my thoughts becomes me best –*

would in other contexts go down well. It would fit his Agincourt speech; General Montgomery might have cited it before El Alamein. But at Harfleur it introduces with what seems a horrifying *relish* the threats with which Henry menaces the town. Perhaps, one reflects, Shakespeare, honest about war's horrors, is shocking the moral sense so that it sees what war means; perhaps, further, he is drawing the tragic contrast between the normally humane man and the enforcedly brutal leader. The trouble is that the speech gives no sign of these assumptions; Henry proudly invokes his soldiership as the warranty for the fiendishness soldiership commits, a warranty accompanied by a disavowal not only of responsibility ('when you yourselves are cause') but even of regret:

> *What is it then to me, if impious war,*
> *Arrayed in flames, like to the prince of fiends,*
> *Do with his smirched complexion all fell feats*
> *Enlinked to waste and desolation?*

War and policy, it is true, call at times for cruelty, as at other times for clemency; moreover, within the terms of the play Henry's threats, however bloodthirsty (and indeed because they are so bloodthirsty), never materialize – the town yields and the townsmen are shown mercy. Henry's ferocity thereby justifies itself as both essential and effective; threats are his ultimate weapon, and they save his army at the moment when 'winter [is] coming on, and sickness growing | Upon our soldiers' (III.3.55–6). Expedient ruthlessness is essential. Is there, then, a valid criticism not against the threat of horrors but against Henry's horrific zest in threatening them, and against what seems Shakespeare's invitation to approve without moral qualms so stirring a leader? 'As the embodiment of worldly success,' an earlier editor of the play remarked, '[Henry is] entitled to our unreserved admiration'. But a proper response is more complex than this. One might argue that, with very serious but very covert irony, Shakespeare here offers a profound criticism of the whole nature of war; and so, in a sense, he does – but it is not a criticism of *Henry's* war. Rather, he presents his King as both a cool and a passionate man. The coolness reckons that threats, if violent enough, will carry the day; the passion generates the extraordinary force of melodramatic realization the speech achieves. Henry is master of his strategy, and speaks with a well-judged purpose. But, as in the great leader they must do, his passions kindle from his judgements and make him, when need requires, in the highest degree bloody, bold, and resolute. As for his

35

apparent relish, which in real life would indicate a sadisti-
cally exciting hysteria, in the simpler conditions of
Elizabethan drama it simply means that Shakespeare is
writing as strongly as he can; any relish is the author's, and
it is an artistic, not a moral (or immoral), relish. Henry
speaks with a frightening urgency; war is a nightmare as
well as an adventure, and if soldiers are heroes they can
also be brutes.

Is there, perhaps, a developing theme in the play's sense
of war, by which it moves from the unintelligent fervour of
prelates and peers (indeed, of the whole nation, as the
choruses interpret it) to the informed realization of
butchery, so that peace, willingly forsaken at the outset,
is again revered at the close, and war, having been pain-
fully experienced, is known for what it is? There is indeed
a general trend of this kind; the play realizes these truths
as it develops through Act III into the grimmer attitudes
of Act IV. Yet the movement is uncertain. Henry is
already conscious in Act I (as who could not be?) of the
sufferings war causes:

> *For God doth know how many now in health*
> *Shall drop their blood in approbation*
> *Of what your reverence shall incite us to.* I.2.18–20

Yet Act IV has not so accepted war's realities as to deny
itself the sentimental-elegiac death-scene of York and
Suffolk. Act V shows Henry carrying into his wooing the
soldierly manner of which he is so proud, and the Epilogue
rejoices in the rewards of victory. One reflects again that
Shakespeare's sources, and popular expectation, allowed
him no real chance of revaluing Henry's war even had he
wished to do so, and the play's splendid vigour does not
in the least suggest that he did. The point is not that he
could or should have rejected Elizabethan notions of a

cherished heroic episode, and the excited attitudes these naturally provoked; it is rather that his treatment of the war shows far more insights into its necessary accompaniments and consequences than do the chronicles or patriotic poems, while still accepting without question the popular case for the war, the popular zest that went with it, and the popular sense of triumph that resulted from it. None of his plays shows him better as the skilled professional, the writer who can measure his material against the interests of his audience and provide the maximum dramatic gratification. He is certainly too captivated by his theme to be *merely* turning out an efficient product; the play is too grand, the poetry too powerful, the realization too moving, for such a limiting judgement to hold good. Yet sheer professional zest in face of so gripping and famous a story makes him write to the top of his bent *for each immediate purpose*, and one understands the play better by recognizing this than by seeking to draw all its parts into convincing psychological, symbolical, or moral coherence. Just this same characteristic, of writing for the greatest immediate effect, marks his treatment also of action and character; this will be the next subject for discussion. The result is a play which works superbly as a dramatic sequence but which, on the moral plane, teasingly offers and then withdraws (as if uncertain whether they belong with the heroic theme) a series of tentatives towards an altogether deeper realization of its subject.

*

The acceptance of the chronicles' popular reading of events results in an enormously effective yet an episodic drama rather than one integrated from a centre. 'Pageant-like' is the word often applied to its practice of showing off each scene as a separate entity, rather than developing the action organically from the impulses of characters who progressively know more about themselves; development of action is something more than mere sequence of actions. Yet 'pageant-like' needs qualifying; the play holds together much better than that word would suggest. To some degree (though a small one), the low comedy satirically reacts to the high history, and so makes a pattern with it. Act II, for instance, shows lofty patriotism in its chorus and second scene but base rapacity in its first and third, and the cynic might say (though Shakespeare would probably reject the view) that these are not quite as antithetical as they seem. Immediately after 'God for Harry, England, and Saint George!' (III.1.34) there enter the discreditable Bardolph, Pistol, and Nym, like a sardonic comment. The degree of such interaction, however, does not go far towards establishing organic form, as it does in *Henry IV*, though certainly it affords a diverting variety of effect. Much more telling in producing coherence is the speed and thrust with which the action drives forward, each episode pressing on and looking towards the event. The play generates unity by its impetus.

Shakespeare shapes the material well. He assumes that the whole significance of Henry's reign is to lead to Agincourt and Troyes, and he uses the choruses brilliantly to link and explain the action. The episodic nature of the plot arises not because the events fall apart – they are connected and consecutive – but because the serious action consists of successive demonstrations rather than a germination and growth of part into part, connected by moral significance, such as make 'dramatic poems' of *Othello* and *Macbeth* and *King Lear* – or, should these comparisons be unfair, of *Richard II* and either part of *Henry IV*. The plot is extremely simple, without an 'inner' dimension.

*

From the nature of plot to that of characterization: how is Henry himself handled? In 1886 R. G. Moulton delivered to the New Shakspere Society a paper comparing the presentation of Henry's character with that of Macbeth's; Henry, he decided, is complete from the beginning, whereas Macbeth 'develops as the seed grows into the tree; the tree may be *potentially* present in the seed, but the passage from that potential to the actual is not a matter depending upon external observation but is a succession of changes in the substance of the organism itself'. This overstates the 'given' nature of Henry; from Act I we should hardly predict the much more interesting figure of Act IV, and Dover Wilson's introduction to the New Cambridge edition, arguing for a deepening personality as Agincourt draws near, provides the right counterbalance. Moulton's point is, though, not precisely that nothing new is revealed about Henry as the play proceeds but that what is presented is a series of stances, each powerful and effective, but not evincing that subtle, inward development of personality we look for in Shakespeare's great figures. King-as-counsellor, King-as-spokesman, King-as-patriot, King-as-warrior, King-as-wooer – these were some of the predetermined attitudes in which Henry needed to be displayed. And there comes to mind what Coleridge said about predetermined (or mechanic) and organic forms, during his lecture, 'Shakespeare a Poet Generally', in the *Lectures and Notes on Shakespeare*. The passage runs:

> *The form is mechanic, when on any given material we impress a predetermined form, not necessarily arising out of the properties of the material. . . . The organic form, on the other hand, is innate; it shapes, as it develops, itself from within, and the fullness of its development is one and*

*the same with the perfection of its outward form. Such as
the life is, such is the form.*

Is Henry V's 'form', or his play's 'form', in this sense
'mechanic'? Has the heroic model King of the chronicles
proved hard to animate as an inwardly-motivated dramatic
person? Holinshed presents the King as beloved, strong,
just, bountiful, diligent, constant in temperament, en-
during and valiant, 'of life without spot', 'of person and
form . . . rightly representing his heroical affects, . . . a
majesty . . . that both lived and died a pattern in prince-
hood, a lode-star' (compare 'This star of England';
Epilogue.6), 'and mirror of magnificence' (compare 'the
mirror of all Christian kings'; 2.Chorus.6).

Such a character might daunt the boldest dramatist,
but Shakespeare is quite undaunted; he seems to welcome
the chance of creating the hero and the man, just as in
Richard III, facing an earlier problem of predetermined
characterization, he had welcomed the chance of creating
the great villain. Within a few months he would tackle the
still harder problem of Caesar, the state figure so commanding that one cannot feel sure what sort of man lives
within the imperial frame. Shakespeare surmounts the
difficulty better with Henry than with Caesar, displaying
him much more fully and variously. But does he mean
Henry to combine majesty and humanity in harmonious
union? Or is the majesty at odds with the humanity? If
so, is the strain treated sympathetically, or objectively,
or ironically? All these positions have been maintained.

Shakespeare's problem is to humanize and animate an
accepted hero, and to show how a man can be a king, a
king a man. What no one could predetermine was the
success with which, in the moving address to Scroop, the
night-scene self-examination before Agincourt, and the

Agincourt speech itself, he would achieve all this, and this achievement gives the play at these moments a deeply human passion. So, designed though it must be to show Henry in this light and in that, *Henry V* is much more than a series of tableaux. It is vigorous in forwarding events, forceful in the asserting and urging of views (there is an intellectual drama as well as a historical one), and at its best successful in presenting not only an able but a deeply human ruler. It remains true, however, that Henry is on exhibition; each scene in which he figures is designed to show his quality, even though this is done not statically but dynamically.

But is there also something subtler going on, a searching critique of power, unillusioned though unsatirical? Some critics have thought so. This critique might, in essence, be summed up in Henry's own words,

> *What infinite heart's ease*
> *Must kings neglect that private men enjoy!* IV.1.229–30

Does the royal office deprive its holder not only of his own private heart's ease but of the common humanity of heart's ease with other men? Presented in the Archbishop's panegyric as the essence of wisdom and grace, Henry must fill the part of the great king, centre of Church and State – yet at what expense of human naturalness and spontaneity? If one may put it so, kings are born free, yet are everywhere to be found in chains. The reverence in which Henry is held (so the argument goes) is vitiated by adulation; the imposing dispositions of his council do not conceal Machiavellianism; the heroics of war involve corruption and cruelty; the kingly authority ('a paradise | T' envelop and contain celestial spirits') must ignore such human attachments as once were felt for Falstaff and Bardolph (the wonderful treatment of Falstaff's death suggests how much has been, even if unavoidably, lost; and Henry's detachment over Bardolph's hanging reflects his now official status); and the King must yield periodically to outbursts of passion which betray the tension between kingly control and human emotion.

All this is interestingly observed. Certainly the difference is profound between a Tamburlaine, superhumanly wielding a heartless command, and Henry, ruling well yet bound to the political and social realities; the good king, working in the human conditions of politics, is affected by them in a way the tyrant is not. He can neither on the one hand override his subjects' rights, nor on the other be swayed from his duty by personal affections. On the whole, *Henry V* recognizes the problems of kingly position but does not stress the tension between office and man; after all, it makes a particular point of the fact that Henry is surrounded by his brothers, his good friends, and his devoted subjects. Certainly a king must sometimes act as ordinary humanity would not; he must reject a Falstaff, hang a Bardolph, threaten innocent citizens, and order prisoners to be killed. Yet the play offers virtually no criticism at these points; if Henry has 'run bad humours' on Falstaff and 'killed his heart' (II.1.116, 84) yet for Nym he is 'a good king' (II.1.120) and for Pistol 'a bawcock, and a heart of gold' (IV.1.44). Had it been Shakespeare's point that kings must forgo their finer feelings he would have made this clear, even if an ironic commentator like Falconbridge in *King John* had been needed to do so. He seems quite satisfied with Henry as he is, and sturdily sure that provided he rules well he is all that could be desired.

In two great scenes, however – that with Scroop, and that leading from the soldiers' debate before the battle (together with Henry's 'ceremony' speech) up to Henry's prayer – Henry as man feels the burdens of kingship profoundly, and the play takes on a moving gravity as he reveals what the loss of his heart's ease means. Yet these are passing phases only, soon superseded by the zest of leadership or by triumph in war and love. Elsewhere, Henry willingly accords with what is expected of a monarch, and indeed his finest quality as commander is the naturalness with which, uncondescingly, he is on terms as man to man with those he leads. A comradely spirit, stemming from him, unites the English army from general to private, while on the French side the bickering leaders are worlds removed from their despised peasants. The play, then, is on the whole about unity (rather than division) between Henry's kingly and human natures, as it is about unity between him and his subjects.

So the theory that Shakespeare here penetrates into the ironic intricacies of politics or of the political man, in a spirit either coolly objective or wisely grave, is too ingenious. Indeed, so little does the play really explore the subtleties of kingship that some critics have judged Shakespeare to be deliberately reducing the witty, sceptical, intelligent Prince Hal into the mere 'king of good fellows' who can deal handily with practical matters and is (whatever the Archbishop says) an average man writ large. So limited did Granville-Barker find Henry, in intellect and psychology, that in 'From *Henry V* to *Hamlet*' he suggested that Shakespeare had lost interest in the man of action and so turned, with Brutus and Hamlet, from the unreflective to the reflective hero. Yet limited though he is in inward interest there is more than enough about Henry to keep one wholly engaged by him. By turns sensitive, violent, and thoughtful, he is frank, honest, confident, shrewd, eminently good-hearted and resilient, and the play fully makes out its case that he is, in war and peace alike, a good king. One comes back, then, repeatedly to a central position among conflicting views, that the play is best interpreted rather simply. It is not quite so plain a tale of heroism as the more complacent used to think; neither on the other hand is it an ironically evaluated critique of ambiguous politics, such as current criticism is inclined to hold. It is essentially a play for the popular taste, but popular taste has now fewer romantic predilections and more toughness of quality than it used to have, and it takes *Henry V* as relating real heroism to the real grimness of war and the real conditions of life.

*

The last question about the play concerns the manner of its writing. Does Shakespeare believe wholeheartedly in his subject, and address himself to it with zest, or does he, as one critic thinks, 'audibly brace himself [for a] not very congenial effort' as he faces a theme and character 'lacking in true humanity'? Is he, as has further been suggested, so uncomfortable that the play hides intellectual paucity behind a façade of oratory, reduces a courtly, witty Prince into a war-machine King, is casual in its comedy, and often falls slack in its verse?

The verse is not, in fact, slack, except in the 'Salic law' rigmarole. It is usually strong and interesting, forthright and uncomplicated, at its best animated, eloquent, and rich. Yet mostly it is the style of speech-making rather than of personal idiosyncrasy, that idiosyncrasy which is felt, for instance, throughout *Henry IV*, where the movement, texture, and meaning of the words simultaneously express inner complexes of feeling. In its attitude to style-making, though not in its particular styles, *Henry V* harks back to *Richard II*, aiming to put the content demonstratively on show. Most of its serious speeches are addresses

44

with an aim in mind. This is appropriate to its material, to the demonstrative nature of plot and character, and it is extremely well done. In a story traditionally so concerned with the King's status, from a King who, it must always be made evident, has emerged into ability and wisdom, the necessary utterance will express not the complexities of personality but a demonstrative eloquence. One fires with admiration and pleasure at it, yet senses that on the whole one is being, as it were, set alight by design.

Henry's speech to the conspirators, and particularly to Scroop, is a case in point. A richly-felt and moving address, it sounds the tenor of tragic emotion as Henry discovers that one so trusted has proved so false. Yet the humiliation of Cambridge, Grey, and Scroop must be a formal public occasion, as that of Falstaff had been, and for the same reason, that the fault committed affects Henry's public station, and the world must understand this. Like much that Henry is bound by his office to do it needs to be set forth. To say this is to define but not to disparage it; it is excellently managed (even if 'managed' is, indeed, the word that significantly comes to mind). It creates a particular tone which the scene needs, that of reconciliation in tragic parting, through grief shared between King and conspirators, so that even their intended treachery ends in prayers for the safety of the land. Henry's speech is heart-felt, tender, and dignified. Yet its unusual length, and the relationship between speaker and hearer it necessarily imposes, that of authority *ex cathedra* and submissive penitent, cannot but promote a sense of occasion, unanswerable and final. The 'ceremony' speech preceding Agincourt has some of the same qualities; though a soliloquy, it is really a public address, eloquent and memorable. Not that it satisfies every reader: John Palmer calls it a 'most ingenuous apologia' and proposes to defend Shakespeare

from the charge of approving 'moral humbug' only on the
grounds that he is making clear, as a matter of natural fact,
the attitudinizing habitual to the political man. Such a
reaction is extravagant; Dr Johnson, who recognized moral
humbug when he saw it, thought the speech 'very striking
and solemn', and observed in his notes on the play,
'Something like this, on less occasions, every breast has
felt'. In face of Agincourt, affected by the scepticism of
Williams, Henry senses the truth underlying common-
places about the 'hard condition, | Twin-born with great-
ness' (IV.1.226–7), and though his speech echoes his
father's sentiment, 'Uneasy lies the head that wears a
crown' (2 *Henry IV*, III.1.31), he speaks from his own
awareness. Yet, eloquent though he is, this again is the
speech of status; even in its very privacy it discourses to
the audience about kingly cares and humble content.
Tell-tale phrases, it is true, betray an unexpected petulance or self-pitying extravagance – phrases like 'every
fool, whose sense no more can feel | But his own wringing'
(this comes coarsely, after the honest realism of Williams),
'horrid night, the child of hell', 'the wretched slave . . .
all night | Sleeps in Elysium' (said of the toiling peasant
dead to the world with weariness in his hovel), or 'with
profitable labour' (said of the peasant's hard-earned pit-
tance). These touches of irrationality may be signs that
Henry is under strain, and the actor may certainly treat
them as such; the speech is not without Shakespeare's
humanizing psychology. Yet on the whole Henry is going
through an understood exercise; even the soliloquy is
oratorical, and occasional false notes suggest that a case is
being made.

The serious speeches must accord with what is expected.
Nevertheless, even through this formidable apparatus of
the demonstrative there shows much of spirited and

brilliant verse; whatever the play's intellectual and psychological conditions, Shakespeare was evidently writing with pleasure. And at important points qualities emerge that, rather than being merely accomplished, are deep and true. Of this, in the smaller compass, all that relates to Falstaff's cronies as they learn of his illness, to the Hostess as she narrates his death, to the Boy as his wit brightens the scene until he goes down in the slaughter, and to Fluellen in everything he says and does is an example. This is all sensitive and humane, not in the least disguised behind the public gesture. In the larger compass, most of what bears upon Henry himself when he is gravely tested is imaginative and right. The fourth chorus is in a different manner from its precursors, superior even to the third in significance of atmosphere and mood. Henry is now to be not only leader but friend, and the language becomes tender in evoking the endangered English and the 'little touch of Harry in the night' which is to hearten them. This crucial eve before Agincourt gives all that could be asked for. The English commanders and soldiers know and fundamentally trust each other (the lifelike lower-rank cynicism is something quite different from disloyalty or untrustworthiness), and Henry's debate with his men is of the greatest interest. Critics who dislike him, or think him only a superb operator, hit him hardest here; for one of them the discussion is disappointingly 'sober and rational'; for another, Henry's arguments are 'squirming sophistry'; for a third, his conscience is 'incapable of even so much as an honest piece of reasoning'. If so, Shakespeare has missed his mark completely, for he gives no sign of meaning the King to show up poorly; leading his men in a cause by definition just, Henry is meant to be morally right and to make his case fairly. In fact, he argues with skill, but lucidly and honestly, even if (as with Scroop) he goes on so long that what began as debate ends in argumentative monopoly. The acuteness with which he follows the argument through and the sharpness and concentration of the argument itself are signs of an unexpectedly earnest engagement with the subject at a level of hypothesis of which one would not have thought him capable. As Dr Johnson observes on the passage, 'the whole argument is well followed, and properly concluded'.

As for the speech before Agincourt, fame has made its every phrase so familiar that one can hardly hope to see it objectively at all. But familiarity breeds compulsion, not contempt. At each re-hearing it reaffirms its sway, almost against one's will, and renews that exultancy which it is its purpose to effect. Is this merely the climactic activation of stock responses? To some degree, yes; these are (and they are no worse for it) those 'images which find a mirror in every mind, and thoughts to which every bosom returns an echo', of which Johnson wrote in the *Life of Gray*. Technically, there is also the excitement of the supreme expected occasion; this is the crowning exercise of all those in which Henry must direct his words to a prescribed end. But as he does so he creates the sense that he is at one with the occasion and with his own truest feelings. The thoughts come with ease and power, borne along infallibly by the rhythmical flow and resonant melody of the lines, and heightened by the heady refrain about St Crispin's day. The daring paradox by which the very fewness of his soldiers is made to sound a source of strength is carried off with irresistible conviction; the mounting vision of victory and fame is offered in words both heroic and human; and from the initial stress on the King's own honour there spread out widening circles of contagious emulation, until all his men feel the spell of brotherhood, their thoughts lifted beyond present peril to the prospect of honour, old age, and brave memories. This comment merely rewrites flatly what Henry says exaltingly; the great thing about the exaltation is that it blends itself with intimate human feeling, with neighbourliness, and humour, and hope, and proper pride.

*

To sum up, then: if this discussion has been a good deal concerned with possible dissatisfactions or critical disagreements that is because the grounds on which, at one point or another, serious critics have disagreed or been dissatisfied need to be recognized. Yet one cannot but conclude that much of the criticism is based on false premisses (such as those of much later historical and moral criteria), or is hypercritical, or springs from seeking more deeply-involved moral judgements than seem to be there. Naïve, in a sense, the play requires one to be, willingly naïve rather than innocent. It would be innocent to rise from it feeling idealistic about policy or war (that 'continuation of policy by other means', as Clausewitz called it); the underside of such things is sufficiently revealed, though at times in an oddly incidental, or accidental, manner. Naïve in a way one needs to be, for the play to work. One must give one's scepticism a day off and let one's gusto serve instead, though it will at times prove a disturbing gusto, as at others exhilarating. There must be a preparedness to go along with the play's fine confidence about what it is doing – it rarely hesitates in its onward action or its compulsive style. If one yields to its conviction, the result will be a slight anaesthetizing of the intellect but a marked exhilaration in the pulse, a stirring of pleasure in eloquence, and a very human sense of what men are like when danger brings out their better natures.

ANYONE working on *Henry V* must owe an especial debt to John Dover Wilson for his New Cambridge edition. His dramatic, linguistic, and historical scholarship illuminates all the play's technical aspects; equally, his generous knowledge of men interprets its spirit and meaning as, surely, Shakespeare meant them to be interpreted. An editor coming after him cannot fail to salute one

> *Who laboured here, though with the greater art.*

Sources and Historical Background

The sources are well presented and analysed in W. G. Boswell-Stone, *Shakespeare's Holinshed* (1896, 1907) and G. Bullough, *Narrative and Dramatic Sources of Shakespeare*, volume iv (1962). A very satisfactory edition for following the historical narrative is *Shakespeare's Holinshed: An Edition of Holinshed's Chronicle (1587)*, selected, edited, and annotated by Richard Hosley (New York, 1968). *The Famous Victories of Henry the Fifth* is available in Bullough (above) or in facsimiles (Shakspere-Quarto series, edited by C. Praetorius and P. A. Daniel, 1887; Tudor Facsimile Texts, edited by J. S. Farmer, 1913). The anonymous play of *Edward III*, which offers points of resemblance, is reprinted by G. C. Moore Smith (Temple Dramatists, 1897), J. S. Farmer (Tudor Facsimile Texts, 1910), C. F. Tucker Brooke, *The Shakespeare Apocrypha* (1918), and W. A. Armstrong, *Elizabethan History Plays* (1965). The actual historical events are related in C. L. Kingsford, *Henry V* (1901), J. H. Wylie, *The Reign of Henry V*, volume ii (1919), and E. F. Jacob, *Henry V and the Invasion of France* (1947). Elizabethan views of this phase of history are surveyed in E. M. W. Tillyard,

Shakespeare's History Plays (1944; Penguin Books, 1962), L. B. Campbell, *Shakespeare's 'Histories': Mirrors of Elizabethan Policy* (1947), K. J. Holzknecht, *The Backgrounds of Shakespeare's Plays* (1950 – a compact account of Elizabethan interest in the past, Shakespeare's treatment of history, and the presentation of kingship), and the editions by J. Dover Wilson (New Cambridge, 1947) and J. H. Walter (Arden, 1954).

Texts

There are facsimiles of the 1600 'Bad' Quarto by C. Praetorius (Shakspere-Quarto series, 1886) and W. W. Greg (Shakespeare Quarto series, 1957); reprints in the (old) Cambridge Shakespeare, volume iv (1864, 1891), and by Brinsley Nicholson for the New Shakspere Society (1875, with the Folio text following; 1877, with Quarto and Folio texts in parallel), and Ernest Roman (*Shakespeare Reprints* iii, Marburg, 1908, with the first and third Quarto and first Folio texts on the same page). Facsimiles of the first Folio text are available in the first Folio facsimiles (for example, edited by Sidney Lee, 1902; edited by Kökeritz and Prouty, 1955; edited by Charlton Hinman (the Norton Facsimile), 1968), and separately (edited by J. Dover Wilson, 1931). There are scholarly analyses of textual matters in E. K. Chambers, *William Shakespeare*, volume i (1930), W. W. Greg, *The Shakespeare First Folio* (1955), and the editions by J. Dover Wilson (New Cambridge, 1947) and J. H. Walter (Arden, 1954); both these editions argue for an original version 'with Sir John in it'. John Munro's London Shakespeare edition, volume iv (1957), skilfully and compactly examines textual matters and the range of critical opinion.

Critical Estimates

Several critics and editors survey the competing views of their precursors; the New Cambridge and London Shakespeare editions (above) do this well. The New Cambridge also offers a fine appraisal of the play's spirit and Henry's qualities, and the Arden usefully sets the play against the conventions of epic and of the Renaissance prince. The New Cambridge is informative also on stage history, but the best account of this is in A. C. Sprague, *Shakespeare's Histories: Plays for the Stage* (1964), a fascinating study of the play in performance, and what actors and critics have made of it. J. Dover Wilson and T. C. Worsley's *Shakespeare's Histories at Stratford, 1951* (1952) is a lively illustrated record of the *Richard II – Henry V* sequence in performance, with a stimulating anthology of critical viewpoints.

Critical studies divide, roughly, into those which accept and those which reject the play's proffered enthusiasm for Henry. Those which accept do so either unreservedly or with the admission of flaws which nevertheless are held to leave Henry largely unimpaired. Those which reject do so because Shakespeare is thought to have failed in percipience (to have succumbed to jingoism, or worship of crude success, or type-casting which he cannot humanize) or because, it is argued, the enthusiasm is merely ostensible and really masks an unillusioned analysis (whether comic, ironic, or tragic) of the inevitable Machiavellianism of 'policy'. A rough tabulation of views would go as follows (the more striking are starred *):

(a) *Unreserved approval of Henry*: G. G. Gervinus, *Shakespeare Commentaries*, volume i (1863); * H. N. Hudson, *Shakespeare: His Life, Art, and Characters*, volume i (1880); F. E. Schelling, *The English Chronicle Play* (1902); John Bailey, *Shakespeare* (1929) – cogent, though rather downright-commonsensical; Charles Williams, 'Henry V', in *Shakespeare Criticism 1919–1935*, edited by Anne Ridler (1936); * J. Middleton Murry, *Shakespeare* (1936) – this brings the play's glowing spirit imaginatively across; * J. Dover Wilson, New Cambridge edition (1947); * Rose A. Zimbardo, 'The Formalism of *Henry V*', in *Shakespeare Encomium*, edited by Anne Paolucci (1964).

(b) *Qualified approval of Henry*: * A. C. Bradley, 'The Rejection of Falstaff', in *Oxford Lectures on Poetry* (1909); * E. E. Stoll, *Poets and Playwrights* (1930); * M. M. Reese, *The Cease of Majesty* (1961) – an extract appears in *Shakespeare's Histories: An Anthology of Modern Criticism*, edited by William A. Armstrong (Penguin Shakespeare Library, 1972); * S. C.

Sen Gupta, *Shakespeare's Historical Plays* (1964); H. M. Richmond, *Shakespeare's Political Plays* (1967) – harsh on Henry at the start, but just to his growing maturity; * Gareth Lloyd Evans, *Shakespeare II* (1969).

(c) *Discontent (moral and/or aesthetic) with Henry:* * W. Hazlitt, *Characters of Shakespeare's Plays* (1817) – Hazlitt, however, praises the poetry; H. Granville-Barker, 'From *Henry V* to *Hamlet*' (1925), revised in *Aspects of Shakespeare* (1933) and *Studies in Shakespeare*, edited by P. Alexander (1964); Mark Van Doren, *Shakespeare* (1939); * U. M. Ellis-Fermor, *The Frontiers of Drama* (1945) – this is a brief but brilliant contention that in Henry the King-as-ruler has entirely displaced the King-as-human-being; * Honor Matthews, *Character and Symbol in Shakespeare's Plays* (1962).

(d) *The play as unillusioned political analysis:* A. C. Swinburne, *A Study of Shakespeare* (1880) – a few pages only; * W. B. Yeats, 'At Stratford-on-Avon', in *Ideas of Good and Evil* (1903); Gerald Gould, 'A New Reading of *Henry V*' (in *The English Review*, vol. 29, 1929) – this takes the play as anti-war satire and Henry as 'the perfect hypocrite'; H. B. Charlton, *Shakespeare, Politics and Politicians* (1929); * J. Palmer, *Political Characters of Shakespeare* (1945); H. C. Goddard, *The Meaning of Shakespeare*, volume i (1951) – a provocative view, very hostile to Henry, spoilt by prejudiced interpretation and the importation of extraneous evidence; * D. A. Traversi, *Shakespeare from 'Richard II' to 'Henry V'* (1957); R. W. Battenhouse, '*Henry V* as Heroic Comedy', in *Essays on Shakespeare and Elizabethan Drama*, edited by R. Hosley (1963) – rather extravagant in comment but interesting in taking the play as 'heroic comedy' when others – for example Traversi – offer it as potential tragedy; * Z. Stříbrný, '*Henry V* and History', in *Shakespeare in a Changing World*, edited by A. Kettle (1964) – an excellent essay.

(e) Brief but interesting comments may be sampled in G. B. Shaw, '*Henry IV*', in *Our Theatre in the Nineties*, volume ii (1931), in *Plays and Players*, selected by A. C. Ward (1952), and in *Shaw on Shakespeare*, edited by Edwin Wilson (1962;

Penguin Shakespeare Library, 1969); A. P. Rossiter, 'Ambivalence: the Dialectic of the Histories', in *Angel with Horns* (1951); P. Alexander, introduction to Collins' Classics edition (1955) – also in *Introductions to Shakespeare* (1964); L. C. Knights, *Shakespeare: the Histories* (1962).

(f) Brian Vickers, *The Artistry of Shakespeare's Prose* (1968), analyses the prose qualities well. * *Shakespeare: 'Henry V': A Casebook* (1969), edited by Michael Quinn, gathers critical commentaries since the eighteenth century: it includes, in full or in part, the discussions listed above by Bradley, Charlton, Ellis-Fermor, Gould, Granville-Barker, Hazlitt, Matthews, Shaw, Sprague, Stoll, Stříbrný, Tillyard, Traversi, Van Doren, Walter, Williams, Yeats, and Zimbardo.

HENRY V

THE CHARACTERS IN THE PLAY

CHORUS

KING HENRY THE FIFTH
DUKE OF GLOUCESTER ⎫
DUKE OF BEDFORD ⎬ brothers of the King
DUKE OF CLARENCE ⎭
DUKE OF EXETER, uncle of the King
DUKE OF YORK, cousin of the King
EARL OF SALISBURY
EARL OF WESTMORLAND
EARL OF WARWICK
EARL OF HUNTINGDON
ARCHBISHOP OF CANTERBURY
BISHOP OF ELY
RICHARD EARL OF CAMBRIDGE ⎫
HENRY LORD SCROOP ⎬ conspirators
SIR THOMAS GREY ⎭ against the King
SIR THOMAS ERPINGHAM ⎫
CAPTAIN FLUELLEN ⎪
CAPTAIN GOWER ⎬ officers in the King's
CAPTAIN JAMY ⎪ army
CAPTAIN MACMORRIS ⎭
JOHN BATES ⎫
ALEXANDER COURT ⎬ soldiers in the King's army
MICHAEL WILLIAMS ⎭
BARDOLPH ⎫
NYM ⎪
PISTOL ⎬ camp-followers in the King's army
BOY ⎭

HOSTESS of an Eastcheap tavern, formerly Mistress Quickly, now married to Pistol

An English Herald

CHARLES THE SIXTH, King of France

LEWIS, the Dauphin

DUKE OF BURGUNDY

DUKE OF ORLEANS

DUKE OF BRITAINE

DUKE OF BOURBON

CHARLES DELABRETH, the Constable of France

GRANDPRÉ ⎫
RAMBURES ⎭ French Lords

THE GOVERNOR OF HARFLEUR

MONTJOY, a French Herald

AMBASSADORS to the King of England

MONSIEUR LE FER, a French soldier

ISABEL, Queen of France

KATHERINE, daughter of the King and Queen of France

ALICE, a lady attending on her

Lords, ladies

Officers, soldiers, citizens, messengers, and attendants

[breaks illusion]

Flourish. Enter Chorus

CHORUS

O for a Muse of fire, that would ascend
The brightest heaven of invention,
A kingdom for a stage, princes to act,
And monarchs to behold the swelling scene!
Then should the warlike Harry, like himself,
Assume the port of Mars, and at his heels,
Leashed in like hounds, should famine, sword, and fire
Crouch for employment. But pardon, gentles all,

Brecht!

The flat unraisèd spirits that hath dared
On this unworthy scaffold to bring forth   10
So great an object. Can this cockpit hold
The vasty fields of France? Or may we cram
Within this wooden O the very casques
That did affright the air at Agincourt?
O, pardon! since a crookèd figure may
Attest in little place a million,
And let us, ciphers to this great account,
On your imaginary forces work.
Suppose within the girdle of these walls
Are now confined two mighty monarchies,   20
Whose high uprearèd and abutting fronts
The perilous narrow ocean parts asunder.
Piece out our imperfections with your thoughts:
Into a thousand parts divide one man,
And make imaginary puissance.
Think, when we talk of horses, that you see them

Printing their proud hoofs i'th'receiving earth;
For 'tis your thoughts that now must deck our kings,
Carry them here and there, jumping o'er times,
30   Turning th'accomplishment of many years
Into an hour-glass: for the which supply,
Admit me Chorus to this history,
Who Prologue-like your humble patience pray,
Gently to hear, kindly to judge, our play.   *Exit*

Enter the Archbishop of Canterbury and the
Bishop of Ely

CANTERBURY

My lord, I'll tell you. That self bill is urged
Which in th'eleventh year of the last King's reign
Was like, and had indeed against us passed,
But that the scambling and unquiet time
Did push it out of farther question.

ELY

But how, my lord, shall we resist it now?

CANTERBURY

It must be thought on. If it pass against us,
We lose the better half of our possession;
For all the temporal lands which men devout
By testament have given to the Church   10
Would they strip from us; being valued thus –
As much as would maintain, to the King's honour,
Full fifteen earls, and fifteen hundred knights,
Six thousand and two hundred good esquires;
And, to relief of lazars and weak age,
Of indigent faint souls past corporal toil,
A hundred almshouses right well supplied;
And, to the coffers of the King beside,
A thousand pounds by th'year. Thus runs the bill.

ELY

This would drink deep.

CANTERBURY   'Twould drink the cup and all.   20

ELY

But what prevention?

CANTERBURY

The King is full of grace and fair regard.

ELY

And a true lover of the holy Church.

CANTERBURY

The courses of his youth promised it not.
The breath no sooner left his father's body
But that his wildness, mortified in him,
Seemed to die too. Yea, at that very moment,
Consideration like an angel came
And whipped th'offending Adam out of him,
30 Leaving his body as a paradise
T'envelop and contain celestial spirits.
Never was such a sudden scholar made;
Never came reformation in a flood
With such a heady currance scouring faults;
Nor never Hydra-headed wilfulness
So soon did lose his seat, and all at once,
As in this King.

ELY   We are blessèd in the change.

CANTERBURY

Hear him but reason in divinity,
And all-admiring, with an inward wish,
40 You would desire the King were made a prelate.
Hear him debate of commonwealth affairs,
You would say it hath been all in all his study.
List his discourse of war, and you shall hear
A fearful battle rendered you in music.
Turn him to any cause of policy,
The Gordian knot of it he will unloose,
Familiar as his garter; that, when he speaks,
The air, a chartered libertine, is still,
And the mute wonder lurketh in men's ears
50 To steal his sweet and honeyed sentences.

So that the art and practic part of life
Must be the mistress to this theoric –
Which is a wonder how his grace should glean it,
Since his addiction was to courses vain,
His companies unlettered, rude, and shallow,
His hours filled up with riots, banquets, sports,
And never noted in him any study,
Any retirement, any sequestration,
From open haunts and popularity.

ELY
The strawberry grows underneath the nettle,   60
And wholesome berries thrive and ripen best
Neighboured by fruit of baser quality:
And so the Prince obscured his contemplation
Under the veil of wildness, which, no doubt,
Grew like the summer grass, fastest by night,
Unseen, yet crescive in his faculty.

CANTERBURY
It must be so, for miracles are ceased;
And therefore we must needs admit the means
How things are perfected.

ELY   But, my good lord,
How now for mitigation of this bill   70
Urged by the Commons? Doth his majesty
Incline to it, or no?

CANTERBURY   He seems indifferent,
Or rather swaying more upon our part
Than cherishing th'exhibiters against us;
For I have made an offer to his majesty –
Upon our spiritual Convocation,
And in regard of causes now in hand,
Which I have opened to his grace at large
As touching France – to give a greater sum
Than ever at one time the clergy yet   80

63

Did to his predecessors part withal.

ELY

How did this offer seem received, my lord?

CANTERBURY

With good acceptance of his majesty,
Save that there was not time enough to hear,
As I perceived his grace would fain have done,
The severals and unhidden passages
Of his true titles to some certain dukedoms,
And generally to the crown and seat of France,
Derived from Edward, his great-grandfather.

ELY

90   What was th'impediment that broke this off?

CANTERBURY

The French ambassador upon that instant
Craved audience, and the hour, I think, is come
To give him hearing. Is it four o'clock?

ELY

It is.

CANTERBURY

Then go we in to know his embassy;
Which I could with a ready guess declare
Before the Frenchman speak a word of it.

ELY

I'll wait upon you, and I long to hear it.

Exeunt

I.2   *Enter the King, Gloucester, Bedford, Clarence,*
         Exeter, Warwick, Westmorland, and attendants

KING HENRY

Where is my gracious Lord of Canterbury?

EXETER

Not here in presence.

KING HENRY   Send for him, good uncle.

WESTMORLAND

Shall we call in th'ambassador, my liege?

KING HENRY

Not yet, my cousin; we would be resolved,
Before we hear him, of some things of weight
That task our thoughts, concerning us and France.
*Enter the Archbishop of Canterbury and the Bishop
of Ely*

CANTERBURY

God and His angels guard your sacred throne,
And make you long become it!

KING HENRY   Sure, we thank you.
My learnèd lord, we pray you to proceed,
And justly and religiously unfold   10
Why the law Salic that they have in France
Or should or should not bar us in our claim.
And God forbid, my dear and faithful lord,
That you should fashion, wrest, or bow your reading,
Or nicely charge your understanding soul
With opening titles miscreate, whose right
Suits not in native colours with the truth;
For God doth know how many now in health
Shall drop their blood in approbation
Of what your reverence shall incite us to.   20
Therefore take heed how you impawn our person,
How you awake our sleeping sword of war.
We charge you in the name of God, take heed;
For never two such kingdoms did contend
Without much fall of blood, whose guiltless drops
Are every one a woe, a sore complaint
'Gainst him whose wrongs gives edge unto the swords
That makes such waste in brief mortality.
Under this conjuration speak, my lord,
For we will hear, note, and believe in heart   30
That what you speak is in your conscience washed

As pure as sin with baptism.

CANTERBURY

Then hear me, gracious sovereign, and you peers,
That owe yourselves, your lives, and services
To this imperial throne. There is no bar
To make against your highness' claim to France
But this, which they produce from Pharamond:
'*In terram Salicam mulieres ne succedant*' –
'No woman shall succeed in Salic land';
40 Which Salic land the French unjustly gloze
To be the realm of France, and Pharamond
The founder of this law and female bar.
Yet their own authors faithfully affirm
That the land Salic is in Germany,
Between the floods of Sala and of Elbe;
Where Charles the Great, having subdued the Saxons,
There left behind and settled certain French,
Who, holding in disdain the German women
For some dishonest manners of their life,
50 Established then this law: to wit, no female
Should be inheritrix in Salic land;
Which Salic, as I said, 'twixt Elbe and Sala,
Is at this day in Germany called Meisen.
Then doth it well appear the Salic law
Was not devisèd for the realm of France;
Nor did the French possess the Salic land
Until four hundred one-and-twenty years
After defunction of King Pharamond,
Idly supposed the founder of this law,
60 Who died within the year of our redemption
Four hundred twenty-six; and Charles the Great
Subdued the Saxons, and did seat the French
Beyond the river Sala, in the year
Eight hundred five. Besides, their writers say,
King Pepin, which deposèd Childeric,

Did, as heir general, being descended
Of Blithild, which was daughter to King Clothair,
Make claim and title to the crown of France.
Hugh Capet also – who usurped the crown
Of Charles the Duke of Lorraine, sole heir male   70
Of the true line and stock of Charles the Great –
To find his title with some shows of truth,
Though in pure truth it was corrupt and naught,
Conveyed himself as th'heir to th'Lady Lingare,
Daughter to Charlemain, who was the son
To Lewis the Emperor, and Lewis the son
Of Charles the Great. Also King Lewis the Tenth,
Who was sole heir to the usurper Capet,
Could not keep quiet in his conscience,
Wearing the crown of France, till satisfied   80
That fair Queen Isabel, his grandmother,
Was lineal of the Lady Ermengare,
Daughter to Charles the foresaid Duke of Lorraine;
By the which marriage the line of Charles the Great
Was re-united to the crown of France.
So that, as clear as is the summer's sun,
King Pepin's title, and Hugh Capet's claim,
King Lewis his satisfaction, all appear
To hold in right and title of the female;
So do the kings of France unto this day,   90
Howbeit they would hold up this Salic law
To bar your highness claiming from the female,
And rather choose to hide them in a net
Than amply to imbare their crookèd titles
Usurped from you and your progenitors.

KING HENRY
    May I with right and conscience make this claim?
CANTERBURY
    The sin upon my head, dread sovereign!
    For in the Book of Numbers is it writ,

When the man dies, let the inheritance
100 Descend unto the daughter. Gracious lord,
Stand for your own, unwind your bloody flag,
Look back into your mighty ancestors.
Go, my dread lord, to your great-grandsire's tomb,
From whom you claim; invoke his warlike spirit,
And your great-uncle's, Edward the Black Prince,
Who on the French ground played a tragedy,
Making defeat on the full power of France,
Whiles his most mighty father on a hill
Stood smiling to behold his lion's whelp
110 Forage in blood of French nobility.
O noble English, that could entertain
With half their forces the full pride of France,
And let another half stand laughing by,
All out of work and cold for action!

ELY

Awake remembrance of these valiant dead,
And with your puissant arm renew their feats.
You are their heir, you sit upon their throne,
The blood and courage that renownèd them
Runs in your veins; and my thrice-puissant liege
120 Is in the very May-morn of his youth,
Ripe for exploits and mighty enterprises.

EXETER

Your brother kings and monarchs of the earth
Do all expect that you should rouse yourself,
As did the former lions of your blood.

WESTMORLAND

They know your grace hath cause and means and
        might –
So hath your highness. Never King of England
Had nobles richer and more loyal subjects,
Whose hearts have left their bodies here in England

And lie pavilioned in the fields of France.

CANTERBURY

O, let their bodies follow, my dear liege, 130
With blood and sword and fire to win your right!
In aid whereof we of the spiritualty
Will raise your highness such a mighty sum
As never did the clergy at one time
Bring in to any of your ancestors.

KING HENRY

We must not only arm t'invade the French
But lay down our proportions to defend
Against the Scot, who will make road upon us
With all advantages.

CANTERBURY

They of those marches, gracious sovereign, 140
Shall be a wall sufficient to defend
Our inland from the pilfering borderers.

KING HENRY

We do not mean the coursing snatchers only,
But fear the main intendment of the Scot,
Who hath been still a giddy neighbour to us;
For you shall read that my great-grandfather
Never went with his forces into France
But that the Scot on his unfurnished kingdom
Came pouring, like the tide into a breach,
With ample and brim fullness of his force, 150
Galling the gleanèd land with hot assays,
Girding with grievous siege castles and towns;
That England, being empty of defence,
Hath shook and trembled at th'ill neighbourhood.

CANTERBURY

She hath been then more feared than harmed, my
      liege;
For hear her but exampled by herself:

69

When all her chivalry hath been in France,
And she a mourning widow of her nobles,
She hath herself not only well defended
160 But taken and impounded as a stray
The King of Scots, whom she did send to France
To fill King Edward's fame with prisoner kings,
And make her chronicle as rich with praise
As is the ooze and bottom of the sea
With sunken wrack and sumless treasuries.

ELY

But there's a saying very old and true:
  'If that you will France win,
   Then with Scotland first begin.'
For once the eagle England being in prey,
170 To her unguarded nest the weasel Scot
Comes sneaking, and so sucks her princely eggs,
Playing the mouse in absence of the cat,
To 'tame and havoc more than she can eat.

EXETER

It follows then the cat must stay at home;
Yet that is but a crushed necessity,
Since we have locks to safeguard necessaries,
And pretty traps to catch the petty thieves.
While that the armèd hand doth fight abroad,
Th'advisèd head defends itself at home;
180 For government, though high, and low, and lower,
Put into parts, doth keep in one consent,
Congreeing in a full and natural close,
Like music.

CANTERBURY True: therefore doth heaven divide
The state of man in divers functions,
Setting endeavour in continual motion;
To which is fixèd as an aim or butt
Obedience; for so work the honey-bees,

Creatures that by a rule in nature teach
The act of order to a peopled kingdom.
They have a king, and officers of sorts,   190
Where some, like magistrates, correct at home;
Others, like merchants, venture trade abroad;
Others, like soldiers, armèd in their stings,
Make boot upon the summer's velvet buds;
Which pillage they with merry march bring home
To the tent-royal of their emperor;
Who, busied in his majesty, surveys
The singing masons building roofs of gold,
The civil citizens kneading up the honey,
The poor mechanic porters crowding in   200
Their heavy burdens at his narrow gate,
The sad-eyed justice, with his surly hum,
Delivering o'er to executors pale
The lazy yawning drone. I this infer,
That many things, having full reference
To one consent, may work contrariously,
As many arrows loosèd several ways
Come to one mark,
As many several ways meet in one town,
As many fresh streams meet in one salt sea,   210
As many lines close in the dial's centre;
So may a thousand actions, once afoot,
End in one purpose, and be all well borne
Without defeat. Therefore to France, my liege!
Divide your happy England into four;
Whereof take you one quarter into France,
And you withal shall make all Gallia shake.
If we, with thrice such powers left at home,
Cannot defend our own doors from the dog,
Let us be worried, and our nation lose   220
The name of hardiness and policy.

KING HENRY

Call in the messengers sent from the Dauphin.

Exeunt some attendants

Now are we well resolved, and by God's help
And yours, the noble sinews of our power,
France being ours, we'll bend it to our awe,
Or break it all to pieces. Or there we'll sit,
Ruling in large and ample empery
O'er France and all her almost kingly dukedoms,
Or lay these bones in an unworthy urn,
230   Tombless, with no remembrance over them.
Either our history shall with full mouth
Speak freely of our acts, or else our grave,
Like Turkish mute, shall have a tongueless mouth,
Not worshipped with a waxen epitaph.

Enter Ambassadors of France

Now are we well prepared to know the pleasure
Of our fair cousin Dauphin; for we hear
Your greeting is from him, not from the King.

AMBASSADOR

May't please your majesty to give us leave
Freely to render what we have in charge,
240   Or shall we sparingly show you far off
The Dauphin's meaning and our embassy?

KING HENRY

We are no tyrant, but a Christian king,
Unto whose grace our passion is as subject
As is our wretches fettered in our prisons:
Therefore with frank and with uncurbèd plainness
Tell us the Dauphin's mind.

AMBASSADOR   Thus then, in few:
Your highness, lately sending into France,
Did claim some certain dukedoms, in the right
Of your great predecessor, King Edward the Third.
250   In answer of which claim, the Prince our master

Says that you savour too much of your youth,
And bids you be advised there's naught in France
That can be with a nimble galliard won;
You cannot revel into dukedoms there.
He therefore sends you, meeter for your spirit,
This tun of treasure; and, in lieu of this,
Desires you let the dukedoms that you claim
Hear no more of you. This the Dauphin speaks.

KING HENRY
What treasure, uncle?

EXETER   Tennis-balls, my liege.

KING HENRY
We are glad the Dauphin is so pleasant with us.   260
His present, and your pains, we thank you for.
When we have matched our rackets to these balls,
We will in France, by God's grace, play a set
Shall strike his father's crown into the hazard.
Tell him he hath made a match with such a wrangler
That all the courts of France will be disturbed
With chases. And we understand him well,
How he comes o'er us with our wilder days,
Not measuring what use we made of them.
We never valued this poor seat of England,   270
And therefore, living hence, did give ourself
To barbarous licence; as 'tis ever common
That men are merriest when they are from home.
But tell the Dauphin I will keep my state,
Be like a king, and show my sail of greatness,
When I do rouse me in my throne of France.
For that I have laid by my majesty,
And plodded like a man for working-days;
But I will rise there with so full a glory
That I will dazzle all the eyes of France,   280
Yea, strike the Dauphin blind to look on us.
And tell the pleasant Prince this mock of his

Hath turned his balls to gun-stones, and his soul
Shall stand sore chargèd for the wasteful vengeance
That shall fly with them: for many a thousand widows
Shall this his mock mock out of their dear husbands;
Mock mothers from their sons, mock castles down;
And some are yet ungotten and unborn
That shall have cause to curse the Dauphin's scorn.
290 But this lies all within the will of God,
To whom I do appeal, and in whose name,
Tell you the Dauphin, I am coming on,
To venge me as I may, and to put forth
My rightful hand in a well-hallowed cause.
So get you hence in peace; and tell the Dauphin
His jest will savour but of shallow wit
When thousands weep more than did laugh at it.
Convey them with safe conduct. Fare you well.

Exeunt Ambassadors

EXETER
This was a merry message.

KING HENRY
300 We hope to make the sender blush at it.
Therefore, my lords, omit no happy hour
That may give furtherance to our expedition;
For we have now no thought in us but France,
Save those to God, that run before our business.
Therefore let our proportions for these wars
Be soon collected, and all things thought upon
That may with reasonable swiftness add
More feathers to our wings; for, God before,
We'll chide this Dauphin at his father's door.
310 Therefore let every man now task his thought
That this fair action may on foot be brought. *Exeunt*

*

CHORUS

Now all the youth of England are on fire,
And silken dalliance in the wardrobe lies.
Now thrive the armourers, and honour's thought
Reigns solely in the breast of every man.
They sell the pasture now to buy the horse,
Following the mirror of all Christian kings
With wingèd heels, as English Mercuries.
For now sits expectation in the air,
And hides a sword from hilts unto the point
With crowns imperial, crowns and coronets,   10
Promised to Harry and his followers.
The French, advised by good intelligence
Of this most dreadful preparation,
Shake in their fear, and with pale policy
Seek to divert the English purposes.
O England! model to thy inward greatness,
Like little body with a mighty heart,
What mightst thou do, that honour would thee do,
Were all thy children kind and natural!
But see, thy fault France hath in thee found out,   20
A nest of hollow bosoms, which he fills
With treacherous crowns; and three corrupted men –
One, Richard Earl of Cambridge, and the second,
Henry Lord Scroop of Masham, and the third,
Sir Thomas Grey, knight, of Northumberland –
Have, for the gilt of France – O guilt indeed! –
Confirmed conspiracy with fearful France;
And by their hands this grace of kings must die,
If hell and treason hold their promises,
Ere he take ship for France, and in Southampton.   30
Linger your patience on, and we'll digest
Th'abuse of distance, force a play.

The sum is paid; the traitors are agreed;
The King is set from London; and the scene
Is now transported, gentles, to Southampton.
There is the playhouse now, there must you sit,
And thence to France shall we convey you safe
And bring you back, charming the narrow seas
To give you gentle pass; for, if we may,

40 We'll not offend one stomach with our play.
But till the King come forth, and not till then,
Unto Southampton do we shift our scene. *Exit*

II.1 *Enter Corporal Nym and Lieutenant Bardolph*

BARDOLPH Well met, Corporal Nym.

NYM Good morrow, Lieutenant Bardolph.

BARDOLPH What, are Ancient Pistol and you friends yet?

NYM For my part, I care not. I say little; but when time shall serve, there shall be smiles – but that shall be as it may. I dare not fight, but I will wink and hold out mine iron. It is a simple one, but what though? It will toast cheese, and it will endure cold as another man's sword will – and there's an end.

10 BARDOLPH I will bestow a breakfast to make you friends, and we'll be all three sworn brothers to France. Let't be so, good Corporal Nym.

NYM Faith, I will live so long as I may, that's the certain of it; and when I cannot live any longer, I will do as I may. That is my rest, that is the rendezvous of it.

BARDOLPH It is certain, Corporal, that he is married to Nell Quickly, and certainly she did you wrong, for you were troth-plight to her.

NYM I cannot tell; things must be as they may. Men may
20 sleep, and they may have their throats about them at that time, and some say knives have edges: it must be as

it may – though patience be a tired mare, yet she will
plod – there must be conclusions – well, I cannot tell.

Enter Pistol and Hostess Quickly

BARDOLPH Here comes Ancient Pistol and his wife. Good
Corporal, be patient here.

NYM How now, mine host Pistol?

PISTOL

Base tike, call'st thou me host?

Now by this hand I swear I scorn the term;

Nor shall my Nell keep lodgers.

HOSTESS No, by my troth, not long; for we cannot lodge 30
and board a dozen or fourteen gentlewomen that live
honestly by the prick of their needles but it will be
thought we keep a bawdy-house straight.

Nym draws his sword

O well-a-day, Lady, if he be not drawn now! We shall
see wilful adultery and murder committed.

BARDOLPH Good Lieutenant! Good Corporal! Offer
nothing here.

NYM Pish!

PISTOL

Pish for thee, Iceland dog! thou prick-eared cur of
Iceland!

HOSTESS Good Corporal Nym, show thy valour, and put 40
up your sword.

NYM Will you shog off? I would have you *solus*.

He sheathes his sword

PISTOL

'*Solus*', egregious dog? O viper vile!

The '*solus*' in thy most mervailous face!

The '*solus*' in thy teeth and in thy throat,

And in thy hateful lungs, yea, in thy maw, perdy!

And, which is worse, within thy nasty mouth!

I do retort the '*solus*' in thy bowels,

For I can take, and Pistol's cock is up,
50 And flashing fire will follow.

NYM I am not Barbason; you cannot conjure me. I have
an humour to knock you indifferently well. If you grow
foul with me, Pistol, I will scour you with my rapier,
as I may, in fair terms. If you would walk off, I would
prick your guts a little, in good terms, as I may, and
that's the humour of it.

PISTOL

O braggart vile, and damnèd furious wight!
The grave doth gape, and doting death is near:
Therefore exhale!

They both draw

60 BARDOLPH Hear me, hear me what I say! He that strikes
the first stroke, I'll run him up to the hilts, as I am a
soldier.

He draws

PISTOL

An oath of mickle might, and fury shall abate.

Pistol and Nym sheathe their swords

Give me thy fist, thy forefoot to me give;
Thy spirits are most tall.

NYM I will cut thy throat one time or other, in fair terms,
that is the humour of it.

PISTOL

'*Couple a gorge!*'
That is the word. I thee defy again!
70 O hound of Crete, think'st thou my spouse to get?
No, to the spital go,
And from the powdering tub of infamy
Fetch forth the lazar kite of Cressid's kind,
Doll Tearsheet she by name, and her espouse.
I have, and I will hold, the quondam Quickly
For the only she; and – *pauca*, there's enough.

Go to!
> *Enter the Boy*

BOY Mine host Pistol, you must come to my master – and
you, Hostess: he is very sick, and would to bed. Good
Bardolph, put thy face between his sheets, and do the 80
office of a warming-pan. Faith, he's very ill.

BARDOLPH Away, you rogue!

HOSTESS By my troth, he'll yield the crow a pudding one
of these days; the King has killed his heart. Good
husband, come home presently.   *Exit with Boy*

BARDOLPH Come, shall I make you two friends? We must
to France together: why the devil should we keep knives
to cut one another's throats?

PISTOL
Let floods o'erswell, and fiends for food howl on!

NYM You'll pay me the eight shillings I won of you at 90
betting?

PISTOL
Base is the slave that pays!

NYM That now I will have; that's the humour of it.

PISTOL
As manhood shall compound. Push home!
> *They draw*

BARDOLPH By this sword, he that makes the first thrust,
I'll kill him! By this sword, I will.

PISTOL
Sword is an oath, and oaths must have their course.
> *He sheathes his sword*

BARDOLPH Corporal Nym, an thou wilt be friends, be
friends: an thou wilt not, why then be enemies with me
too. Prithee put up.   100

NYM I shall have my eight shillings I won of you at betting?

PISTOL
A noble shalt thou have, and present pay;

And liquor likewise will I give to thee,
And friendship shall combine, and brotherhood.
I'll live by Nym, and Nym shall live by me.
Is not this just? For I shall sutler be
Unto the camp, and profits will accrue.
Give me thy hand.

Nym sheathes his sword

NYM I shall have my noble?

PISTOL

110 In cash most justly paid.

NYM Well then, that's the humour of't.

Enter Hostess

HOSTESS As ever you came of women, come in quickly
to Sir John. Ah, poor heart! he is so shaked of a burning
quotidian tertian that it is most lamentable to behold.
Sweet men, come to him.

NYM The King hath run bad humours on the knight, that's
the even of it.

PISTOL

Nym, thou hast spoke the right;
His heart is fracted and corroborate.

120 NYM The King is a good king, but it must be as it may: he
passes some humours and careers.

PISTOL

Let us condole the knight; for, lambkins, we will live.

Exeunt

II.2   *Enter Exeter, Bedford, and Westmorland*

BEDFORD

Fore God, his grace is bold to trust these traitors.

EXETER

They shall be apprehended by and by.

WESTMORLAND

How smooth and even they do bear themselves!

As if allegiance in their bosoms sat,
Crownèd with faith and constant loyalty.

BEDFORD

The King hath note of all that they intend,
By interception which they dream not of.

EXETER

Nay, but the man that was his bedfellow,
Whom he hath dulled and cloyed with gracious
      favours –
That he should, for a foreign purse, so sell   10
His sovereign's life to death and treachery!
    Sound trumpets. Enter the King, Scroop, Cambridge,
    Grey, and attendants

KING HENRY

Now sits the wind fair, and we will aboard.
My Lord of Cambridge, and my kind Lord of
      Masham,
And you, my gentle knight, give me your thoughts.
Think you not that the powers we bear with us
Will cut their passage through the force of France,
Doing the execution and the act
For which we have in head assembled them?

SCROOP

No doubt, my liege, if each man do his best.

KING HENRY

I doubt not that, since we are well persuaded   20
We carry not a heart with us from hence
That grows not in a fair consent with ours,
Nor leave not one behind that doth not wish
Success and conquest to attend on us.

CAMBRIDGE

Never was monarch better feared and loved
Than is your majesty. There's not, I think, a subject
That sits in heart-grief and uneasiness

Under the sweet shade of your government.

GREY

True: those that were your father's enemies
30 Have steeped their galls in honey, and do serve you
With hearts create of duty and of zeal.

KING HENRY

We therefore have great cause of thankfulness,
And shall forget the office of our hand
Sooner than quittance of desert and merit
According to the weight and worthiness.

SCROOP

So service shall with steelèd sinews toil,
And labour shall refresh itself with hope
To do your grace incessant services.

KING HENRY

We judge no less. Uncle of Exeter,
40 Enlarge the man committed yesterday
That railed against our person. We consider
It was excess of wine that set him on,
And on his more advice we pardon him.

SCROOP

That's mercy, but too much security.
Let him be punished, sovereign, lest example
Breed, by his sufferance, more of such a kind.

KING HENRY

O, let us yet be merciful.

CAMBRIDGE

So may your highness, and yet punish too.

GREY

Sir,
50 You show great mercy if you give him life
After the taste of much correction.

KING HENRY

Alas, your too much love and care of me

Are heavy orisons 'gainst this poor wretch!
If little faults, proceeding on distemper,
Shall not be winked at, how shall we stretch our eye
When capital crimes, chewed, swallowed, and digested,
Appear before us? We'll yet enlarge that man,
Though Cambridge, Scroop, and Grey, in their dear
        care
And tender preservation of our person
Would have him punished. And now to our French   60
        causes:
Who are the late commissioners?

CAMBRIDGE
    I one, my lord.
Your highness bade me ask for it today.

SCROOP
    So did you me, my liege.

GREY
    And I, my royal sovereign.

KING HENRY
    Then, Richard Earl of Cambridge, there is yours;
There yours, Lord Scroop of Masham; and, sir knight,
Grey of Northumberland, this same is yours.
Read them, and know I know your worthiness.
My Lord of Westmorland, and uncle Exeter,   70
We will aboard tonight. – Why, how now, gentlemen?
What see you in those papers, that you lose
So much complexion? Look ye, how they change!
Their cheeks are paper. – Why, what read you there
That have so cowarded and chased your blood
Out of appearance?

CAMBRIDGE   I do confess my fault,
And do submit me to your highness' mercy.

GREY, SCROOP
    To which we all appeal.

KING HENRY

The mercy that was quick in us but late
80　By your own counsel is suppressed and killed.
You must not dare, for shame, to talk of mercy,
For your own reasons turn into your bosoms
As dogs upon their masters, worrying you.
See you, my Princes, and my noble peers,
These English monsters! My Lord of Cambridge here –
You know how apt our love was to accord
To furnish him with all appertinents
Belonging to his honour; and this man
Hath, for a few light crowns, lightly conspired,
90　And sworn unto the practices of France,
To kill us here in Hampton: to the which
This knight, no less for bounty bound to us
Than Cambridge is, hath likewise sworn. But O,
What shall I say to thee, Lord Scroop, thou cruel,
Ingrateful, savage, and inhuman creature?
Thou that didst bear the key of all my counsels,
That knew'st the very bottom of my soul,
That almost mightst have coined me into gold,
Wouldst thou have practised on me, for thy use?
100　May it be possible that foreign hire
Could out of thee extract one spark of evil
That might annoy my finger? 'Tis so strange
That, though the truth of it stands off as gross
As black and white, my eye will scarcely see it.
Treason and murder ever kept together,
As two yoke-devils sworn to either's purpose,
Working so grossly in a natural cause
That admiration did not whoop at them.
But thou, 'gainst all proportion, didst bring in
110　Wonder to wait on treason and on murder:
And whatsoever cunning fiend it was

That wrought upon thee so preposterously
Hath got the voice in hell for excellence.
All other devils that suggest by treasons
Do botch and bungle up damnation
With patches, colours, and with forms, being fetched
From glistering semblances of piety;
But he that tempered thee bade thee stand up,
Gave thee no instance why thou shouldst do treason,
Unless to dub thee with the name of traitor.   120
If that same demon that hath gulled thee thus
Should with his lion gait walk the whole world,
He might return to vasty Tartar back,
And tell the legions, 'I can never win
A soul so easy as that Englishman's.'
O, how hast thou with jealousy infected
The sweetness of affiance! Show men dutiful?
Why, so didst thou. Seem they grave and learnèd?
Why, so didst thou. Come they of noble family?
Why, so didst thou. Seem they religious?   130
Why, so didst thou. Or are they spare in diet,
Free from gross passion or of mirth or anger,
Constant in spirit, not swerving with the blood,
Garnished and decked in modest complement,
Not working with the eye without the ear,
And but in purgèd judgement trusting neither?
Such and so finely bolted didst thou seem:
And thus thy fall hath left a kind of blot
To mark the full-fraught man and best endued
With some suspicion. I will weep for thee;   140
For this revolt of thine, methinks, is like
Another fall of man. Their faults are open.
Arrest them to the answer of the law;
And God acquit them of their practices!
EXETER I arrest thee of high treason, by the name of

85

Richard Earl of Cambridge.
I arrest thee of high treason, by the name of Henry Lord
Scroop of Masham.
I arrest thee of high treason, by the name of Thomas
150 Grey, knight, of Northumberland.

SCROOP

Our purposes God justly hath discovered,
And I repent my fault more than my death,
Which I beseech your highness to forgive,
Although my body pay the price of it.

CAMBRIDGE

For me, the gold of France did not seduce,
Although I did admit it as a motive
The sooner to effect what I intended.
But God be thankèd for prevention,
Which I in sufferance heartily will rejoice,
160 Beseeching God and you to pardon me.

GREY

Never did faithful subject more rejoice
At the discovery of most dangerous treason
Than I do at this hour joy o'er myself,
Prevented from a damnèd enterprise.
My fault, but not my body, pardon, sovereign.

KING HENRY

God quit you in His mercy! Hear your sentence.
You have conspired against our royal person,
Joined with an enemy proclaimed, and from his coffers
Received the golden earnest of our death;
170 Wherein you would have sold your King to slaughter,
His princes and his peers to servitude,
His subjects to oppression and contempt,
And his whole kingdom into desolation.
Touching our person seek we no revenge,
But we our kingdom's safety must so tender,

Whose ruin you have sought, that to her laws
We do deliver you. Get you therefore hence,
Poor miserable wretches, to your death;
The taste whereof God of His mercy give
You patience to endure, and true repentance   180
Of all your dear offences. Bear them hence.

Exeunt Cambridge, Scroop, and Grey, guarded
Now, lords, for France; the enterprise whereof
Shall be to you, as us, like glorious.
We doubt not of a fair and lucky war,
Since God so graciously hath brought to light
This dangerous treason lurking in our way
To hinder our beginnings. We doubt not now
But every rub is smoothèd on our way.
Then forth, dear countrymen! Let us deliver
Our puissance into the hand of God,   190
Putting it straight in expedition.
Cheerly to sea! The signs of war advance!
No King of England if not King of France!

Flourish. Exeunt

Enter Pistol, Hostess, Nym, Bardolph, and Boy   II.3
HOSTESS Prithee, honey-sweet husband, let me bring thee
to Staines.
PISTOL
No, for my manly heart doth earn.
Bardolph, be blithe! Nym, rouse thy vaunting veins!
Boy, bristle thy courage up! For Falstaff, he is dead,
And we must earn therefor.
BARDOLPH Would I were with him, wheresome'er he is,
either in heaven or in hell!
HOSTESS Nay, sure, he's not in hell: he's in Arthur's
bosom, if ever man went to Arthur's bosom. 'A made 10

87

a finer end, and went away an it had been any christom
child; 'a parted e'en just between twelve and one, e'en
at the turning o'th'tide; for after I saw him fumble with
the sheets, and play with flowers, and smile upon his
fingers' ends, I knew there was but one way; for his
nose was as sharp as a pen, and 'a babbled of green
fields. 'How now, Sir John?' quoth I, 'What, man, be
o'good cheer!' So 'a cried out, 'God, God, God!' three
or four times. Now I, to comfort him, bid him 'a should
20 not think of God – I hoped there was no need to
trouble himself with any such thoughts yet. So 'a bade
me lay more clothes on his feet; I put my hand into the
bed, and felt them, and they were as cold as any stone;
then I felt to his knees, and so up'ard and up'ard, and
all was as cold as any stone.

NYM They say he cried out of sack.

HOSTESS Ay, that 'a did.

BARDOLPH And of women.

HOSTESS Nay, that 'a did not.

30 BOY Yes, that 'a did, and said they were devils incarnate.

HOSTESS 'A could never abide carnation, 'twas a colour
he never liked.

BOY 'A said once, the devil would have him about women.

HOSTESS 'A did in some sort, indeed, handle women; but
then he was rheumatic, and talked of the Whore of
Babylon.

BOY Do you not remember, 'a saw a flea stick upon Bardolph's nose, and 'a said it was a black soul burning in
hell?

40 BARDOLPH Well, the fuel is gone that maintained that
fire – that's all the riches I got in his service.

NYM Shall we shog? The King will be gone from Southampton.

PISTOL
Come, let's away. My love, give me thy lips.

Look to my chattels and my movables.
Let senses rule. The word is 'Pitch and pay!'
Trust none;
For oaths are straws, men's faiths are wafer-cakes,
And Holdfast is the only dog, my duck.
Therefore, *Caveto* be thy counsellor.   50
Go, clear thy crystals. Yoke-fellows in arms,
Let us to France, like horse-leeches, my boys,
To suck, to suck, the very blood to suck!
BOY And that's but unwholesome food, they say.
PISTOL
  Touch her soft mouth, and march.
BARDOLPH Farewell, Hostess.
      He kisses her
NYM I cannot kiss, that is the humour of it; but adieu.
PISTOL
  Let housewifery appear. Keep close, I thee command.
HOSTESS Farewell! Adieu!   *Exeunt*

      Flourish. Enter the French King, the Dauphin, the II.4
      Dukes of Berri and Britaine, the Constable and others
FRENCH KING
  Thus comes the English with full power upon us,
  And more than carefully it us concerns
  To answer royally in our defences.
  Therefore the Dukes of Berri and of Britaine,
  Of Brabant and of Orleans, shall make forth,
  And you, Prince Dauphin, with all swift dispatch,
  To line and new repair our towns of war
  With men of courage and with means defendant;
  For England his approaches makes as fierce
  As waters to the sucking of a gulf.   10
  It fits us then to be as provident
  As fear may teach us, out of late examples

Left by the fatal and neglected English
Upon our fields.

DAUPHIN   My most redoubted father,
It is most meet we arm us 'gainst the foe;
For peace itself should not so dull a kingdom,
Though war nor no known quarrel were in question,
But that defences, musters, preparations,
Should be maintained, assembled, and collected,
20 As were a war in expectation.
Therefore, I say, 'tis meet we all go forth
To view the sick and feeble parts of France:
And let us do it with no show of fear –
No, with no more than if we heard that England
Were busied with a Whitsun morris-dance;
For, my good liege, she is so idly kinged,
Her sceptre so fantastically borne
By a vain, giddy, shallow, humorous youth,
That fear attends her not.

CONSTABLE   O, peace, Prince Dauphin!
30 You are too much mistaken in this King.
Question your grace the late ambassadors,
With what great state he heard their embassy,
How well supplied with noble counsellors,
How modest in exception, and withal
How terrible in constant resolution,
And you shall find his vanities forespent
Were but the outside of the Roman Brutus,
Covering discretion with a coat of folly;
As gardeners do with ordure hide those roots
40 That shall first spring and be most delicate.

DAUPHIN
Well, 'tis not so, my Lord High Constable;
But though we think it so, it is no matter.
In cases of defence, 'tis best to weigh

The enemy more mighty than he seems.
So the proportions of defence are filled;
Which of a weak and niggardly projection
Doth like a miser spoil his coat with scanting
A little cloth.

FRENCH KING Think we King Harry strong;
And, Princes, look you strongly arm to meet him.
The kindred of him hath been fleshed upon us,   50
And he is bred out of that bloody strain
That haunted us in our familiar paths.
Witness our too much memorable shame
When Crécy battle fatally was struck,
And all our princes captived by the hand
Of that black name, Edward, Black Prince of Wales;
Whiles that his mountain sire, on mountain standing,
Up in the air, crowned with the golden sun,
Saw his heroical seed, and smiled to see him,
Mangle the work of nature, and deface   60
The patterns that by God and by French fathers
Had twenty years been made. This is a stem
Of that victorious stock; and let us fear
The native mightiness and fate of him.

    Enter a Messenger

MESSENGER
Ambassadors from Harry King of England
Do crave admittance to your majesty.

FRENCH KING
We'll give them present audience. Go and bring them.
                Exeunt Messenger and certain lords
You see this chase is hotly followed, friends.

DAUPHIN
Turn head, and stop pursuit, for coward dogs
Most spend their mouths when what they seem to   70
    threaten

Runs far before them. Good my sovereign,
Take up the English short, and let them know
Of what a monarchy you are the head.
Self-love, my liege, is not so vile a sin
As self-neglecting.

Enter lords, with Exeter and train

FRENCH KING   From our brother of England?

EXETER

From him; and thus he greets your majesty:
He wills you, in the name of God Almighty,
That you divest yourself, and lay apart
The borrowed glories that by gift of heaven,
80   By law of nature and of nations, 'longs
To him and to his heirs – namely, the crown,
And all wide-stretchèd honours that pertain
By custom and the ordinance of times
Unto the crown of France. That you may know
'Tis no sinister nor no awkward claim
Picked from the worm-holes of long-vanished days,
Nor from the dust of old oblivion raked,
He sends you this most memorable line,
In every branch truly demonstrative,
90   Willing you overlook this pedigree;
And when you find him evenly derived
From his most famed of famous ancestors,
Edward the Third, he bids you then resign
Your crown and kingdom, indirectly held
From him, the native and true challenger.

FRENCH KING

Or else what follows?

EXETER

Bloody constraint; for if you hide the crown
Even in your hearts, there will he rake for it.
Therefore in fierce tempest is he coming,

In thunder and in earthquake, like a Jove, 100
That, if requiring fail, he will compel;
And bids you, in the bowels of the Lord,
Deliver up the crown, and to take mercy
On the poor souls for whom this hungry war
Opens his vasty jaws; and on your head
Turning the widows' tears, the orphans' cries,
The dead men's blood, the privèd maidens' groans,
For husbands, fathers, and betrothèd lovers
That shall be swallowed in this controversy.
This is his claim, his threatening, and my message – 110
Unless the Dauphin be in presence here,
To whom expressly I bring greeting too.

FRENCH KING

For us, we will consider of this further.
Tomorrow shall you bear our full intent
Back to our brother of England.

DAUPHIN   For the Dauphin,
I stand here for him. What to him from England?

EXETER

Scorn and defiance, slight regard, contempt,
And anything that may not misbecome
The mighty sender, doth he prize you at.
Thus says my King: an if your father's highness 120
Do not, in grant of all demands at large,
Sweeten the bitter mock you sent his majesty,
He'll call you to so hot an answer of it
That caves and womby vaultages of France
Shall chide your trespass, and return your mock
In second accent of his ordinance.

DAUPHIN

Say, if my father render fair return,
It is against my will, for I desire
Nothing but odds with England. To that end,

130 As matching to his youth and vanity,
I did present him with the Paris balls.

EXETER
He'll make your Paris Louvre shake for it,
Were it the mistress court of mighty Europe:
And, be assured, you'll find a difference,
As we his subjects have in wonder found,
Between the promise of his greener days
And these he masters now. Now he weighs time
Even to the utmost grain; that you shall read
In your own losses, if he stay in France.

FRENCH KING
140 Tomorrow shall you know our mind at full.
Flourish

EXETER
Dispatch us with all speed, lest that our King
Come here himself to question our delay,
For he is footed in this land already.

FRENCH KING
You shall be soon dispatched with fair conditions.
A night is but small breath and little pause
To answer matters of this consequence.   *Exeunt*

*

III   *Flourish. Enter Chorus*
CHORUS
Thus with imagined wing our swift scene flies
In motion of no less celerity
Than that of thought. Suppose that you have seen
The well-appointed King at Hampton pier
Embark his royalty, and his brave fleet
With silken streamers the young Phoebus fanning.

Play with your fancies, and in them behold
Upon the hempen tackle ship-boys climbing;
Hear the shrill whistle which doth order give
To sounds confused; behold the threaden sails,   10
Borne with th'invisible and creeping wind,
Draw the huge bottoms through the furrowed sea,
Breasting the lofty surge. O, do but think
You stand upon the rivage and behold
A city on th'inconstant billows dancing;
For so appears this fleet majestical,
Holding due course to Harfleur. Follow, follow!
Grapple your minds to sternage of this navy,
And leave your England, as dead midnight still,
Guarded with grandsires, babies, and old women,   20
Either past or not arrived to pith and puissance.
For who is he whose chin is but enriched
With one appearing hair that will not follow
These culled and choice-drawn cavaliers to France?
Work, work your thoughts, and therein see a siege:
Behold the ordnance on their carriages,
With fatal mouths gaping on girded Harfleur.
Suppose th'ambassador from the French comes back;
Tells Harry that the King doth offer him
Katherine his daughter, and with her, to dowry,   30
Some petty and unprofitable dukedoms.
The offer likes not; and the nimble gunner
With linstock now the devilish cannon touches,
    Alarum, and chambers go off
And down goes all before them. Still be kind,
And eke out our performance with your mind.   *Exit*

Alarum. Enter the King, Exeter, Bedford, Gloucester,
        other lords, and soldiers with scaling-ladders

KING HENRY

    Once more unto the breach, dear friends, once more,
    Or close the wall up with our English dead!
    In peace there's nothing so becomes a man
    As modest stillness and humility:
    But when the blast of war blows in our ears,
    Then imitate the action of the tiger;
    Stiffen the sinews, conjure up the blood,
    Disguise fair nature with hard-favoured rage;
    Then lend the eye a terrible aspect;
10   Let it pry through the portage of the head
    Like the brass cannon; let the brow o'erwhelm it
    As fearfully as doth a gallèd rock
    O'erhang and jutty his confounded base,
    Swilled with the wild and wasteful ocean.
    Now set the teeth, and stretch the nostril wide,
    Hold hard the breath, and bend up every spirit
    To his full height! On, on, you noblest English,
    Whose blood is fet from fathers of war-proof! –
    Fathers that, like so many Alexanders,
20   Have in these parts from morn till even fought,
    And sheathed their swords for lack of argument.
    Dishonour not your mothers; now attest
    That those whom you called fathers did beget you!
    Be copy now to men of grosser blood,
    And teach them how to war. And you, good yeomen,
    Whose limbs were made in England, show us here
    The mettle of your pasture; let us swear
    That you are worth your breeding – which I doubt not;
    For there is none of you so mean and base
30   That hath not noble lustre in your eyes.
    I see you stand like greyhounds in the slips,

Straining upon the start. The game's afoot!
Follow your spirit, and upon this charge
Cry, 'God for Harry, England, and Saint George!'
Exeunt. Alarum, and chambers go off

Enter Nym, Bardolph, Pistol, and Boy

BARDOLPH On, on, on, on, on! To the breach, to the
breach!

NYM Pray thee, Corporal, stay – the knocks are too hot,
and, for mine own part, I have not a case of lives. The
humour of it is too hot, that is the very plainsong of it.

PISTOL
The plainsong is most just; for humours do abound.
Knocks go and come; God's vassals drop and die;
And sword and shield,
In bloody field,
Doth win immortal fame.   10

BOY Would I were in an alehouse in London! I would
give all my fame for a pot of ale, and safety.

PISTOL And I:
If wishes would prevail with me,
My purpose should not fail with me,
But thither would I hie.

BOY   As duly,
But not as truly,
As bird doth sing on bough.
Enter Fluellen

FLUELLEN Up to the breach, you dogs! Avaunt, you 20
cullions!
He drives them forward

PISTOL
Be merciful, great Duke, to men of mould!
Abate thy rage, abate thy manly rage,

III.2

Abate thy rage, great Duke!

Good bawcock, bate thy rage! Use lenity, sweet chuck!

NYM These be good humours! Your honour wins bad humours.   *Exeunt all but the Boy*

BOY As young as I am, I have observed these three swashers. I am boy to them all three, but all they three, though they would serve me, could not be man to me; for indeed three such antics do not amount to a man. For Bardolph, he is white-livered and red-faced; by the means whereof 'a faces it out, but fights not. For Pistol, he hath a killing tongue, and a quiet sword; by the means whereof 'a breaks words, and keeps whole weapons. For Nym, he hath heard that men of few words are the best men; and therefore he scorns to say his prayers, lest 'a should be thought a coward; but his few bad words are matched with as few good deeds, for 'a never broke any man's head but his own, and that was against a post, when he was drunk. They will steal anything, and call it purchase. Bardolph stole a lute-case, bore it twelve leagues, and sold it for three half-pence. Nym and Bardolph are sworn brothers in filching, and in Calais they stole a fire-shovel – I knew by that piece of service the men would carry coals. They would have me as familiar with men's pockets as their gloves or their handkerchers: which makes much against my manhood, if I should take from another's pocket to put into mine; for it is plain pocketing up of wrongs. I must leave them, and seek some better service. Their villainy goes against my weak stomach, and therefore I must cast it up.   *Exit*

Enter Fluellen, Gower following

GOWER Captain Fluellen, you must come presently to the mines. The Duke of Gloucester would speak with you.

FLUELLEN To the mines? Tell you the Duke, it is not so

good to come to the mines, for, look you, the mines is
not according to the disciplines of the war. The con-
cavities of it is not sufficient; for, look you, th'athversary,
you may discuss unto the Duke, look you, is digt him- 60
self four yard under the countermines. By Cheshu, I
think 'a will plow up all, if there is not better directions.

GOWER The Duke of Gloucester, to whom the order of the
siege is given, is altogether directed by an Irishman, a
very valiant gentleman, i'faith.

FLUELLEN It is Captain Macmorris, is it not?

GOWER I think it be.

FLUELLEN By Cheshu, he is an ass, as in the world; I
will verify as much in his beard. He has no more
directions in the true disciplines of the wars, look you, 70
of the Roman disciplines, than is a puppy-dog.

Enter Captain Macmorris and Captain Jamy

GOWER Here 'a comes, and the Scots captain, Captain
Jamy, with him.

FLUELLEN Captain Jamy is a marvellous falorous gentleman, that is certain, and of great expedition and
knowledge in th'aunchient wars, upon my particular
knowledge of his directions. By Cheshu, he will maintain
his argument as well as any military man in the world, in
the disciplines of the pristine wars of the Romans.

JAMY I say gud-day, Captain Fluellen.   80

FLUELLEN Good-e'en to your worship, good Captain
James.

GOWER How now, Captain Macmorris, have you quit the
mines? Have the pioneers given o'er?

MACMORRIS By Chrish, la, 'tish ill done! The work ish
give over, the trompet sound the retreat. By my hand
I swear, and my father's soul, the work ish ill done: it
ish give over. I would have blowed up the town, so
Chrish save me, la, in an hour. O, 'tish ill done, 'tish ill

90   done – by my hand, 'tish ill done!

   FLUELLEN Captain Macmorris, I beseech you now, will
you voutsafe me, look you, a few disputations with you,
as partly touching or concerning the disciplines of the
war, the Roman wars, in the way of argument, look you,
and friendly communication? – partly to satisfy my
opinion, and partly for the satisfaction, look you, of my
mind – as touching the direction of the military discipline, that is the point.

   JAMY It sall be vary gud, gud feith, gud captens bath, and
100   I sall quit you with gud leve, as I may pick occasion: that
sall I, marry.

   MACMORRIS It is no time to discourse, so Chrish save me!
The day is hot, and the weather, and the wars, and the
King, and the Dukes – it is no time to discourse, the
town is beseeched, and the trumpet call us to the breach,
and we talk, and, be Chrish, do nothing; 'tis shame for us
all: so God sa' me, 'tis shame to stand still, it is shame, by
my hand – and there is throats to be cut, and works to be
done, and there ish nothing done, so Chrish sa' me, la!

110   JAMY By the mess, ere theise eyes of mine take themselves to slomber, ay'll de gud service, or ay'll lig
i'th'grund for it, ay, or go to death! And ay'll pay't as
valorously as I may, that sall I suerly do, that is the
breff and the long. Marry, I wad full fain hear some
question 'tween you tway.

   FLUELLEN Captain Macmorris, I think, look you, under
your correction, there is not many of your nation –

   MACMORRIS Of my nation? What ish my nation? Ish a
villain, and a bastard, and a knave, and a rascal. What
120   ish my nation? Who talks of my nation?

   FLUELLEN Look you, if you take the matter otherwise
than is meant, Captain Macmorris, peradventure I shall
think you do not use me with that affability as in dis-

cretion you ought to use me, look you, being as good a
man as yourself, both in the disciplines of war, and in
the derivation of my birth, and in other particularities.

MACMORRIS I do not know you so good a man as myself.
So Chrish save me, I will cut off your head.

GOWER Gentlemen both, you will mistake each other.

JAMY Ah, that's a foul fault! 130

A parley is sounded

GOWER The town sounds a parley.

FLUELLEN Captain Macmorris, when there is more
better opportunity to be required, look you, I will be
so bold as to tell you, I know the disciplines of war; and
there is an end. *Exeunt*

Some citizens of Harfleur appear on the walls. Enter III.3
the King and all his train before the gates

KING HENRY
How yet resolves the Governor of the town?
This is the latest parle we will admit:
Therefore to our best mercy give yourselves,
Or, like to men proud of destruction,
Defy us to our worst; for, as I am a soldier,
A name that in my thoughts becomes me best,
If I begin the battery once again,
I will not leave the half-achievèd Harfleur
Till in her ashes she lie burièd.
The gates of mercy shall be all shut up, 10
And the fleshed soldier, rough and hard of heart,
In liberty of bloody hand shall range
With conscience wide as hell, mowing like grass
Your fresh fair virgins, and your flowering infants.
What is it then to me, if impious war,
Arrayed in flames, like to the prince of fiends,

Do, with his smirched complexion, all fell feats
Enlinked to waste and desolation?
What is't to me, when you yourselves are cause,
20 If your pure maidens fall into the hand
Of hot and forcing violation?
What rein can hold licentious wickedness
When down the hill he holds his fierce career?
We may as bootless spend our vain command
Upon th'enragèd soldiers in their spoil
As send precepts to the leviathan
To come ashore. Therefore, you men of Harfleur,
Take pity of your town and of your people
Whiles yet my soldiers are in my command,
30 Whiles yet the cool and temperate wind of grace
O'erblows the filthy and contagious clouds
Of heady murder, spoil, and villainy.
If not, why, in a moment look to see
The blind and bloody soldier with foul hand
Defile the locks of your shrill-shrieking daughters;
Your fathers taken by the silver beards,
And their most reverend heads dashed to the walls;
Your naked infants spitted upon pikes,
Whiles the mad mothers with their howls confused
40 Do break the clouds, as did the wives of Jewry
At Herod's bloody-hunting slaughtermen.
What say you? Will you yield, and this avoid?
Or, guilty in defence, be thus destroyed?
Enter the Governor on the wall

GOVERNOR
Our expectation hath this day an end.
The Dauphin, whom of succours we entreated,
Returns us that his powers are yet not ready
To raise so great a siege. Therefore, great King,
We yield our town and lives to thy soft mercy.

Enter our gates, dispose of us and ours,
For we no longer are defensible.   50

KING HENRY
Open your gates.   *Exit Governor*
     Come, uncle Exeter,
Go you and enter Harfleur; there remain,
And fortify it strongly 'gainst the French.
Use mercy to them all. For us, dear uncle,
The winter coming on, and sickness growing
Upon our soldiers, we will retire to Calais.
Tonight in Harfleur will we be your guest;
Tomorrow for the march are we addressed.
  Flourish, and enter the town

  Enter Katherine and Alice, an old gentlewoman III.4

KATHERINE Alice, tu as été en Angleterre, et tu parles
 bien le langage.

ALICE Un peu, madame.

KATHERINE Je te prie, m'enseignez – il faut que j'apprenne
 à parler. Comment appelez-vous la main en anglais?

ALICE La main? Elle est appelée de hand.

KATHERINE De hand. Et les doigts?

ALICE Les doigts? Ma foi, j'oublie les doigts, mais je me
 souviendrai. Les doigts? Je pense qu'ils sont appelés
 de fingres; oui, de fingres.   10

KATHERINE La main, de hand; les doigts, de fingres. Je
 pense que je suis le bon écolier; j'ai gagné deux mots
 d'anglais vitement. Comment appelez-vous les ongles?

ALICE Les ongles? Nous les appelons de nailès.

KATHERINE De nailès. Écoutez: dites-moi si je parle
 bien – de hand, de fingres, et de nailès.

ALICE C'est bien dit, madame. Il est fort bon anglais.

KATHERINE Dites-moi l'anglais pour le bras.

ALICE De arm, madame.

20 KATHERINE Et le coude?

ALICE D'elbow.

KATHERINE D'elbow. Je m'en fais la répétition de tous
les mots que vous m'avez appris dès à présent.

ALICE Il est trop difficile, madame, comme je pense.

KATHERINE Excusez-moi, Alice; écoutez – d'hand, de
fingre, de nailès, d'arma, de bilbow.

ALICE D'elbow, madame.

KATHERINE O Seigneur Dieu, je m'en oublie! D'elbow.
Comment appelez-vous le col?

30 ALICE De nick, madame.

KATHERINE De nick. Et le menton?

ALICE De chin.

KATHERINE De sin. Le col, de nick; le menton, de sin.

ALICE Oui. Sauf votre honneur, en vérité, vous prononcez
les mots aussi droit que les natifs d'Angleterre.

KATHERINE Je ne doute point d'apprendre, par la grace
de Dieu, et en peu de temps.

ALICE N'avez-vous pas déjà oublié ce que je vous ai
enseigné?

40 KATHERINE Non, je réciterai à vous promptement: d'hand,
de fingre, de mailès –

ALICE De nailès, madame.

KATHERINE De nailès, de arm, de ilbow –

ALICE Sauf votre honneur, d'elbow.

KATHERINE Ainsi dis-je: d'elbow, de nick, et de sin.
Comment appelez-vous le pied et la robe?

ALICE Le foot, madame, et le count.

KATHERINE Le foot, et le count? O Seigneur Dieu! Ils
sont mots de son mauvais, corruptible, gros, et impu-
50 dique, et non pour les dames d'honneur d'user. Je ne
voudrais prononcer ces mots devant les seigneurs de
France pour tout le monde. Foh! Le foot et le count!

Néanmoins, je réciterai une autre fois ma leçon en-
semble: d'hand, de fingre, de nailès, d'arm, d'elbow, de
nick, de sin, de foot, le count.

ALICE Excellent, madame!

KATHERINE C'est assez pour une fois. Allons-nous à
dîner. *Exeunt*

Enter the King of France, the Dauphin, the Duke of III.5
Britaine, the Constable of France, and others

FRENCH KING
'Tis certain he hath passed the River Somme.

CONSTABLE
And if he be not fought withal, my lord,
Let us not live in France: let us quit all,
And give our vineyards to a barbarous people.

DAUPHIN
O Dieu vivant! Shall a few sprays of us,
The emptying of our fathers' luxury,
Our scions, put in wild and savage stock,
Spirt up so suddenly into the clouds,
And overlook their grafters?

BRITAINE
Normans, but bastard Normans, Norman bastards!   10
Mort Dieu! Ma vie! If they march along
Unfought withal, but I will sell my dukedom
To buy a slobbery and a dirty farm
In that nook-shotten isle of Albion.

CONSTABLE
Dieu de batailles! Where have they this mettle?
Is not their climate foggy, raw, and dull,
On whom, as in despite, the sun looks pale,
Killing their fruit with frowns? Can sodden water,
A drench for sur-reined jades, their barley broth,

20 Decoct their cold blood to such valiant heat?
  And shall our quick blood, spirited with wine,
  Seem frosty? O, for honour of our land,
  Let us not hang like roping icicles
  Upon our houses' thatch, whiles a more frosty people
  Sweat drops of gallant youth in our rich fields! –
  Lest poor we call them in their native lords.

DAUPHIN

  By faith and honour,
  Our madams mock at us, and plainly say
  Our mettle is bred out, and they will give
30 Their bodies to the lust of English youth,
  To new-store France with bastard warriors.

BRITAINE

  They bid us to the English dancing-schools,
  And teach lavoltas high and swift corantos,
  Saying our grace is only in our heels,
  And that we are most lofty runaways.

FRENCH KING

  Where is Montjoy the Herald? Speed him hence,
  Let him greet England with our sharp defiance.
  Up, Princes, and with spirit of honour edged,
  More sharper than your swords, hie to the field!
40 Charles Delabreth, High Constable of France,
  You Dukes of Orleans, Bourbon, and of Berri,
  Alençon, Brabant, Bar, and Burgundy,
  Jaques Chatillon, Rambures, Vaudemont,
  Beaumont, Grandpré, Roussi, and Faulconbridge,
  Foix, Lestrake, Bouciqualt, and Charolois,
  High Dukes, great Princes, Barons, Lords, and
        Knights,
  For your great seats, now quit you of great shames.
  Bar Harry England, that sweeps through our land
  With pennons painted in the blood of Harfleur!

Rush on his host, as doth the melted snow   50
Upon the valleys, whose low vassal seat
The Alps doth spit and void his rheum upon!
Go down upon him, you have power enough,
And in a captive chariot into Rouen
Bring him our prisoner.

CONSTABLE   This becomes the great.
Sorry am I his numbers are so few,
His soldiers sick, and famished in their march;
For I am sure, when he shall see our army,
He'll drop his heart into the sink of fear,
And for achievement offer us his ransom.   60

FRENCH KING
Therefore, Lord Constable, haste on Montjoy,
And let him say to England that we send
To know what willing ransom he will give.
Prince Dauphin, you shall stay with us in Rouen.

DAUPHIN
Not so, I do beseech your majesty.

FRENCH KING
Be patient, for you shall remain with us.
Now forth, Lord Constable, and Princes all,
And quickly bring us word of England's fall.   *Exeunt*

Enter Captains, English and Welsh (*Gower and Fluellen*)   III.6
GOWER How now, Captain Fluellen? Come you from the
    bridge?
FLUELLEN I assure you, there is very excellent services
    committed at the bridge.
GOWER Is the Duke of Exeter safe?
FLUELLEN The Duke of Exeter is as magnanimous as
    Agamemnon, and a man that I love and honour with my
    soul, and my heart, and my duty, and my live, and my

living, and my uttermost power. He is not – God be
praised and blessed! – any hurt in the world, but keeps
the bridge most valiantly, with excellent discipline.
There is an aunchient lieutenant there at the pridge, I
think in my very conscience he is as valiant a man as
Mark Antony, and he is a man of no estimation in the
world, but I did see him do as gallant service.

GOWER What do you call him?

FLUELLEN He is called Aunchient Pistol.

GOWER I know him not.

Enter Pistol

FLUELLEN Here is the man.

PISTOL

Captain, I thee beseech to do me favours.

The Duke of Exeter doth love thee well.

FLUELLEN Ay, I praise God, and I have merited some love
at his hands.

PISTOL

Bardolph, a soldier firm and sound of heart,

And of buxom valour, hath, by cruel fate,

And giddy Fortune's furious fickle wheel,

That goddess blind,

That stands upon the rolling restless stone –

FLUELLEN By your patience, Aunchient Pistol: Fortune
is painted blind, with a muffler afore her eyes, to signify
to you that Fortune is blind; and she is painted also
with a wheel, to signify to you, which is the moral of it,
that she is turning, and inconstant, and mutability, and
variation; and her foot, look you, is fixed upon a
spherical stone, which rolls, and rolls, and rolls. In
good truth, the poet makes a most excellent description
of it: Fortune is an excellent moral.

PISTOL

Fortune is Bardolph's foe, and frowns on him;

For he hath stolen a pax, and hangèd must 'a be –
A damnèd death!   40
Let gallows gape for dog; let man go free,
And let not hemp his windpipe suffocate.
But Exeter hath given the doom of death
For pax of little price.
Therefore go speak – the Duke will hear thy voice;
And let not Bardolph's vital thread be cut
With edge of penny cord and vile reproach.
Speak, Captain, for his life, and I will thee requite.

FLUELLEN Aunchient Pistol, I do partly understand your
meaning.   50

PISTOL
Why then, rejoice therefor!

FLUELLEN Certainly, Aunchient, it is not a thing to
rejoice at, for if, look you, he were my brother, I would
desire the Duke to use his good pleasure, and put him to
execution; for discipline ought to be used.

PISTOL
Die and be damned! and *figo* for thy friendship.

FLUELLEN It is well.

PISTOL
The fig of Spain!   *Exit*

FLUELLEN Very good.

GOWER Why, this is an arrant counterfeit rascal, I 60
remember him now – a bawd, a cutpurse.

FLUELLEN I'll assure you, 'a uttered as prave words at
the pridge as you shall see in a summer's day. But it is
very well; what he has spoke to me, that is well, I
warrant you, when time is serve.

GOWER Why, 'tis a gull, a fool, a rogue, that now and then
goes to the wars, to grace himself at his return into
London under the form of a soldier. And such fellows
are perfect in the great commanders' names, and they

70   will learn you by rote where services were done: at such
and such a sconce, at such a breach, at such a convoy;
who came off bravely, who was shot, who disgraced,
what terms the enemy stood on; and this they con
perfectly in the phrase of war, which they trick up with
new-tuned oaths: and what a beard of the general's
cut and a horrid suit of the camp will do among foaming
bottles and ale-washed wits is wonderful to be thought
on. But you must learn to know such slanders of the
age, or else you may be marvellously mistook.

80 FLUELLEN I tell you what, Captain Gower; I do perceive
he is not the man that he would gladly make show to
the world he is. If I find a hole in his coat, I will tell
him my mind. (*Drum within*) Hark you, the King is
coming, and I must speak with him from the pridge.

> *Drum and colours. Enter the King and his poor*
> *soldiers, with Gloucester*

God pless your majesty!

KING HENRY

How now, Fluellen, cam'st thou from the bridge?

FLUELLEN Ay, so please your majesty. The Duke of
Exeter has very gallantly maintained the pridge. The
French is gone off, look you, and there is gallant and
90 most prave passages. Marry, th'athversary was have
possession of the pridge, but he is enforced to retire,
and the Duke of Exeter is master of the pridge. I can
tell your majesty, the Duke is a prave man.

KING HENRY What men have you lost, Fluellen?

FLUELLEN The perdition of th'athversary hath been very
great, reasonable great. Marry, for my part, I think the
Duke hath lost never a man, but one that is like to be
executed for robbing a church, one Bardolph, if your
majesty know the man: his face is all bubukles, and
100 whelks, and knobs, and flames o'fire; and his lips blows

at his nose, and it is like a coal of fire, sometimes plue,
and sometimes red; but his nose is executed, and his
fire's out.

KING HENRY We would have all such offenders so cut
off: and we give express charge, that in our marches
through the country there be nothing compelled from
the villages, nothing taken but paid for, none of the
French upbraided or abused in disdainful language;
for when lenity and cruelty play for a kingdom, the
gentler gamester is the soonest winner.   110

    Tucket. Enter Montjoy

MONTJOY You know me by my habit.

KING HENRY Well then, I know thee: what shall I know
of thee?

MONTJOY My master's mind.

KING HENRY Unfold it.

MONTJOY Thus says my King: 'Say thou to Harry of
England, Though we seemed dead, we did but sleep.
Advantage is a better soldier than rashness. Tell him
we could have rebuked him at Harfleur, but that we
thought not good to bruise an injury till it were full   120
ripe. Now we speak upon our cue, and our voice is
imperial: England shall repent his folly, see his weakness,
and admire our sufferance. Bid him therefore consider
of his ransom, which must proportion the losses we
have borne, the subjects we have lost, the disgrace we
have digested; which in weight to re-answer, his petti-
ness would bow under. For our losses, his exchequer is
too poor; for th'effusion of our blood, the muster of his
kingdom too faint a number; and for our disgrace, his
own person kneeling at our feet but a weak and worth-   130
less satisfaction. To this add defiance: and tell him for
conclusion, he hath betrayed his followers, whose
condemnation is pronounced.' So far my King and

    master; so much my office.

KING HENRY

    What is thy name? I know thy quality.

MONTJOY Montjoy.

KING HENRY

    Thou dost thy office fairly. Turn thee back,
    And tell thy King I do not seek him now,
    But could be willing to march on to Calais
140   Without impeachment: for, to say the sooth,
    Though 'tis no wisdom to confess so much
    Unto an enemy of craft and vantage,
    My people are with sickness much enfeebled,
    My numbers lessened, and those few I have
    Almost no better than so many French;
    Who when they were in health, I tell thee, Herald,
    I thought upon one pair of English legs
    Did march three Frenchmen. Yet forgive me, God,
    That I do brag thus! This your air of France
150   Hath blown that vice in me – I must repent.
    Go, therefore, tell thy master here I am;
    My ransom is this frail and worthless trunk;
    My army but a weak and sickly guard:
    Yet, God before, tell him we will come on,
    Though France himself, and such another neighbour,
    Stand in our way. There's for thy labour, Montjoy.
    Go bid thy master well advise himself:
    If we may pass, we will; if we be hindered,
    We shall your tawny ground with your red blood
160   Discolour: and so, Montjoy, fare you well.
    The sum of all our answer is but this:
    We would not seek a battle as we are,
    Nor, as we are, we say we will not shun it.
    So tell your master.

MONTJOY

    I shall deliver so. Thanks to your highness.   *Exit*

GLOUCESTER

  I hope they will not come upon us now.

KING HENRY

  We are in God's hand, brother, not in theirs.

  March to the bridge; it now draws toward night.

  Beyond the river we'll encamp ourselves,

  And on tomorrow bid them march away.   170

Exeunt

Enter the Constable of France, the Lord Rambures, III.7
Orleans, Dauphin, with others

CONSTABLE Tut! I have the best armour of the world. Would it were day!

ORLEANS You have an excellent armour; but let my horse have his due.

CONSTABLE It is the best horse of Europe.

ORLEANS Will it never be morning?

DAUPHIN My Lord of Orleans, and my Lord High Constable, you talk of horse and armour?

ORLEANS You are as well provided of both as any prince in the world.   10

DAUPHIN What a long night is this! I will not change my horse with any that treads but on four pasterns. *Ça, ha!* He bounds from the earth as if his entrails were hairs – *le cheval volant*, the Pegasus, *chez les narines de feu!* When I bestride him, I soar, I am a hawk. He trots the air; the earth sings when he touches it; the basest horn of his hoof is more musical than the pipe of Hermes.

ORLEANS He's of the colour of the nutmeg.

DAUPHIN And of the heat of the ginger. It is a beast for Perseus: he is pure air and fire; and the dull elements of 20 earth and water never appear in him, but only in patient stillness while his rider mounts him. He is indeed a horse, and all other jades you may call beasts.

CONSTABLE Indeed, my lord, it is a most absolute and excellent horse.

DAUPHIN It is the prince of palfreys; his neigh is like the bidding of a monarch, and his countenance enforces homage.

ORLEANS No more, cousin.

30 DAUPHIN Nay, the man hath no wit that cannot, from the rising of the lark to the lodging of the lamb, vary deserved praise on my palfrey. It is a theme as fluent as the sea: turn the sands into eloquent tongues, and my horse is argument for them all. 'Tis a subject for a sovereign to reason on, and for a sovereign's sovereign to ride on; and for the world, familiar to us and unknown, to lay apart their particular functions and wonder at him. I once writ a sonnet in his praise, and began thus: 'Wonder of nature –'.

40 ORLEANS I have heard a sonnet begin so to one's mistress.

DAUPHIN Then did they imitate that which I composed to my courser, for my horse is my mistress.

ORLEANS Your mistress bears well.

DAUPHIN Me well, which is the prescript praise and perfection of a good and particular mistress.

CONSTABLE Nay, for methought yesterday your mistress shrewdly shook your back.

DAUPHIN So perhaps did yours.

CONSTABLE Mine was not bridled.

50 DAUPHIN O, then belike she was old and gentle, and you rode like a kern of Ireland, your French hose off, and in your strait strossers.

CONSTABLE You have good judgement in horsemanship.

DAUPHIN Be warned by me, then: they that ride so, and ride not warily, fall into foul bogs. I had rather have my horse to my mistress.

CONSTABLE I had as lief have my mistress a jade.

DAUPHIN I tell thee, Constable, my mistress wears his own hair.

CONSTABLE I could make as true a boast as that, if I had 60 a sow to my mistress.

DAUPHIN '*Le chien est retourné à son propre vomissement, et la truie lavée au bourbier*': thou mak'st use of anything.

CONSTABLE Yet do I not use my horse for my mistress, or any such proverb so little kin to the purpose.

RAMBURES My Lord Constable, the armour that I saw in your tent tonight – are those stars or suns upon it?

CONSTABLE Stars, my lord.

DAUPHIN Some of them will fall tomorrow, I hope.

CONSTABLE And yet my sky shall not want. 70

DAUPHIN That may be, for you bear a many super-fluously, and 'twere more honour some were away.

CONSTABLE E'en as your horse bears your praises, who would trot as well were some of your brags dis-mounted.

DAUPHIN Would I were able to load him with his desert! Will it never be day? I will trot tomorrow a mile, and my way shall be paved with English faces.

CONSTABLE I will not say so, for fear I should be faced out of my way; but I would it were morning, for I 80 would fain be about the ears of the English.

RAMBURES Who will go to hazard with me for twenty prisoners?

CONSTABLE You must first go yourself to hazard ere you have them.

DAUPHIN 'Tis midnight: I'll go arm myself. *Exit*

ORLEANS The Dauphin longs for morning.

RAMBURES He longs to eat the English.

CONSTABLE I think he will eat all he kills.

ORLEANS By the white hand of my lady, he's a gallant 90 prince.

CONSTABLE Swear by her foot, that she may tread out
the oath.

ORLEANS He is simply the most active gentleman of
France.

CONSTABLE Doing is activity, and he will still be doing.

ORLEANS He never did harm, that I heard of.

CONSTABLE Nor will do none tomorrow: he will keep that
good name still.

100 ORLEANS I know him to be valiant.

CONSTABLE I was told that, by one that knows him better
than you.

ORLEANS What's he?

CONSTABLE Marry, he told me so himself, and he said he
cared not who knew it.

ORLEANS He needs not; it is no hidden virtue in him.

CONSTABLE By my faith, sir, but it is; never anybody
saw it but his lackey. 'Tis a hooded valour, and when it
appears it will bate.

110 ORLEANS Ill will never said well.

CONSTABLE I will cap that proverb with 'There is flattery
in friendship.'

ORLEANS And I will take up that with 'Give the devil his
due!'

CONSTABLE Well placed! There stands your friend for the
devil. Have at the very eye of that proverb with 'A pox
of the devil!'

ORLEANS You are the better at proverbs by how much 'A
fool's bolt is soon shot.'

120 CONSTABLE You have shot over.

ORLEANS 'Tis not the first time you were overshot.

Enter a Messenger

MESSENGER My Lord High Constable, the English lie
within fifteen hundred paces of your tents.

CONSTABLE Who hath measured the ground?

MESSENGER The Lord Grandpré.

CONSTABLE A valiant and most expert gentleman. Would
it were day! Alas, poor Harry of England! He longs not
for the dawning as we do.

ORLEANS What a wretched and peevish fellow is this King
of England, to mope with his fat-brained followers so far 130
out of his knowledge.

CONSTABLE If the English had any apprehension, they
would run away.

ORLEANS That they lack; for if their heads had any
intellectual armour, they could never wear such heavy
head-pieces.

RAMBURES That island of England breeds very valiant
creatures: their mastiffs are of unmatchable courage.

ORLEANS Foolish curs, that run winking into the mouth
of a Russian bear, and have their heads crushed like 140
rotten apples! You may as well say that's a valiant flea
that dare eat his breakfast on the lip of a lion.

CONSTABLE Just, just: and the men do sympathize with
the mastiffs in robustious and rough coming on,
leaving their wits with their wives; and then, give them
great meals of beef, and iron and steel; they will eat
like wolves, and fight like devils.

ORLEANS Ay, but these English are shrewdly out of beef.

CONSTABLE Then shall we find tomorrow they have only
stomachs to eat, and none to fight. Now is it time to 150
arm. Come, shall we about it?

ORLEANS

It is now two o'clock: but, let me see – by ten
We shall have each a hundred Englishmen.   *Exeunt*

*

Flourish. Enter Chorus

CHORUS

Now entertain conjecture of a time
When creeping murmur and the poring dark
Fills the wide vessel of the universe.
From camp to camp, through the foul womb of night,
The hum of either army stilly sounds,
That the fixed sentinels almost receive
The secret whispers of each other's watch.
Fire answers fire, and through their paly flames
Each battle sees the other's umbered face.
10 Steed threatens steed, in high and boastful neighs,
Piercing the night's dull ear; and from the tents
The armourers, accomplishing the knights,
With busy hammers closing rivets up,
Give dreadful note of preparation.
The country cocks do crow, the clocks do toll,
And the third hour of drowsy morning name.
Proud of their numbers, and secure in soul,
The confident and over-lusty French
Do the low-rated English play at dice,
20 And chide the cripple tardy-gaited night
Who like a foul and ugly witch doth limp
So tediously away. The poor condemnèd English,
Like sacrifices, by their watchful fires
Sit patiently, and inly ruminate
The morning's danger; and their gesture sad,
Investing lank-lean cheeks and war-worn coats,
Presenteth them unto the gazing moon
So many horrid ghosts. O now, who will behold
The royal Captain of this ruined band
30 Walking from watch to watch, from tent to tent,
Let him cry, 'Praise and glory on his head!'
For forth he goes and visits all his host,

Bids them good morrow with a modest smile,
And calls them brothers, friends, and countrymen.
Upon his royal face there is no note
How dread an army hath enrounded him,
Nor doth he dedicate one jot of colour
Unto the weary and all-watchèd night,
But freshly looks, and overbears attaint
With cheerful semblance and sweet majesty;   40
That every wretch, pining and pale before,
Beholding him, plucks comfort from his looks.
A largess universal, like the sun,
His liberal eye doth give to every one,
Thawing cold fear, that mean and gentle all
Behold, as may unworthiness define,
A little touch of Harry in the night.
And so our scene must to the battle fly;
Where – O for pity! – we shall much disgrace,
With four or five most vile and ragged foils,   50
Right ill-disposed in brawl ridiculous,
The name of Agincourt. Yet sit and see,
Minding true things by what their mockeries be.   *Exit*

Enter the King, Bedford, and Gloucester   IV.1
KING HENRY
Gloucester, 'tis true that we are in great danger:
The greater therefore should our courage be.
Good morrow, brother Bedford. God Almighty!
There is some soul of goodness in things evil,
Would men observingly distil it out;
For our bad neighbour makes us early stirrers,
Which is both healthful, and good husbandry.
Besides, they are our outward consciences,
And preachers to us all, admonishing

10 That we should dress us fairly for our end.
Thus may we gather honey from the weed,
And make a moral of the devil himself.

    Enter Erpingham

Good morrow, old Sir Thomas Erpingham!
A good soft pillow for that good white head
Were better than a churlish turf of France.

ERPINGHAM

Not so, my liege – this lodging likes me better,
Since I may say, 'Now lie I like a king.'

KING HENRY

'Tis good for men to love their present pains
Upon example: so the spirit is eased;
20 And when the mind is quickened, out of doubt
The organs, though defunct and dead before,
Break up their drowsy grave and newly move
With casted slough and fresh legerity.
Lend me thy cloak, Sir Thomas. Brothers both,
Commend me to the princes in our camp;
Do my good morrow to them, and anon
Desire them all to my pavilion.

GLOUCESTER We shall, my liege.

ERPINGHAM

Shall I attend your grace?

KING HENRY   No, my good knight.
30 Go with my brothers to my lords of England.
I and my bosom must debate awhile,
And then I would no other company.

ERPINGHAM

The Lord in heaven bless thee, noble Harry!

        Exeunt all but the King

KING HENRY

God-a-mercy, old heart, thou speak'st cheerfully.

    Enter Pistol

PISTOL

  Qui va là?

KING HENRY A friend.

PISTOL

  Discuss unto me, art thou officer,

  Or art thou base, common, and popular?

KING HENRY I am a gentleman of a company.

PISTOL

  Trail'st thou the puissant pike? 40

KING HENRY Even so. What are you?

PISTOL

  As good a gentleman as the Emperor.

KING HENRY Then you are a better than the King.

PISTOL

  The King's a bawcock, and a heart of gold,

  A lad of life, an imp of fame;

  Of parents good, of fist most valiant.

  I kiss his dirty shoe, and from heartstring

  I love the lovely bully. What is thy name?

KING HENRY Harry le Roy.

PISTOL

  Le Roy? A Cornish name. Art thou of Cornish crew? 50

KING HENRY No, I am a Welshman.

PISTOL

  Know'st thou Fluellen?

KING HENRY Yes.

PISTOL

  Tell him I'll knock his leek about his pate

  Upon Saint Davy's day.

KING HENRY Do not you wear your dagger in your cap

  that day, lest he knock that about yours.

PISTOL

  Art thou his friend?

KING HENRY And his kinsman too.

PISTOL

60　The *figo* for thee then!

KING HENRY I thank you. God be with you!

PISTOL

My name is Pistol called.　　　　　　　　　　　*Exit*

KING HENRY It sorts well with your fierceness.

Enter Fluellen and Gower

GOWER Captain Fluellen!

FLUELLEN So! In the name of Jesu Christ, speak fewer.
It is the greatest admiration in the universal world,
when the true and aunchient prerogatifes and laws of
the wars is not kept. If you would take the pains but to
examine the wars of Pompey the Great, you shall find,

70　I warrant you, that there is no tiddle-taddle nor pibble-
pabble in Pompey's camp. I warrant you, you shall
find the ceremonies of the wars, and the cares of it, and
the forms of it, and the sobriety of it, and the modesty
of it, to be otherwise.

GOWER Why, the enemy is loud, you hear him all night.

FLUELLEN If the enemy is an ass, and a fool, and a
prating coxcomb, is it meet, think you, that we should
also, look you, be an ass, and a fool, and a prating coxcomb? In your own conscience now?

80 GOWER I will speak lower.

FLUELLEN I pray you and beseech you that you will.

Exeunt Gower and Fluellen

KING HENRY

Though it appear a little out of fashion,

There is much care and valour in this Welshman.

*Enter three soldiers, John Bates, Alexander Court,
and Michael Williams*

COURT Brother John Bates, is not that the morning which
breaks yonder?

BATES I think it be; but we have no great cause to desire
the approach of day.

WILLIAMS We see yonder the beginning of the day, but I
    think we shall never see the end of it. Who goes there?

KING HENRY A friend.   90

WILLIAMS Under what captain serve you?

KING HENRY Under Sir Thomas Erpingham.

WILLIAMS A good old commander, and a most kind
    gentleman. I pray you, what thinks he of our estate?

KING HENRY Even as men wrecked upon a sand, that
    look to be washed off the next tide.

BATES He hath not told his thought to the King?

KING HENRY No, nor it is not meet he should. For
    though I speak it to you, I think the King is but a man,
    as I am: the violet smells to him as it doth to me; the   100
    element shows to him as it doth to me; all his senses have
    but human conditions. His ceremonies laid by, in his
    nakedness he appears but a man; and though his
    affections are higher mounted than ours, yet when they
    stoop, they stoop with the like wing. Therefore, when
    he sees reason of fears, as we do, his fears, out of doubt,
    be of the same relish as ours are: yet, in reason, no
    man should possess him with any appearance of fear,
    lest he, by showing it, should dishearten his army.

BATES He may show what outward courage he will, but I   110
    believe, as cold a night as 'tis, he could wish himself in
    Thames up to the neck; and so I would he were, and
    I by him, at all adventures, so we were quit here.

KING HENRY By my troth, I will speak my conscience of
    the King: I think he would not wish himself anywhere
    but where he is.

BATES Then I would he were here alone; so should he be
    sure to be ransomed, and a many poor men's lives
    saved.

KING HENRY I dare say you love him not so ill to wish   120
    him here alone, howsoever you speak this to feel other
    men's minds. Methinks I could not die anywhere so

contented as in the King's company, his cause being
just and his quarrel honourable.

WILLIAMS That's more than we know.

BATES Ay, or more than we should seek after; for we know
enough if we know we are the King's subjects. If his
cause be wrong, our obedience to the King wipes the
crime of it out of us.

130 WILLIAMS But if the cause be not good, the King himself
hath a heavy reckoning to make, when all those legs,
and arms, and heads, chopped off in a battle, shall join
together at the latter day, and cry all, 'We died at such
a place'; some swearing, some crying for a surgeon,
some upon their wives left poor behind them, some upon
the debts they owe, some upon their children rawly left.
I am afeard there are few die well that die in a battle,
for how can they charitably dispose of anything when
blood is their argument? Now, if these men do not die
140 well, it will be a black matter for the King that led them
to it, who to disobey were against all proportion of
subjection.

KING HENRY So, if a son that is by his father sent about
merchandise do sinfully miscarry upon the sea, the
imputation of his wickedness, by your rule, should be
imposed upon his father that sent him; or if a servant,
under his master's command, transporting a sum of
money, be assailed by robbers, and die in many irreconciled iniquities, you may call the business of the master
150 the author of the servant's damnation. But this is not so.
The King is not bound to answer the particular endings
of his soldiers, the father of his son, nor the master of
his servant; for they purpose not their death when they
purpose their services. Besides, there is no king, be
his cause never so spotless, if it come to the arbitrement
of swords, can try it out with all unspotted soldiers.
157 Some, peradventure, have on them the guilt of pre-

meditated and contrived murder; some, of beguiling
virgins with the broken seals of perjury; some, making
the wars their bulwark, that have before gored the 160
gentle bosom of peace with pillage and robbery. Now,
if these men have defeated the law, and outrun native
punishment, though they can outstrip men they have no
wings to fly from God. War is His beadle, war is His
vengeance; so that here men are punished for before-
breach of the King's laws, in now the King's quarrel.
Where they feared the death, they have borne life away;
and where they would be safe, they perish. Then if
they die unprovided, no more is the King guilty of their
damnation than he was before guilty of those impieties 170
for the which they are now visited. Every subject's duty
is the King's, but every subject's soul is his own. Therefore should every soldier in the wars do as every sick
man in his bed, wash every mote out of his conscience;
and dying so, death is to him advantage; or not dying,
the time was blessedly lost wherein such preparation
was gained; and in him that escapes, it were not sin to
think that, making God so free an offer, He let him
outlive that day to see His greatness, and to teach others
how they should prepare.   180

WILLIAMS 'Tis certain, every man that dies ill, the ill
upon his own head – the King is not to answer it.

BATES I do not desire he should answer for me, and yet I
determine to fight lustily for him.

KING HENRY I myself heard the King say he would not be
ransomed.

WILLIAMS Ay, he said so, to make us fight cheerfully:
but when our throats are cut he may be ransomed, and
we ne'er the wiser.

KING HENRY If I live to see it, I will never trust his word 190
after.

WILLIAMS You pay him then! That's a perilous shot out

IV.1

of an elder-gun, that a poor and a private displeasure
can do against a monarch! You may as well go about to
turn the sun to ice, with fanning in his face with a pea-
cock's feather. You'll never trust his word after! Come,
'tis a foolish saying.

KING HENRY Your reproof is something too round. I
should be angry with you, if the time were convenient.

200 WILLIAMS Let it be a quarrel between us, if you live.

KING HENRY I embrace it.

WILLIAMS How shall I know thee again?

KING HENRY Give me any gage of thine, and I will wear
it in my bonnet: then, if ever thou dar'st acknowledge it,
I will make it my quarrel.

WILLIAMS Here's my glove: give me another of thine.

KING HENRY There.

WILLIAMS This will I also wear in my cap. If ever thou
come to me and say, after tomorrow, 'This is my glove,'
210 by this hand, I will take thee a box on the ear.

KING HENRY If ever I live to see it, I will challenge it.

WILLIAMS Thou dar'st as well be hanged.

KING HENRY Well, I will do it, though I take thee in the
King's company.

WILLIAMS Keep thy word. Fare thee well.

BATES Be friends, you English fools, be friends! We have
French quarrels enow, if you could tell how to reckon.

KING HENRY Indeed, the French may lay twenty French
crowns to one they will beat us, for they bear them on
220 their shoulders; but it is no English treason to cut
French crowns, and tomorrow the King himself will be
a clipper.   *Exeunt Soldiers*

Upon the King! Let us our lives, our souls,
Our debts, our careful wives,
Our children, and our sins, lay on the King!
We must bear all. O hard condition,

126

Twin-born with greatness, subject to the breath
Of every fool, whose sense no more can feel
But his own wringing! What infinite heart's ease
Must kings neglect that private men enjoy!
And what have kings that privates have not too,
Save ceremony, save general ceremony?
And what art thou, thou idol ceremony?
What kind of god art thou, that suffer'st more
Of mortal griefs than do thy worshippers?
What are thy rents? What are thy comings-in?
O ceremony, show me but thy worth!
What is thy soul of adoration?
Art thou aught else but place, degree, and form,
Creating awe and fear in other men?
Wherein thou art less happy, being feared,
Than they in fearing.
What drink'st thou oft, instead of homage sweet,
But poisoned flattery? O, be sick, great greatness,
And bid thy ceremony give thee cure!
Thinks thou the fiery fever will go out
With titles blown from adulation?
Will it give place to flexure and low bending?
Canst thou, when thou command'st the beggar's knee,
Command the health of it? No, thou proud dream,   250
That play'st so subtly with a king's repose.
I am a king that find thee, and I know
'Tis not the balm, the sceptre, and the ball,
The sword, the mace, the crown imperial,
The intertissued robe of gold and pearl,
The farcèd title running fore the king,
The throne he sits on, nor the tide of pomp
That beats upon the high shore of this world –
No, not all these, thrice-gorgeous ceremony,
Not all these, laid in bed majestical,   260

Can sleep so soundly as the wretched slave,
Who, with a body filled, and vacant mind,
Gets him to rest, crammed with distressful bread;
Never sees horrid night, the child of hell,
But, like a lackey, from the rise to set,
Sweats in the eye of Phoebus, and all night
Sleeps in Elysium; next day after dawn
Doth rise and help Hyperion to his horse;
And follows so the ever-running year
270   With profitable labour to his grave:
And but for ceremony, such a wretch,
Winding up days with toil, and nights with sleep,
Had the fore-hand and vantage of a king.
The slave, a member of the country's peace,
Enjoys it, but in gross brain little wots
What watch the king keeps to maintain the peace,
Whose hours the peasant best advantages.

Enter Erpingham

ERPINGHAM
My lord, your nobles, jealous of your absence,
Seek through your camp to find you.
KING HENRY   Good old knight,
280   Collect them all together at my tent.
I'll be before thee.
ERPINGHAM   I shall do't, my lord.   *Exit*
KING HENRY
O God of battles, steel my soldiers' hearts;
Possess them not with fear; take from them now
The sense of reckoning, if th'opposèd numbers
Pluck their hearts from them. Not today, O Lord,
O not today, think not upon the fault
My father made in compassing the crown!
I Richard's body have interrèd new,
And on it have bestowed more contrite tears

128

Than from it issued forcèd drops of blood.   290
Five hundred poor I have in yearly pay,
Who twice a day their withered hands hold up
Toward heaven, to pardon blood: and I have built
Two chantries where the sad and solemn priests
Sing still for Richard's soul. More will I do,
Though all that I can do is nothing worth,
Since that my penitence comes after all,
Imploring pardon.

Enter Gloucester

GLOUCESTER
  My liege!
KING HENRY My brother Gloucester's voice? Ay,
  I know thy errand, I will go with thee.   300
  The day, my friends, and all things stay for me.

                                            Exeunt

          Enter the Dauphin, Orleans, Rambures, and others   IV.2
ORLEANS
  The sun doth gild our armour: up, my lords!
DAUPHIN
  Montez à cheval! My horse! *Varlet! Lacquais!*
  Ha!
ORLEANS
    O brave spirit!
DAUPHIN   *Via! Les eaux et la terre!*
ORLEANS
  Rien puis? L'air et le feu?
DAUPHIN   *Ciel,* cousin Orleans!
      Enter the Constable
  Now, my Lord Constable!
CONSTABLE
  Hark how our steeds for present service neigh!

DAUPHIN

    Mount them and make incision in their hides,
    That their hot blood may spin in English eyes
    And dout them with superfluous courage, ha!

RAMBURES

10   What, will you have them weep our horses' blood?
    How shall we then behold their natural tears?
        Enter a Messenger

MESSENGER

    The English are embattled, you French peers.

CONSTABLE

    To horse, you gallant Princes, straight to horse!
    Do but behold yon poor and starvèd band,
    And your fair show shall suck away their souls,
    Leaving them but the shales and husks of men.
    There is not work enough for all our hands,
    Scarce blood enough in all their sickly veins
    To give each naked curtle-axe a stain
20   That our French gallants shall today draw out,
    And sheathe for lack of sport. Let us but blow on
        them,
    The vapour of our valour will o'erturn them.
    'Tis positive 'gainst all exceptions, lords,
    That our superfluous lackeys, and our peasants,
    Who in unnecessary action swarm
    About our squares of battle, were enow
    To purge this field of such a hilding foe,
    Though we upon this mountain's basis by
    Took stand for idle speculation:
30   But that our honours must not. What's to say?
    A very little little let us do,
    And all is done. Then let the trumpets sound
    The tucket sonance and the note to mount;
    For our approach shall so much dare the field

That England shall couch down in fear and yield.
Enter Grandpré

GRANDPRÉ

Why do you stay so long, my lords of France?
Yon island carrions, desperate of their bones,
Ill-favouredly become the morning field.
Their ragged curtains poorly are let loose,
And our air shakes them passing scornfully.   40
Big Mars seems bankrupt in their beggared host,
And faintly through a rusty beaver peeps.
The horsemen sit like fixèd candlesticks,
With torch-staves in their hand; and their poor jades
Lob down their heads, dropping the hides and hips,
The gum down-roping from their pale-dead eyes,
And in their pale dull mouths the gimmaled bit
Lies foul with chawed grass, still and motionless;
And their executors, the knavish crows,
Fly o'er them all, impatient for their hour.   50
Description cannot suit itself in words
To demonstrate the life of such a battle
In life so lifeless as it shows itself.

CONSTABLE

They have said their prayers, and they stay for death.

DAUPHIN

Shall we go send them dinners, and fresh suits,
And give their fasting horses provender,
And after fight with them?

CONSTABLE

I stay but for my guidon. To the field!
I will the banner from a trumpet take,
And use it for my haste. Come, come away!   60
The sun is high, and we outwear the day.   *Exeunt*

*Enter Gloucester, Bedford, Exeter, Erpingham with
all his host; Salisbury and Westmorland*

GLOUCESTER
Where is the King?

BEDFORD
The King himself is rode to view their battle.

WESTMORLAND
Of fighting men they have full three-score thousand.

EXETER
There's five to one: besides, they all are fresh.

SALISBURY
God's arm strike with us! 'Tis a fearful odds.
God bye you, Princes all: I'll to my charge.
If we no more meet till we meet in heaven,
Then joyfully, my noble Lord of Bedford,
My dear Lord Gloucester, and my good Lord Exeter,
10   And my kind kinsman, warriors all, adieu!

BEDFORD
Farewell, good Salisbury, and good luck go with thee!

EXETER
Farewell, kind lord: fight valiantly today –
And yet I do thee wrong to mind thee of it,
For thou art framed of the firm truth of valour.

> *Exit Salisbury*

BEDFORD
He is as full of valour as of kindness,
Princely in both.

> *Enter the King*

WESTMORLAND   O that we now had here
But one ten thousand of those men in England
That do no work today!

KING HENRY   What's he that wishes so?
My cousin Westmorland? No, my fair cousin.
20   If we are marked to die, we are enow

To do our country loss: and if to live,
The fewer men, the greater share of honour.
God's will! I pray thee wish not one man more.
By Jove, I am not covetous for gold,
Nor care I who doth feed upon my cost;
It yearns me not if men my garments wear;
Such outward things dwell not in my desires.
But if it be a sin to covet honour,
I am the most offending soul alive.
No, faith, my coz, wish not a man from England: 30
God's peace! I would not lose so great an honour
As one man more methinks would share from me
For the best hope I have. O, do not wish one more!
Rather proclaim it, Westmorland, through my host,
That he which hath no stomach to this fight,
Let him depart: his passport shall be made,
And crowns for convoy put into his purse.
We would not die in that man's company
That fears his fellowship to die with us.
This day is called the Feast of Crispian: 40
He that outlives this day, and comes safe home,
Will stand a-tiptoe when this day is named,
And rouse him at the name of Crispian.
He that shall see this day, and live old age,
Will yearly on the vigil feast his neighbours,
And say, 'Tomorrow is Saint Crispian.'
Then will he strip his sleeve, and show his scars,
And say, 'These wounds I had on Crispin's day.'
Old men forget; yet all shall be forgot,
But he'll remember, with advantages, 50
What feats he did that day. Then shall our names,
Familiar in his mouth as household words,
Harry the King, Bedford and Exeter,
Warwick and Talbot, Salisbury and Gloucester,

Be in their flowing cups freshly remembered.
This story shall the good man teach his son;
And Crispin Crispian shall ne'er go by,
From this day to the ending of the world,
But we in it shall be rememberèd –
60   We few, we happy few, we band of brothers:
For he today that sheds his blood with me
Shall be my brother; be he ne'er so vile,
This day shall gentle his condition;
And gentlemen in England now abed
Shall think themselves accursed they were not here,
And hold their manhoods cheap, whiles any speaks
That fought with us upon Saint Crispin's day.

Enter Salisbury

SALISBURY

My sovereign lord, bestow yourself with speed.
The French are bravely in their battles set,
70   And will with all expedience charge on us.

KING HENRY

All things are ready, if our minds be so.

WESTMORLAND

Perish the man whose mind is backward now!

KING HENRY

Thou dost not wish more help from England, coz?

WESTMORLAND

God's will, my liege, would you and I alone,
Without more help, could fight this royal battle!

KING HENRY

Why, now thou hast unwished five thousand men,
Which likes me better than to wish us one.
You know your places. God be with you all!

Tucket. Enter Montjoy

MONTJOY

Once more I come to know of thee, King Harry,

If for thy ransom thou wilt now compound,   80
Before thy most assurèd overthrow:
For certainly thou art so near the gulf
Thou needs must be englutted. Besides, in mercy,
The Constable desires thee thou wilt mind
Thy followers of repentance, that their souls
May make a peaceful and a sweet retire
From off these fields, where, wretches, their poor
    bodies
Must lie and fester.

KING HENRY   Who hath sent thee now?

MONTJOY

The Constable of France.

KING HENRY

I pray thee bear my former answer back: 90
Bid them achieve me, and then sell my bones.
Good God, why should they mock poor fellows thus?
The man that once did sell the lion's skin
While the beast lived, was killed with hunting him.
A many of our bodies shall no doubt
Find native graves; upon the which, I trust,
Shall witness live in brass of this day's work.
And those that leave their valiant bones in France,
Dying like men, though buried in your dunghills,
They shall be famed; for there the sun shall greet them,   100
And draw their honours reeking up to heaven,
Leaving their earthly parts to choke your clime,
The smell whereof shall breed a plague in France.
Mark then abounding valour in our English,
That being dead, like to the bullet's crasing,
Break out into a second course of mischief,
Killing in relapse of mortality.
Let me speak proudly: tell the Constable
We are but warriors for the working-day;

110 Our gayness and our gilt are all besmirched
With rainy marching in the painful field.
There's not a piece of feather in our host –
Good argument, I hope, we will not fly –
And time hath worn us into slovenry.
But, by the mass, our hearts are in the trim;
And my poor soldiers tell me, yet ere night
They'll be in fresher robes, or they will pluck
The gay new coats o'er the French soldiers' heads,
And turn them out of service. If they do this –
120 As, if God please, they shall – my ransom then
Will soon be levied. Herald, save thou thy labour;
Come thou no more for ransom, gentle Herald.
They shall have none, I swear, but these my joints,
Which if they have as I will leave 'em them
Shall yield them little, tell the Constable.

MONTJOY
I shall, King Harry. And so fare thee well:
Thou never shalt hear herald any more.   *Exit*

KING HENRY
I fear thou wilt once more come again for a ransom.
        Enter York

YORK
130 My lord, most humbly on my knee I beg
The leading of the vaward.

KING HENRY
Take it, brave York. Now, soldiers, march away:
And how Thou pleasest, God, dispose the day!
                                        Exeunt

IV.4   *Alarum. Excursions. Enter Pistol, French Soldier, Boy*
PISTOL
    Yield, cur!

FRENCH SOLDIER *Je pense que vous êtes le gentilhomme de bonne qualité.*

PISTOL

    Calitie! 'Calen o custure me!'

    Art thou a gentleman? What is thy name? Discuss.

FRENCH SOLDIER *O Seigneur Dieu!*

PISTOL

    O Signieur Dew should be a gentleman:

    Perpend my words, O Signieur Dew, and mark.

    O Signieur Dew, thou diest on point of fox,

    Except, O Signieur, thou do give to me   10

    Egregious ransom.

FRENCH SOLDIER *O, prenez miséricorde! Ayez pitié de moy!*

PISTOL

    Moy shall not serve: I will have forty moys,

    Or I will fetch thy rim out at thy throat

    In drops of crimson blood!

FRENCH SOLDIER *Est-il impossible d'échapper la force de ton bras?*

PISTOL

    Brass, cur?

    Thou damnèd and luxurious mountain goat,   20

    Offer'st me brass?

FRENCH SOLDIER *O, pardonne-moy!*

PISTOL

    Say'st thou me so? Is that a ton of moys?

    Come hither, boy: ask me this slave in French

    What is his name.

BOY *Écoutez: comment êtes-vous appelé?*

FRENCH SOLDIER *Monsieur le Fer.*

BOY He says his name is Master Fer.

PISTOL Master Fer! I'll fer him, and firk him, and ferret him. Discuss the same in French unto him.   30

BOY I do not know the French for fer, and ferret, and firk.

PISTOL

    Bid him prepare, for I will cut his throat.

FRENCH SOLDIER *Que dit-il, monsieur?*

BOY *Il me commande à vous dire que vous faites vous prêt,*
car ce soldat içi est disposé tout à cette heure de couper
votre gorge.

PISTOL

    Owy, cuppele gorge, permafoy,

    Peasant, unless thou give me crowns, brave crowns;

    Or mangled shalt thou be by this my sword.

40 FRENCH SOLDIER *O, je vous supplie, pour l'amour de Dieu,*
me pardonner! Je suis le gentilhomme de bonne maison.
Gardez ma vie, et je vous donnerai deux cents écus.

PISTOL

    What are his words?

BOY He prays you to save his life. He is a gentleman of a
    good house, and for his ransom he will give you two
    hundred crowns.

PISTOL

    Tell him my fury shall abate, and I

    The crowns will take.

FRENCH SOLDIER *Petit monsieur, que dit-il?*

50 BOY *Encore qu'il est contre son jurement de pardonner aucun*
prisonnier; néanmoins, pour les écus que vous l'avez
promis, il est content à vous donner la liberté, le franchise-
ment.

FRENCH SOLDIER *Sur mes genoux je vous donne mille*
remercîments; et je m'estime heureux que je suis tombé
entre les mains d'un chevalier, je pense, le plus brave,
vaillant, et très distingué seigneur d'Angleterre.

PISTOL

    Expound unto me, boy.

BOY He gives you upon his knees a thousand thanks; and

he esteems himself happy that he hath fallen into the 60
hands of one – as he thinks – the most brave, valorous,
and thrice-worthy signieur of England.

PISTOL

As I suck blood, I will some mercy show.
Follow me!   *Exit*

BOY *Suivez-vous le grand capitaine.* (*Exit French Soldier*)
I did never know so full a voice issue from so empty a
heart; but the saying is true, 'The empty vessel makes
the greatest sound.' Bardolph and Nym had ten times
more valour than this roaring devil i'th'old play, that
everyone may pare his nails with a wooden dagger; and 70
they are both hanged – and so would this be, if he durst
steal anything adventurously. I must stay with the
lackeys, with the luggage of our camp. The French
might have a good prey of us, if he knew of it, for there
is none to guard it but boys.

                                                         Exit

Enter the Constable, Orleans, Bourbon, Dauphin, IV.5
and Rambures

CONSTABLE *O diable!*

ORLEANS *O Seigneur! Le jour est perdu, tout est perdu!*

DAUPHIN

Mort Dieu! Ma vie! All is confounded, all!
Reproach and everlasting shame
Sits mocking in our plumes. *O méchante fortune!*
        A short alarum
Do not run away!

CONSTABLE   Why, all our ranks are broke.

DAUPHIN

O perdurable shame! Let's stab ourselves.
Be these the wretches that we played at dice for?

                                 139

ORLEANS

Is this the King we sent to for his ransom?

BOURBON

10 Shame, and eternal shame, nothing but shame!
Let's die in honour! Once more back again!
And he that will not follow Bourbon now,
Let him go hence, and with his cap in hand,
Like a base pander, hold the chamber-door
Whilst by a slave, no gentler than my dog,
His fairest daughter is contaminated.

CONSTABLE

Disorder that hath spoiled us, friend us now!
Let us on heaps go offer up our lives.

ORLEANS

We are enow yet living in the field
20 To smother up the English in our throngs,
If any order might be thought upon.

BOURBON

The devil take order now! I'll to the throng.
Let life be short, else shame will be too long.   *Exeunt*

IV.6   *Alarum. Enter the King and his train, Exeter and*
              others, with prisoners

KING HENRY

Well have we done, thrice-valiant countrymen;
But all's not done – yet keep the French the field.

EXETER

The Duke of York commends him to your majesty.

KING HENRY

Lives he, good uncle? Thrice within this hour
I saw him down; thrice up again, and fighting.
From helmet to the spur all blood he was.

EXETER

In which array, brave soldier, doth he lie,

Larding the plain; and by his bloody side,
Yoke-fellow to his honour-owing wounds,
The noble Earl of Suffolk also lies.   10
Suffolk first died; and York, all haggled over,
Comes to him, where in gore he lay insteeped,
And takes him by the beard, kisses the gashes
That bloodily did yawn upon his face.
He cries aloud, 'Tarry, my cousin Suffolk!
My soul shall thine keep company to heaven.
Tarry, sweet soul, for mine, then fly abreast,
As in this glorious and well-foughten field
We kept together in our chivalry!'
Upon these words I came and cheered him up;   20
He smiled me in the face, raught me his hand,
And, with a feeble grip, says, 'Dear my lord,
Commend my service to my sovereign.'
So did he turn, and over Suffolk's neck
He threw his wounded arm, and kissed his lips,
And so espoused to death, with blood he sealed
A testament of noble-ending love.
The pretty and sweet manner of it forced
Those waters from me which I would have stopped;
But I had not so much of man in me,   30
And all my mother came into mine eyes
And gave me up to tears.
KING HENRY   I blame you not;
For, hearing this, I must perforce compound
With mistful eyes, or they will issue too.
        Alarum
But hark! what new alarum is this same?
The French have reinforced their scattered men.
Then every soldier kill his prisoners!
Give the word through.   *Exeunt*

FLUELLEN Kill the poys and the luggage? 'Tis expressly
against the law of arms; 'tis as arrant a piece of knavery,
mark you now, as can be offert – in your conscience now,
is it not?

GOWER 'Tis certain there's not a boy left alive, and the
cowardly rascals that ran from the battle ha' done this
slaughter. Besides, they have burnt and carried away
all that was in the King's tent, wherefore the King most
worthily hath caused every soldier to cut his prisoner's
10   throat. O, 'tis a gallant King!

FLUELLEN Ay, he was porn at Monmouth, Captain
Gower. What call you the town's name where Alexander
the Pig was born?

GOWER Alexander the Great.

FLUELLEN Why, I pray you, is not 'pig' great? The pig,
or the great, or the mighty, or the huge, or the magnanimous, are all one reckonings, save the phrase is a little
variations.

GOWER I think Alexander the Great was born in Macedon;
20   his father was called Philip of Macedon, as I take it.

FLUELLEN I think it is in Macedon where Alexander is
porn. I tell you, Captain, if you look in the maps of the
'orld, I warrant you sall find, in the comparisons between
Macedon and Monmouth, that the situations, look you,
is both alike. There is a river in Macedon, and there is
also moreover a river at Monmouth – it is called Wye
at Monmouth, but it is out of my prains what is the
name of the other river; but 'tis all one, 'tis alike as my
fingers is to my fingers, and there is salmons in both.
30   If you mark Alexander's life well, Harry of Monmouth's
life is come after it indifferent well; for there is figures in
all things. Alexander, God knows and you know, in his
rages, and his furies, and his wraths, and his cholers,

and his moods, and his displeasures, and his indigna-
tions, and also being a little intoxicates in his prains,
did in his ales and his angers, look you, kill his best
friend Cleitus.

GOWER Our King is not like him in that: he never killed
any of his friends.

FLUELLEN It is not well done, mark you now, to take the 40
tales out of my mouth, ere it is made and finished. I
speak but in the figures and comparisons of it. As
Alexander killed his friend Cleitus, being in his ales
and his cups, so also Harry Monmouth, being in his
right wits and his good judgements, turned away the
fat knight with the great-belly doublet – he was full of
jests, and gipes, and knaveries, and mocks: I have forgot
his name.

GOWER Sir John Falstaff.

FLUELLEN That is he. I'll tell you, there is good men porn 50
at Monmouth.

GOWER Here comes his majesty.

*Alarum. Enter King Henry and Bourbon, with
prisoners; also Warwick, Gloucester, Exeter, and
others. Flourish*

KING HENRY

I was not angry since I came to France
Until this instant. Take a trumpet, Herald;
Ride thou unto the horsemen on yon hill.
If they will fight with us, bid them come down,
Or void the field: they do offend our sight.
If they'll do neither, we will come to them,
And make them skirr away as swift as stones
Enforcèd from the old Assyrian slings.   60
Besides, we'll cut the throats of those we have,
And not a man of them that we shall take
Shall taste our mercy. Go and tell them so.

Enter Montjoy

EXETER

Here comes the Herald of the French, my liege.

GLOUCESTER

His eyes are humbler than they used to be.

KING HENRY

How now, what means this, Herald? Know'st thou not
That I have fined these bones of mine for ransom?
Com'st thou again for ransom?

MONTJOY   No, great King;
I come to thce for charitable licence,

70   That we may wander o'er this bloody field
To book our dead, and then to bury them,
To sort our nobles from our common men.
For many of our princes – woe the while! –
Lie drowned and soaked in mercenary blood;
So do our vulgar drench their peasant limbs
In blood of princes, and their wounded steeds
Fret fetlock-deep in gore, and with wild rage
Yerk out their armèd heels at their dead masters,
Killing them twice. O, give us leave, great King,

80   To view the field in safety, and dispose
Of their dead bodies!

KING HENRY   I tell thee truly, Herald,
I know not if the day be ours or no;
For yet a many of your horsemen peer
And gallop o'er the field.

MONTJOY   The day is yours.

KING HENRY

Praisèd be God, and not our strength, for it!
What is this castle called that stands hard by?

MONTJOY

They call it Agincourt.

KING HENRY

Then call we this the field of Agincourt,

Fought on the day of Crispin Crispianus.

FLUELLEN Your grandfather of famous memory, an't 90
please your majesty, and your great-uncle Edward the
Plack Prince of Wales, as I have read in the chronicles,
fought a most prave pattle here in France.

KING HENRY They did, Fluellen.

FLUELLEN Your majesty says very true. If your majesties
is remembered of it, the Welshmen did good service in a
garden where leeks did grow, wearing leeks in their
Monmouth caps, which your majesty know to this hour
is an honourable badge of the service; and I do believe
your majesty takes no scorn to wear the leek upon Saint 100
Tavy's day.

KING HENRY
I wear it for a memorable honour;
For I am Welsh, you know, good countryman.

FLUELLEN All the water in Wye cannot wash your
majesty's Welsh plood out of your pody, I can tell you
that. God pless it and preserve it, as long as it pleases
His grace, and His majesty too!

KING HENRY Thanks, good my countryman.

FLUELLEN By Jeshu, I am your majesty's countryman, I
care not who know it; I will confess it to all the 'orld. 110
I need not to be ashamed of your majesty, praised be
God, so long as your majesty is an honest man.

KING HENRY
God keep me so!
                Enter Williams
                    Our heralds go with him.
Bring me just notice of the numbers dead
On both our parts.   *Exeunt Heralds with Montjoy*
                    Call yonder fellow hither.

EXETER Soldier, you must come to the King.

KING HENRY Soldier, why wear'st thou that glove in thy
cap?

WILLIAMS An't please your majesty, 'tis the gage of one
120 that I should fight withal, if he be alive.

KING HENRY An Englishman?

WILLIAMS An't please your majesty, a rascal that
swaggered with me last night: who, if 'a live and ever
dare to challenge this glove, I have sworn to take him a
box o'th'ear: or if I can see my glove in his cap, which he
swore as he was a soldier he would wear if alive, I will
strike it out soundly.

KING HENRY What think you, Captain Fluellen, is it
fit this soldier keep his oath?

130 FLUELLEN He is a craven and a villain else, an't please
your majesty, in my conscience.

KING HENRY It may be his enemy is a gentleman of
great sort, quite from the answer of his degree.

FLUELLEN Though he be as good a gentleman as the
devil is, as Lucifer and Belzebub himself, it is necessary,
look your grace, that he keep his vow and his oath. If
he be perjured, see you now, his reputation is as arrant
a villain and a Jack-sauce as ever his black shoe trod
upon God's ground and His earth, in my conscience, la!

140 KING HENRY Then keep thy vow, sirrah, when thou
meet'st the fellow.

WILLIAMS So I will, my liege, as I live.

KING HENRY Who serv'st thou under?

WILLIAMS Under Captain Gower, my liege.

FLUELLEN Gower is a good captain, and is good knowledge
and literatured in the wars.

KING HENRY Call him hither to me, soldier.

WILLIAMS I will, my liege.   *Exit*

KING HENRY Here, Fluellen, wear thou this favour for
150 me, and stick it in thy cap. When Alençon and myself
were down together, I plucked this glove from his
helm. If any man challenge this, he is a friend to Alençon,

and an enemy to our person: if thou encounter any such,
apprehend him, an thou dost me love.

FLUELLEN Your grace doo's me as great honours as can
be desired in the hearts of his subjects. I would fain see
the man that has but two legs that shall find himself
aggriefed at this glove, that is all: but I would fain see it
once, and please God of His grace that I might see.

KING HENRY Know'st thou Gower?   160

FLUELLEN He is my dear friend, an please you.

KING HENRY Pray thee go seek him, and bring him to
my tent.

FLUELLEN I will fetch him.   *Exit*

KING HENRY
My Lord of Warwick, and my brother Gloucester,
Follow Fluellen closely at the heels.
The glove which I have given him for a favour
May haply purchase him a box o'th'ear.
It is the soldier's: I by bargain should
Wear it myself. Follow, good cousin Warwick.   170
If that the soldier strike him, as I judge
By his blunt bearing he will keep his word,
Some sudden mischief may arise of it;
For I do know Fluellen valiant,
And, touched with choler, hot as gunpowder,
And quickly will return an injury.
Follow, and see there be no harm between them.
Go you with me, uncle of Exeter.   *Exeunt*

Enter Gower and Williams   IV.8

WILLIAMS I warrant it is to knight you, Captain.
    Enter Fluellen

FLUELLEN God's will and His pleasure, Captain, I
beseech you now, come apace to the King. There is

more good toward you, peradventure, than is in your
knowledge to dream of.

WILLIAMS Sir, know you this glove?

FLUELLEN Know the glove? I know the glove is a glove.

WILLIAMS I know this; and thus I challenge it.

He strikes him

FLUELLEN 'Sblood! an arrant traitor as any's in the
10 universal world, or in France, or in England!

GOWER How now, sir? You villain!

WILLIAMS Do you think I'll be forsworn?

FLUELLEN Stand away, Captain Gower: I will give treason
his payment into plows, I warrant you.

WILLIAMS I am no traitor.

FLUELLEN That's a lie in thy throat. I charge you in his
majesty's name, apprehend him: he's a friend of the
Duke Alençon's.

Enter Warwick and Gloucester

WARWICK How now, how now, what's the matter?

20 FLUELLEN My Lord of Warwick, here is – praised be
God for it! – a most contagious treason come to light,
look you, as you shall desire in a summer's day. Here is
his majesty.

Enter the King and Exeter

KING HENRY How now, what's the matter?

FLUELLEN My liege, here is a villain and a traitor, that,
look your grace, has struck the glove which your majesty
is take out of the helmet of Alençon.

WILLIAMS My liege, this was my glove, here is the fellow
of it; and he that I gave it to in change promised to wear
30 it in his cap. I promised to strike him if he did. I met
this man with my glove in his cap, and I have been as
good as my word.

FLUELLEN Your majesty hear now, saving your majesty's
manhood, what an arrant, rascally, beggarly, lousy knave

it is. I hope your majesty is pear me testimony and witness, and will avouchment, that this is the glove of Alençon that your majesty is give me, in your conscience, now.

KING HENRY Give me thy glove, soldier. Look, here is the fellow of it.   40

'Twas I indeed thou promisèd'st to strike,
And thou hast given me most bitter terms.

FLUELLEN An please your majesty, let his neck answer for it, if there is any martial law in the world.

KING HENRY How canst thou make me satisfaction?

WILLIAMS All offences, my lord, come from the heart: never came any from mine that might offend your majesty.

KING HENRY It was ourself thou didst abuse.

WILLIAMS Your majesty came not like yourself: you   50
appeared to me but as a common man – witness the night, your garments, your lowliness; and what your highness suffered under that shape, I beseech you take it for your own fault, and not mine; for had you been as I took you for, I made no offence: therefore, I beseech your highness, pardon me.

KING HENRY

Here, uncle Exeter, fill this glove with crowns,
And give it to this fellow. Keep it, fellow,
And wear it for an honour in thy cap
Till I do challenge it. Give him the crowns;   60
And, Captain, you must needs be friends with him.

FLUELLEN By this day and this light, the fellow has mettle enough in his belly. Hold, there is twelve pence for you, and I pray you to serve God, and keep you out of prawls, and prabbles, and quarrels, and dissensions, and I warrant you it is the better for you.

WILLIAMS I will none of your money.

FLUELLEN It is with a good will: I can tell you it will serve
you to mend your shoes. Come, wherefore should you
70 be so pashful? – your shoes is not so good; 'tis a good
silling, I warrant you, or I will change it.
   Enter an English Herald
KING HENRY Now, Herald, are the dead numbered?
HERALD
   Here is the number of the slaughtered French.
      He gives him a paper
KING HENRY
   What prisoners of good sort are taken, uncle?
EXETER
   Charles Duke of Orleans, nephew to the King;
   John Duke of Bourbon, and Lord Bouciqualt;
   Of other lords and barons, knights and squires,
   Full fifteen hundred, besides common men.
KING HENRY
   This note doth tell me of ten thousand French
80 That in the field lie slain. Of princes, in this number,
   And nobles bearing banners, there lie dead
   One hundred twenty-six: added to these,
   Of knights, esquires, and gallant gentlemen,
   Eight thousand and four hundred; of the which,
   Five hundred were but yesterday dubbed knights.
   So that, in these ten thousand they have lost,
   There are but sixteen hundred mercenaries;
   The rest are princes, barons, lords, knights, squires,
   And gentlemen of blood and quality.
90 The names of those their nobles that lie dead:
   Charles Delabreth, High Constable of France,
   Jaques of Chatillon, Admiral of France,
   The Master of the Cross-bows, Lord Rambures,
   Great Master of France, the brave Sir Guichard
      Dauphin,

John Duke of Alençon, Antony Duke of Brabant,
The brother to the Duke of Burgundy,
And Edward Duke of Bar: of lusty earls,
Grandpré and Roussi, Faulconbridge and Foix,
Beaumont and Marle, Vaudemont and Lestrake.
Here was a royal fellowship of death!   100
Where is the number of our English dead?

The Herald gives him another paper

Edward the Duke of York, the Earl of Suffolk,
Sir Richard Kikely, Davy Gam, esquire;
None else of name; and of all other men
But five-and-twenty. O God, Thy arm was here!
And not to us, but to Thy arm alone,
Ascribe we all! When, without stratagem,
But in plain shock and even play of battle,
Was ever known so great and little loss
On one part and on th'other? Take it, God,   110
For it is none but Thine!

EXETER   'Tis wonderful!

KING HENRY

Come, go we in procession to the village:
And be it death proclaimèd through our host
To boast of this, or take that praise from God
Which is His only.

FLUELLEN Is it not lawful, an please your majesty, to tell
how many is killed?

KING HENRY

Yes, Captain, but with this acknowledgement,
That God fought for us.

FLUELLEN Yes, my conscience, He did us great good.   120

KING HENRY

Do we all holy rites:
Let there be sung *Non Nobis* and *Te Deum*,
The dead with charity enclosed in clay;

And then to Calais, and to England then,
Where ne'er from France arrived more happy men.

Exeunt

*

V   *Flourish. Enter Chorus*

CHORUS

Vouchsafe to those that have not read the story
That I may prompt them; and of such as have,
I humbly pray them to admit th'excuse
Of time, of numbers, and due course of things,
Which cannot in their huge and proper life
Be here presented. Now we bear the King
Toward Calais. Grant him there: there seen,
Heave him away upon your wingèd thoughts
Athwart the sea. Behold, the English beach
10 Pales in the flood with men, with wives, and boys,
Whose shouts and claps outvoice the deep-mouthed
      sea,
Which like a mighty whiffler fore the King
Seems to prepare his way. So let him land,
And solemnly see him set on to London.
So swift a pace hath thought that even now
You may imagine him upon Blackheath,
Where that his lords desire him to have borne
His bruisèd helmet and his bended sword
Before him through the city. He forbids it,
20 Being free from vainness and self-glorious pride,
Giving full trophy, signal, and ostent
Quite from himself to God. But now behold,
In the quick forge and working-house of thought,
How London doth pour out her citizens:
The Mayor and all his brethren in best sort,

Like to the senators of th'antique Rome,
With the plebeians swarming at their heels,
Go forth and fetch their conquering Caesar in:
As, by a lower but loving likelihood,
Were now the General of our gracious Empress –   30
As in good time he may – from Ireland coming,
Bringing rebellion broachèd on his sword,
How many would the peaceful city quit
To welcome him! Much more, and much more cause,
Did they this Harry. Now in London place him –
As yet the lamentation of the French
Invites the King of England's stay at home.
The Emperor's coming in behalf of France
To order peace between them; and omit
All the occurrences, whatever chanced,   40
Till Harry's back-return again to France.
There must we bring him; and myself have played
The interim, by remembering you 'tis past.
Then brook abridgement, and your eyes advance,
After your thoughts, straight back again to France.

Exit

Enter Fluellen and Gower   V.1

GOWER Nay, that's right; but why wear you your leek
today? Saint Davy's day is past.

FLUELLEN There is occasions and causes why and wherefore in all things. I will tell you ass my friend, Captain
Gower: the rascally, scauld, beggarly, lousy, pragging
knave Pistol – which you and yourself and all the world
know to be no petter than a fellow, look you now, of no
merits – he is come to me and prings me pread and salt
yesterday, look you, and bid me eat my leek. It was in a
place where I could not breed no contention with him;   10

but I will be so bold as to wear it in my cap till I see
him once again, and then I will tell him a little piece of
my desires.

Enter Pistol

GOWER Why, here he comes, swelling like a turkey-cock.

FLUELLEN 'Tis no matter for his swellings nor his turkey-
cocks. God pless you, Aunchient Pistol! you scurvy,
lousy knave, God pless you!

PISTOL

Ha, art thou bedlam? Dost thou thirst, base Troyan,
To have me fold up Parca's fatal web?

20 Hence! I am qualmish at the smell of leek.

FLUELLEN I peseech you heartily, scurvy, lousy knave,
at my desires, and my requests, and my petitions, to eat,
look you, this leek. Because, look you, you do not love
it, nor your affections, and your appetites, and your
digestions, doo's not agree with it, I would desire you to
eat it.

PISTOL

Not for Cadwallader and all his goats!

FLUELLEN There is one goat for you. (*He strikes him*)
Will you be so good, scauld knave, as eat it?

PISTOL

30 Base Troyan, thou shalt die!

FLUELLEN You say very true, scauld knave, when God's
will is. I will desire you to live in the meantime, and
eat your victuals – come, there is sauce for it. (*He strikes
him again*) You called me yesterday mountain-squire,
but I will make you today a squire of low degree. I pray
you fall to – if you can mock a leek, you can eat a leek.

GOWER Enough, Captain, you have astonished him.

FLUELLEN I say, I will make him eat some part of my leek,
or I will peat his pate four days. Bite, I pray you, it is

40 good for your green wound and your ploody coxcomb.

PISTOL Must I bite?

FLUELLEN Yes, certainly, and out of doubt, and out of
question too, and ambiguities.

PISTOL By this leek, I will most horribly revenge – I eat
and eat, I swear –

FLUELLEN Eat, I pray you; will you have some more
sauce to your leek? There is not enough leek to swear
by.

PISTOL Quiet thy cudgel, thou dost see I eat.

FLUELLEN Much good do you, scauld knave, heartily. 50
Nay, pray you throw none away, the skin is good for
your broken coxcomb. When you take occasions to see
leeks hereafter, I pray you mock at 'em, that is all.

PISTOL Good!

FLUELLEN Ay, leeks is good. Hold you, there is a groat to
heal your pate.

PISTOL Me a groat?

FLUELLEN Yes, verily and in truth you shall take it, or I
have another leek in my pocket which you shall eat.

PISTOL I take thy groat in earnest of revenge. 60

FLUELLEN If I owe you anything, I will pay you in
cudgels – you shall be a woodmonger, and buy nothing
of me but cudgels. God bye you, and keep you, and heal
your pate. *Exit*

PISTOL
All hell shall stir for this!

GOWER Go, go, you are a counterfeit cowardly knave.
Will you mock at an ancient tradition, begun upon an
honourable respect, and worn as a memorable trophy
of predeceased valour, and dare not avouch in your
deeds any of your words? I have seen you gleeking and 70
galling at this gentleman twice or thrice. You thought,
because he could not speak English in the native garb,
he could not therefore handle an English cudgel. You

find it otherwise, and henceforth let a Welsh correction
teach you a good English condition. Fare ye well. *Exit*

PISTOL

Doth Fortune play the housewife with me now?
News have I that my Doll is dead i'th'spital
Of malady of France,
And there my rendezvous is quite cut off.
80 Old I do wax, and from my weary limbs
Honour is cudgellèd. Well, bawd I'll turn,
And something lean to cutpurse of quick hand.
To England will I steal, and there I'll – steal;
And patches will I get unto these cudgelled scars,
And swear I got them in the Gallia wars.

Exit

V.2   *Enter, at one door, King Henry, Exeter, Bedford,*
Gloucester, Clarence, Warwick, Westmorland, Hunt-
ingdon, and other Lords; at another, the French King,
Queen Isabel, the Princess Katherine, Alice, and
other French; the Duke of Burgundy and his train

KING HENRY

Peace to this meeting, wherefor we are met!
Unto our brother France, and to our sister,
Health and fair time of day. Joy and good wishes
To our most fair and princely cousin Katherine;
And, as a branch and member of this royalty,
By whom this great assembly is contrived,
We do salute you, Duke of Burgundy;
And, Princes French, and peers, health to you all!

FRENCH KING

Right joyous are we to behold your face,
10 Most worthy brother England: fairly met!
So are you, Princes English, every one.

156

QUEEN ISABEL

So happy be the issue, brother England,
Of this good day, and of this gracious meeting,
As we are now glad to behold your eyes –
Your eyes which hitherto have borne in them,
Against the French that met them in their bent,
The fatal balls of murdering basilisks.
The venom of such looks, we fairly hope,
Have lost their quality, and that this day
Shall change all griefs and quarrels into love.   20

KING HENRY

To cry 'Amen' to that, thus we appear.

QUEEN ISABEL

You English Princes all, I do salute you.

BURGUNDY

My duty to you both, on equal love,
Great Kings of France and England! That I have
            laboured
With all my wits, my pains, and strong endeavours,
To bring your most imperial majesties
Unto this bar and royal interview,
Your mightiness on both parts best can witness.
Since, then, my office hath so far prevailed
That face to face, and royal eye to eye,   30
You have congreeted, let it not disgrace me
If I demand, before this royal view,
What rub or what impediment there is
Why that the naked, poor, and mangled peace,
Dear nurse of arts, plenties, and joyful births,
Should not in this best garden of the world,
Our fertile France, put up her lovely visage?
Alas, she hath from France too long been chased,
And all her husbandry doth lie on heaps,
Corrupting in it own fertility.   40

Her vine, the merry cheerer of the heart,
Unprunèd dies; her hedges even-pleached,
Like prisoners wildly overgrown with hair,
Put forth disordered twigs; her fallow leas
The darnel, hemlock, and rank fumitory
Doth root upon, while that the coulter rusts
That should deracinate such savagery.
The even mead, that erst brought sweetly forth
The freckled cowslip, burnet, and green clover,
50 Wanting the scythe, all uncorrected, rank,
Conceives by idleness, and nothing teems
But hateful docks, rough thistles, kecksies, burs,
Losing both beauty and utility;
And as our vineyards, fallows, meads, and hedges,
Defective in their natures, grow to wildness,
Even so our houses and ourselves and children
Have lost, or do not learn for want of time,
The sciences that should become our country,
But grow like savages – as soldiers will
60 That nothing do but meditate on blood –
To swearing and stern looks, diffused attire,
And everything that seems unnatural.
Which to reduce into our former favour
You are assembled; and my speech entreats
That I may know the let why gentle peace
Should not expel these inconveniences,
And bless us with her former qualities.

KING HENRY

If, Duke of Burgundy, you would the peace
Whose want gives growth to th'imperfections
70 Which you have cited, you must buy that peace
With full accord to all our just demands,
Whose tenors and particular effects
You have, enscheduled briefly, in your hands.

BURGUNDY

   The King hath heard them, to the which as yet
   There is no answer made.

KING HENRY   Well then, the peace
   Which you before so urged lies in his answer.

FRENCH KING

   I have but with a cursitory eye
   O'erglanced the articles. Pleaseth your grace
   To appoint some of your Council presently
   To sit with us once more, with better heed   80
   To re-survey them, we will suddenly
   Pass our accept and peremptory answer.

KING HENRY

   Brother, we shall. Go, uncle Exeter,
   And brother Clarence, and you, brother Gloucester,
   Warwick, and Huntingdon, go with the King;
   And take with you free power to ratify,
   Augment, or alter, as your wisdoms best
   Shall see advantageable for our dignity,
   Anything in or out of our demands,
   And we'll consign thereto. Will you, fair sister,   90
   Go with the Princes, or stay here with us?

QUEEN ISABEL

   Our gracious brother, I will go with them.
   Haply a woman's voice may do some good,
   When articles too nicely urged be stood on.

KING HENRY

   Yet leave our cousin Katherine here with us;
   She is our capital demand, comprised
   Within the fore-rank of our articles.

QUEEN ISABEL

   She hath good leave.

               Exeunt all but Henry, Katherine, and Alice

KING HENRY   Fair Katherine, and most fair,

Will you vouchsafe to teach a soldier terms
100 Such as will enter at a lady's ear
And plead his love-suit to her gentle heart?

KATHERINE Your majesty shall mock at me; I cannot speak your England.

KING HENRY O fair Katherine, if you will love me soundly with your French heart, I will be glad to hear you confess it brokenly with your English tongue. Do you like me, Kate?

KATHERINE *Pardonnez-moi*, I cannot tell wat is 'like me'.

KING HENRY An angel is like you, Kate, and you are like
110 an angel.

KATHERINE *Que dit-il? que je suis semblable à les anges?*

ALICE *Oui, vraiment, sauf votre grâce, ainsi dit-il.*

KING HENRY I said so, dear Katherine, and I must not blush to affirm it.

KATHERINE *O bon Dieu! Les langues des hommes sont pleines de tromperies.*

KING HENRY What says she, fair one? that the tongues of men are full of deceits?

ALICE *Oui*, dat de tongues of de mans is be full of deceits –
120 dat is de *Princesse*.

KING HENRY The Princess is the better Englishwoman. I'faith, Kate, my wooing is fit for thy understanding. I am glad thou canst speak no better English; for if thou couldst, thou wouldst find me such a plain king that thou wouldst think I had sold my farm to buy my crown. I know no ways to mince it in love, but directly to say, 'I love you': then if you urge me farther than to say, 'Do you, in faith?' I wear out my suit. Give me your answer, i'faith, do; and so clap hands, and a bargain.
130 How say you, lady?

KATHERINE *Sauf votre honneur*, me understand well.

KING HENRY Marry, if you would put me to verses, or to

dance for your sake, Kate, why, you undid me. For the
one, I have neither words nor measure; and for the
other, I have no strength in measure, yet a reasonable
measure in strength. If I could win a lady at leapfrog,
or by vaulting into my saddle with my armour on my
back, under the correction of bragging be it spoken, I
should quickly leap into a wife. Or if I might buffet for
my love, or bound my horse for her favours, I could lay 140
on like a butcher, and sit like a jackanapes, never off.
But, before God, Kate, I cannot look greenly, nor gasp
out my eloquence, nor I have no cunning in protestation:
only downright oaths, which I never use till urged, nor
never break for urging. If thou canst love a fellow of this
temper, Kate, whose face is not worth sunburning, that
never looks in his glass for love of anything he sees
there, let thine eye be thy cook. I speak to thee plain
soldier. If thou canst love me for this, take me; if not,
to say to thee that I shall die is true – but for thy love, 150
by the Lord, no – yet I love thee too. And while thou
liv'st, dear Kate, take a fellow of plain and uncoined
constancy; for he perforce must do thee right, because
he hath not the gift to woo in other places. For these
fellows of infinite tongue, that can rhyme themselves
into ladies' favours, they do always reason themselves
out again. What! A speaker is but a prater, a rhyme is
but a ballad. A good leg will fall; a straight back will
stoop; a black beard will turn white; a curled pate will
grow bald; a fair face will wither; a full eye will wax 160
hollow: but a good heart, Kate, is the sun and the moon
– or rather, the sun, and not the moon; for it shines
bright and never changes, but keeps his course truly.
If thou would have such a one, take me; and take me,
take a soldier; take a soldier, take a king. And what
say'st thou then to my love? Speak, my fair, and fairly,

I pray thee.

KATHERINE Is it possible dat I sould love de *ennemi* of France?

170 KING HENRY No, it is not possible you should love the enemy of France, Kate; but in loving me you should love the friend of France, for I love France so well that I will not part with a village of it – I will have it all mine: and Kate, when France is mine, and I am yours, then yours is France, and you are mine.

KATHERINE I cannot tell wat is dat.

KING HENRY No, Kate? I will tell thee in French, which I am sure will hang upon my tongue like a new-married wife about her husband's neck, hardly to be shook off.

180 *Je – quand sur le possession de France, et quand vous avez le possession de moi, –* let me see, what then? Saint Denis be my speed! *– donc vôtre est France, et vous êtes mienne.* It is as easy for me, Kate, to conquer the kingdom as to speak so much more French. I shall never move thee in French, unless it be to laugh at me.

KATHERINE *Sauf votre honneur, le français que vous parlez, il est meilleur que l'anglais lequel je parle.*

KING HENRY No, faith, is't not, Kate; but thy speaking of my tongue, and I thine, most truly-falsely, must 190 needs be granted to be much at one. But Kate, dost thou understand thus much English – canst thou love me?

KATHERINE I cannot tell.

KING HENRY Can any of your neighbours tell, Kate? I'll ask them. Come, I know thou lovest me; and at night, when you come into your closet, you'll question this gentlewoman about me; and I know, Kate, you will to her dispraise those parts in me that you love with your heart. But, good Kate, mock me mercifully; the 200 rather, gentle Princess, because I love thee cruelly.

If ever thou beest mine, Kate, as I have a saving faith within me tells me thou shalt, I get thee with scambling, and thou must therefore needs prove a good soldier-breeder. Shall not thou and I, between Saint Denis and Saint George, compound a boy, half French, half English, that shall go to Constantinople and take the Turk by the beard? Shall we not? What say'st thou, my fair flower-de-luce?

KATHERINE I do not know dat.

KING HENRY No, 'tis hereafter to know, but now to 210 promise. Do but now promise, Kate, you will endeavour for your French part of such a boy, and for my English moiety take the word of a king and a bachelor. How answer you, *la plus belle Katherine du monde, mon très cher et devin déesse*?

KATHERINE Your majestee 'ave *fausse* French enough to deceive de most *sage demoiselle* dat is *en France*.

KING HENRY Now fie upon my false French! By mine honour, in true English, I love thee, Kate: by which honour I dare not swear thou lovest me, yet my blood 220 begins to flatter me that thou dost, notwithstanding the poor and untempering effect of my visage. Now beshrew my father's ambition! He was thinking of civil wars when he got me; therefore was I created with a stubborn outside, with an aspect of iron, that when I come to woo ladies I fright them. But in faith, Kate, the elder I wax, the better I shall appear. My comfort is, that old age, that ill layer-up of beauty, can do no more spoil upon my face. Thou hast me, if thou hast me, at the worst; and thou shalt wear me, if thou wear me, better and 230 better; and therefore tell me, most fair Katherine, will you have me? Put off your maiden blushes, avouch the thoughts of your heart with the looks of an empress, take me by the hand, and say, 'Harry of England, I am

thine': which word thou shalt no sooner bless mine ear withal but I will tell thee aloud, 'England is thine, Ireland is thine, France is thine, and Henry Plantagenet is thine' – who, though I speak it before his face, if he be not fellow with the best king, thou shalt find the best
240 king of good fellows. Come, your answer in broken music – for thy voice is music, and thy English broken; therefore, Queen of all, Katherine, break thy mind to me in broken English – wilt thou have me?

KATHERINE Dat is as it shall please de *Roi mon père*.

KING HENRY Nay, it will please him well, Kate – it shall please him, Kate.

KATHERINE Den it sall also content me.

KING HENRY Upon that I kiss your hand, and I call you my Queen.

250 KATHERINE *Laissez, mon seigneur, laissez, laissez! Ma foi, je ne veux point que vous abaissiez votre grandeur en baisant la main d'une – notre Seigneur – indigne serviteur. Excusez-moi, je vous supplie, mon très puissant seigneur.*

KING HENRY Then I will kiss your lips, Kate.

KATHERINE *Les dames et demoiselles pour être baisées devant leurs noces, il n'est pas la coutume de France.*

KING HENRY Madam my interpreter, what says she?

ALICE Dat it is not be de fashion *pour les* ladies of *France* – I cannot tell wat is *baiser en* Anglish.

260 KING HENRY To kiss.

ALICE Your majestee *entendre* bettre *que moi.*

KING HENRY It is not a fashion for the maids in France to kiss before they are married, would she say?

ALICE *Oui, vraiment.*

KING HENRY O Kate, nice customs curtsy to great kings. Dear Kate, you and I cannot be confined within the weak list of a country's fashion. We are the makers of manners, Kate, and the liberty that follows our places

stops the mouth of all find-faults – as I will do yours for
upholding the nice fashion of your country in denying 270
me a kiss; therefore, patiently, and yielding. (*He kisses
her*) You have witchcraft in your lips, Kate: there is
more eloquence in a sugar touch of them than in the
tongues of the French Council, and they should sooner
persuade Harry of England than a general petition of
monarchs. Here comes your father.

*Enter the French King and Queen, Burgundy, and
English and French Lords*

BURGUNDY God save your majesty! My royal cousin,
teach you our Princess English?

KING HENRY I would have her learn, my fair cousin, how
perfectly I love her, and that is good English.   280

BURGUNDY Is she not apt?

KING HENRY Our tongue is rough, coz, and my condition
is not smooth; so that, having neither the voice nor the
heart of flattery about me, I cannot so conjure up the
spirit of love in her that he will appear in his true
likeness.

BURGUNDY Pardon the frankness of my mirth, if I answer
you for that. If you would conjure in her, you must
make a circle; if conjure up love in her in his true likeness, he must appear naked and blind. Can you blame 290
her, then, being a maid yet rosed over with the virgin
crimson of modesty, if she deny the appearance of a
naked blind boy in her naked seeing self? It were, my
lord, a hard condition for a maid to consign to.

KING HENRY Yet they do wink and yield, as love is blind
and enforces.

BURGUNDY They are then excused, my lord, when they
see not what they do.

KING HENRY Then, good my lord, teach your cousin to
consent winking.   300

BURGUNDY I will wink on her to consent, my lord, if you
will teach her to know my meaning: for maids, well
summered and warm kept, are like flies at Bartholomew-
tide, blind, though they have their eyes, and then they
will endure handling, which before would not abide
looking on.

KING HENRY This moral ties me over to time and a hot
summer; and so I shall catch the fly, your cousin, in the
latter end, and she must be blind too.

310 BURGUNDY As love is, my lord, before it loves.

KING HENRY It is so; and you may, some of you, thank
love for my blindness, who cannot see many a fair
French city for one fair French maid that stands in my
way.

FRENCH KING Yes, my lord, you see them perspectively,
the cities turned into a maid; for they are all girdled
with maiden walls, that war hath never entered.

KING HENRY Shall Kate be my wife?

FRENCH KING So please you.

320 KING HENRY I am content, so the maiden cities you talk
of may wait on her: so the maid that stood in the way
for my wish shall show me the way to my will.

FRENCH KING
We have consented to all terms of reason.

KING HENRY
Is't so, my lords of England?

WESTMORLAND
The King hath granted every article:
His daughter first, and then, in sequel, all,
According to their firm proposèd natures.

EXETER
Only he hath not yet subscribèd this:
Where your majesty demands that the King of France,
330 having any occasion to write for matter of grant, shall

name your highness in this form, and with this addition,
in French, *Notre très cher fils Henri, Roi d'Angleterre,
Héritier de France*: and thus in Latin, *Praeclarissimus
filius noster Henricus, Rex Angliae et Haeres Franciae.*

FRENCH KING

Nor this I have not, brother, so denied
But your request shall make me let it pass.

KING HENRY

I pray you then, in love and dear alliance,
Let that one article rank with the rest,
And thereupon give me your daughter.

FRENCH KING

Take her, fair son, and from her blood raise up   340
Issue to me, that the contending kingdoms
Of France and England, whose very shores look pale
With envy of each other's happiness,
May cease their hatred, and this dear conjunction
Plant neighbourhood and Christian-like accord
In their sweet bosoms, that never war advance
His bleeding sword 'twixt England and fair France.

LORDS Amen!

KING HENRY

Now welcome, Kate; and bear me witness all
That here I kiss her as my sovereign Queen.   350
    Flourish

QUEEN ISABEL

God, the best maker of all marriages,
Combine your hearts in one, your realms in one!
As man and wife, being two, are one in love,
So be there 'twixt your kingdoms such a spousal
That never may ill office, or fell jealousy,
Which troubles oft the bed of blessèd marriage,
Thrust in between the paction of these kingdoms
To make divorce of their incorporate league;

That English may as French, French Englishmen,
360   Receive each other, God speak this 'Amen'!

ALL Amen!

KING HENRY

Prepare we for our marriage; on which day,
My Lord of Burgundy, we'll take your oath,
And all the peers', for surety of our leagues.
Then shall I swear to Kate, and you to me,
And may our oaths well kept and prosperous be!

Sennet. Exeunt

Enter Chorus

CHORUS
  Thus far, with rough and all-unable pen,
    Our bending author hath pursued the story,
  In little room confining mighty men,
    Mangling by starts the full course of their glory.
  Small time, but in that small most greatly lived
    This star of England. Fortune made his sword,
  By which the world's best garden he achieved,
    And of it left his son imperial lord.
  Henry the Sixth, in infant bands crowned King
    Of France and England, did this King succeed,   10
  Whose state so many had the managing
    That they lost France, and made his England bleed:
  Which oft our stage hath shown; and, for their sake,
  In your fair minds let this acceptance take.   *Exit*

COMMENTARY

REFERENCES to plays by Shakespeare not yet available in the New Penguin Shakespeare are to Peter Alexander's edition of the *Complete Works*, London, 1951.

The Characters in the Play
No list of these is provided in the Quarto or Folio. Many editions omit the Duke of Clarence and the Earl of Huntingdon, since, though they are passingly addressed in the final scene (V.2.84–5), neither is given anything at all to say. They are included here as having at least an action to perform, whereas Talbot, mentioned at IV.3.54, says and does nothing whatever, and so is omitted from this list.

The action takes place in England and France.

Prologue
Shakespeare has various formal conclusions to his plays (songs, dances, and epilogues), but formal openings occur only (apart from probably unShakespearian examples in *Henry VIII* and *Pericles*) in *Romeo and Juliet*, *2 Henry IV*, *Henry V*, and *Troilus and Cressida*. That to *Romeo and Juliet*, a sonnet, is followed by a second chorus-sonnet to Act II, and then by nothing further. That to *Troilus and Cressida* provides a lofty introduction to the theme and (as in *Henry V*) admits that a play is limited in what it can show. *2 Henry IV* is the only play other than *Henry V* to have an authentic Shakespearian prologue and epilogue; from it Shakespeare may have realized that in a history play a prologue surveying a great sweep of events could have a special value. He puts this realization to splendid use in *Henry V* by furnishing every Act with a chorus and by using his epilogue (as he does not in *2 Henry IV*) to sum up the great story, thus stressing the play's epic nature.

(stage direction) *Flourish* fanfare. The Folio has flourishes before Acts II and III only; they are inserted here before each Act for uniformity.

1   *a Muse of fire* inspiration as brilliant and aspiring as the highest and brightest of the four elements. At III.7. 20–21 the Dauphin's horse is 'pure air and fire', as contrasted with the 'dull elements of earth and water'; and in a famous phrase Drayton described Marlowe's poetic 'raptures' as 'All air, and fire' (*Epistle to Henry Reynolds, Esquire, Of Poets and Poesie*).

5   *like himself* with all his true attributes

6   *port* bearing

7   *Leashed in.* A 'leash' was a trio of dogs on a lead.
famine, sword, and fire. In Holinshed the Archbishop urges Henry to wage war with blood, sword, and fire, and replying to the French ambassador Henry threatens to do so. The presentation of the King here perhaps echoes Henry's declaration, when besieging Rouen, 'that the goddess of battle, called Bellona, had three handmaidens, ever of necessity attending upon her, as blood, fire, and famine' (Holinshed, *Chronicles of England*, 1587, III.567); similarly *1 Henry VI*, IV.2.11 – 'Lean famine, quartering steel, and climbing fire'.

8   *gentles* gentlefolk

9   *hath.* Plural nouns with singular verbs, and vice versa, are frequent in Elizabethan English.

11   *cockpit* round theatre (the 'wooden O' of line 13). Shakespeare may refer to the existing Curtain Theatre or to the Globe, which was under construction while he was writing the play.

12   *vasty* spacious

15   *crookèd* curved (like the nought which turns 100,000 into 1,000,000)

17   *ciphers* figures of no value
account (1) sum total; (2) narrative

28   *deck our kings* adorn our supposed kings like real ones

30   *many years.* The play covers events between 1414 and 1420.

The Play

I.1.4   *scambling* turbulent. Because of civil disorders, a bill
         proposed by Lollard lords to dispossess the clergy was
         withdrawn from Parliament in 1413.

14   *esquires* candidates for knighthood, attending on a
         knight

15   *lazars* lepers

22   *full of grace.* The chronicles present Henry as reformed
         from his wild youth by a deeply religious redemption;
         the play reflects this throughout.

26   *mortified.* This is the accepted word for the old sinning
         self ('th'offending Adam') dying before the onset of
         grace. The Archbishop uses many Biblical and theo-
         logical phrases.

28   *Consideration* spiritual self-examination (a stronger
         sense than the modern one)

28-31   *like an angel came ... T'envelop and contain celestial
         spirits* (like the angel sent by God to drive the sinning
         Adam – and Eve – out of Eden or Paradise, which
         thereafter was left to blessed spirits only)

34   *currance* current

35   '*Hydra-headed* manifold and proliferating. The Hydra
         was a many-headed monster encountered by Hercules;
         each head, when cut off, grew two more, until a burning
         brand was thrust into the stump.

38   *reason in divinity.* Henry, according to Holinshed, was
         an able theological disputant; he argued matters of
         faith with the Lollard Sir John Oldcastle, imprisoned
         for heresy.

46   *Gordian knot* seemingly insoluble problem. The
         peasant Gordius devised so intricate a knot that,
         tradition held, whoever undid it would rule over Asia:
         Alexander cut it with his sword. By implication,
         Henry outdoes Alexander by untying it, and that
         easily.

48   *The air, a chartered libertine, is still.* 'This line is ex-
         quisitely beautiful' (Johnson). The rich eloquence of

this eulogy does much to save the Archbishop's hyperboles from seeming specious.

chartered libertine free spirit licensed to roam abroad

51–2 *the art and practic part of life | Must be the mistress to this theoric* practical skill and experience must govern his theoretical knowledge

55 *rude* coarse

58–9 *sequestration, | From open haunts and popularity* keeping aloof from places of common resort and from mixing with the people

60–62 *The strawberry grows underneath the nettle ... of baser quality.* The Bishops of Ely had a celebrated strawberry-garden in Holborn, referred to in *Richard III* (III. 4.32–3). T. Hill's *Profitable Arte of Gardeninge* (1572) observes that 'Strawberry ... aptly groweth in shadowy places, and rather joyeth under the shadow of other herbs, than by growing alone'; and Montaigne describes refined plants as growing best near coarse ones, since the latter absorb the 'ill savours' of the ground (*Essays*, III.9).

66 *crescive in his faculty* increasing through its natural capacity

72 *indifferent* impartial

74 *exhibiters* proposers of the bill

86 *severals* details

unhidden passages clear lines of descent

I.2.4 *cousin.* The word is often used loosely for 'kinsman', but in fact Westmorland was Henry's cousin by marriage.

be resolved come to a solution

9–32 *My learnèd lord, we pray you to proceed. . . . As pure as sin with baptism.* The religious note is evidence of Henry's earnest moral sense. Holinshed stresses his care before embarking on a course of action – 'He never enterprised anything before he had fully debated and

174

forecast all the main chances that might happen, which done, with all diligence and courage he set his purpose forward.'

11   *the law Salic.* This was the supposed law by which the crown of France could descend only through males. *Edward III* (I.1.11–41) also has a discourse on the Salic law in relation to Edward's claim to France.

15   *nicely charge your understanding soul* sophistically burden your soul with guilt by knowingly misrepresenting the case

19   *approbation* putting to the proof

20   *incite* induce (without the present sense of instigation). This is an example of the ambiguous diction which haunts this diplomacy – Henry can hardly be implying that the Archbishop is wilfully persuading him into war, yet the modern sense of the word creates suspicions about the Archbishop's proceedings.

21   *impawn* pledge, commit (by offering a guarantee of moral justification)

26–8   *sore complaint ... mortality* grave accusation against him who wrongfully wages war, so destroying the brief lives of men

33–95   *Then hear me, gracious sovereign, and you peers ... Usurped from you and your progenitors.* This address follows Holinshed so closely as to become quite tiresome, yet one need not assume that Shakespeare is satirizing the Archbishop or statecraft. Tedious though it is to modern ears, it conveyed to Elizabethan hearers all the facts needed to prove that Henry was right in his claim, and absolute faith in the rightness of his claim is the play's very basis.

37   *Pharamond* (legendary king of the Salian Franks)

49   *dishonest* unchaste

66   *heir general* legal heir whether through male or female line

72   *find* provide
     shows specious appearances

74   *Conveyed himself* passed himself off

75   *Charlemain*. Hall and Holinshed, followed by Shake-speare, give this name in error for Charles the Bald.

77   *Lewis the Tenth*. This is an error, in Holinshed and Shakespeare, for Louis the Ninth. Hall is correct.

88   *appear* are plainly seen

94   *imbare* reveal to view. This explanation, though not very satisfactory, seems the best one can do with the Quarto's 'imbace' and the first Folio's 'imbarre'. Some editions read 'imbar' and interpret it as 'fence around', but it is hard to think that the French kings preferred to hide behind deceit rather than take steps to defend their title. In a comparable situation in *Edward III* (I.1.76), Edward rejects the King of France's claim, saying 'Truth hath pulled the visard from his face.'

99–100   *When the man dies, let the inheritance | Descend unto the daughter*. Numbers 27.8 reads, 'If a man die and have no son, then ye shall turn his inheritance unto his daughter.' Shakespeare omits 'and have no son'.

103   *great-grandsire* Edward III. Victorious at Crécy in 1346, he died in 1377.

108   *on a hill*. Holinshed tells how Edward III watched from 'a windmill hill', as the Black Prince waged the battle of Crécy: the play of *Edward III* treats of the incident (III.5.1–2).

114   *for action* for want of action

120   *the very May-morn of his youth*. Henry was 27; the prime of youth (the Roman *juventus*) was held to lie between 20 and 35.

123–4   *rouse ... lions*. To 'rouse' was a hunting term for disturbing a large animal from its lair, as in *1 Henry IV* – 'rouse a lion' (I.3.198); *Titus Andronicus* – 'rouse the proudest panther' (II.2.21); Marlowe, *Tamburlaine*, Part One – 'As princely lions when they rouse them-selves' (I.2.52).

126   *So hath your highness* so indeed you *have* (with an emphasis on 'hath')

136-9 *We must not only arm t'invade the French . . . With all advantages.* Henry's moral sense is satisfied; his practical sense must now ensure his kingdom's safety.

140 *marches* borders

145 *still* constantly

151 *gleanèd* stripped (of defenders)
assays assaults

155 *feared* frightened

156 *hear her but exampled by herself* note the examples she can provide from her own history

160 *taken and impounded as a stray* taken into custody like a strayed animal

161-2 *The King of Scots, whom she did send to France . . . kings.* King David II of Scotland was captured at Neville's Cross in 1346 while the main English army was in France. A story circulated, not in fact true, that he was sent to Edward III's camp at Calais, and the supposed episode occurs in the play of *Edward III* (V.1.63).

166-73 *But there's a saying very old and true . . . than she can eat.* In the Quarto this is spoken by '*Lord*', in the Folio by the Bishop of Ely. The corresponding speech in Holinshed is by Westmorland, and in *The Famous Victories* both the Archbishop and the Earl of Oxford have versions of it. In view of this uncertainty it seems best to follow the Folio, though many editors change to Westmorland.

173 *'tame* attame, broach, break into (a sense still current in country usage; compare Wright, *English Dialect Dictionary*, 'tame')

175 *Yet that is but a crushed necessity* yet the conclusion that that is necessary is a forced one

180-83 *For government, though high, and low, and lower . . . Like music.* These lines seem echoes of Elyot's *The Boke named the Governour* – 'In everything is order, and without order may be nothing stable or permanent: and it may not be called order, except it do contain in it degrees, high and base, according to the merit or estimation of the thing that is ordered' (Book I, chapter i), and 'Music, . . . how necessary it is for the better attaining the knowledge of a public weal: which . . . is made of an order of estates and degrees, and by reason thereof containeth in it a perfect harmony' (Book I, chapter vii).

181-2 *parts . . . consent . . . close.* These are musical terms for the separate melodies combining in a concluding cadence; *consent* unites the senses of 'agreement' and 'concent' (singing together). There may be an echo of Lyly's *Euphues* (see following note also), for, telling how bees delight in 'sweet and sound music', Lyly says they are called the Muses' birds, 'because they follow not the sound but the consent' (*Works*, ed. Bond, II.45).

187 *the honey-bees.* Elyot illustrates the need for a just ruler and obedient subjects from 'a little beast, which of all others is most to be marvelled at, I mean the bee' (*The Governour*, Book I, chapter ii), and he describes the ordered hive in a way which closely anticipates Shakespeare. But Lyly, in *Euphues*, may be the source; he tells how the commonwealth of bees 'live under a law' and 'choose a King, whose palace they frame both brave in show, and stronger in substance'. They call a parliament 'for laws, statutes, penalties, choosing officers', and 'every one hath his office, some trimming the honey, some working the wax, one framing hives, another the combs'. They 'keep watch and ward, as living in a camp to others', and their King 'goeth up and down, entreating, threatening, commanding' (*Works*, ed. Bond, II.45). Shakespeare's bees are still more anthropomorphic, performing all the functions of citizens; but the degree of similarity is striking. The idea goes back to Plato, Virgil, and Pliny.

188-9 *Creatures that by a rule in nature teach . . . to a peopled kingdom.* Elyot describes the bee as 'left to man by nature, as it seemeth, a perpetual figure of a just governance or rule' (*The Governour*, Book I, chapter ii).

190   *sorts* different ranks

207   *loosèd several ways* shot from several directions

211   *dial's* sundial's

220   *worried* shaken, savaged (as by a dog; see also II.2.83)

221   *hardiness and policy* courage and statesmanship

225   *ours* our just possession

234   *Not worshipped with a waxen epitaph* not honoured with even the most perishable memorial

243   *grace* spiritual virtue (as being a *Christian* king)

244   *is our wretches* (singular verb and plural subject again)

253   *galliard* dance (in lively triple time)

255   *meeter* more fitting

262   *rackets* (1) tennis-rackets; (2) noises (of gunfire)

264   *crown* (1) coin; (2) royal crown
    hazard (1) aperture in a tennis-court into which if the ball was struck it was unplayable; (2) jeopardy

265   *wrangler* (1) opponent; (2) disputant. (The 'hazard' in tennis was a great source of contention.)

266   *courts* (1) tennis-courts; (2) royal courts

267   *chases* (1) points forfeited at tennis when a ball was allowed to bounce twice; (2) pursuits

274   *keep my state* live up to my royal dignity

275   *sail* full swell

279   *I will rise there with so full a glory.* The metaphor is the frequent sun-image of royalty.

282   *pleasant* jocular

283   *gun-stones* cannon-balls (originally of stone)

290–94   *But this lies all within the will of God . . . well-hallowed cause.* Shakespeare continually brings Henry back to reverence for God's will; the religious references are not at all meant as perfunctory – they establish the war as a 'well-hallowed cause', approved by God.

305   *proportions* appointed forces

308   *God before* with God leading us

II. *Chorus*

2   *silken dalliance* silk-robed pleasure and idleness

6   *the mirror of all Christian kings.* Hall calls Henry the 'mirror of Christendom', Holinshed 'a lode-star in honour' (compare Epilogue.6 – 'This star of England') and 'mirror of magnificence'.

8–11   *For now sits expectation in the air ... Harry and his followers.* The motives here, of personal aggrandisement, are less altruistic than the 'honour's thought' of line 3 but no irony seems intended; the honour sought is worldly renown and its accompaniment of worldly splendour.

9   *hilts.* Since the hilt was made of several parts it was often spoken of in the plural, as it is also at II.1.61.

14   *policy* intrigue (the subversion of lines 20–30)

16   *model* image in miniature

19   *kind.* The senses of 'filial' and 'loving' are combined.

27   *fearful* frightened

28   *this grace of kings* this king who most honours the title (an echo, perhaps, of Chapman, *Seaven Bookes of the Iliades of Homere*, 1598, Book I, sig. C2^r – 'with her [Chryseis] the grace of kings | wise Ithacus ascended too')

29   *hell and treason.* Henry being the mirror of all Christian kings, treason against him is diabolic.

31–2   *digest | Th'abuse* stomach the flouting

32   *force a play* produce a play by cramming its events into a small compass

41–2   *But till the King come forth, and not till then ... our scene.* This looks like an afterthought; possibly the chorus ended at line 40 and was followed by scene 2, scene 1 being inserted later and the extra couplet being added to explain the delay in reaching Southampton. Needing to dispose of Falstaff before the King embarks for France, Shakespeare may have felt that a low-life scene was wanted here to prepare for scene 3.

II.1   (stage direction) *Corporal Nym.* Nym occurs in *The Merry Wives of Windsor* (date uncertain) but not in *Henry IV*. The name means 'taker', 'thief'; compare the pun at line 105.

    Lieutenant Bardolph. Bardolph was a corporal in *2 Henry IV* and becomes one again at III.2.3.

3   *Ancient* ensign, standard-bearer. Thomas Digges in *Stratioticos* (1579) defines the qualifications of an ensign, and Pistol should be measured against these: 'above all other [he ought] to have honourable respect of his charge, and to be no less careful and jealous thereof, than every honest and honourable gentleman should be of his wife. . . . Let the Ensign be a man of good account, honest and virtuous' (pages 93–4).

6   *wink* close my eyes

7   *what though* what of that

8   *endure cold.* When not hot (toasting cheese) it stays cold (with inactivity).

11   *sworn brothers* faithful comrades (in thieving; strictly, companions-in-arms sworn to the laws of chivalry)

15   *rest* stake in the game

    rendezvous last resort

26   *How now, mine host Pistol!* In the Folio, this forms the end of Bardolph's speech, but the Quarto allots the corresponding words to Nym, and he rather than the inoffensive Bardolph seems the proper target of Pistol's wrath.

27–9   *Base tike, call'st thou me host . . . lodgers.* The first Folio gives most of Pistol's verses as prose: see Collation lists on pages 225–6, 228–9.

36   *Lieutenant.* As an ensign, Pistol was in effect a sub-lieutenant; at III.6.12 he is 'aunchient lieutenant'.

39   *Iceland dog.* Nym is evidently shaggy: 'Iceland dogs, curled and rough all over, . . . by reason of the length of their hair, make show neither of face nor of body' (A. Fleming, *Of English Dogges*, 1576). They were kept as lap-dogs.

40–41   *show thy valour, and put up your sword.* The Hostess is given, in this play and in *2 Henry IV*, to self-contradictory remarks.

42   *solus* alone (theatre Latin). Pistol, a shaky linguist, takes it as an insult; or he may take Nym to mean 'I'd prefer you unmarried' (compare line 70).

44   *mervailous.* F1's form is worth retaining as more fitting to the metre than 'marvellous'. The spelling may be Shakespeare's normal one (similar spellings occur in other Shakespeare plays) or it may represent Pistol's idiosyncratic diction.

49   *take* (1) take offence, or take fire; (2) strike
     cock is up trigger is cocked (with a bawdy quibble)

51   *Barbason.* This also occurs in *The Merry Wives of Windsor* (II.2.265) among 'the names of fiends'; it is of uncertain origin. Reginald Scot's *Discoverie of Witchcraft* (1584) names among principal devils one 'Marbas *alias* Barbas', who 'appeareth in the form of a mighty lion; but at the commandment of a conjuror cometh up in the form of a man and answereth fully as touching anything which is hidden or secret' (page 378). Shakespeare may have half-recalled this.
     conjure exorcize. (Pistol's threats in lines 43–8 sound like the rigmaroles used for conjuring or exorcizing devils.)

53   *foul* (1) abusive; (2) dirty (of a pistol barrel)
     scour (1) thrash; (2) clean out. (Nym will run his sword through Pistol as if it were a scouring-rod.)

59   *exhale* draw (a Pistolian extravagance; used normally of the sun drawing phosphorescent vapours from the earth)

63   *mickle* much

65   *tall* valiant

68   *Couple a gorge!* Pistol has prepared some useful tags for the campaign; compare IV.4.37 and end of note to IV.6.37.

70   *hound of Crete* (species of shaggy dog, like 'Iceland dog', II.1.39)

72 *powdering tub* (properly) vat for salting meat; (colloquially) sweating tub used in treating venereal disease

73 *lazar kite of Cressid's kind* leprous whore. In Henryson's *Testament of Cresseid* (written late fifteenth century; printed 1532) the God of Love strikes the faithless Cressida with leprosy; 'kites of Cressid's kind' was a proverbial phrase, kites being birds of prey. In *2 Henry IV* Doll is haled off to prison for brothel-violence with Pistol.

76 *pauca* in few words

77 (stage direction) *Enter the Boy.* The Boy is Falstaff's page, given him by Prince Hal in *2 Henry IV* (I.2.15).

81 *warming-pan.* Bardolph's red nose is the subject of repeated jests in *Henry IV* and *Henry V*.

83 *yield the crow a pudding* die (a proverbial phrase, originally applied to a dead animal whose flesh the crows would peck; *pudding* = stuffed guts, as in 'black pudding')

85 *presently* at once

92 *Base is the slave that pays!* The phrase was proverbial.

94 *As manhood shall compound* in the way a brave man settles such differences

101 *I shall have my eight shillings I won of you at betting?* This is not in the Folio but editors supply it from the Quarto as necessary to Pistol's reply.

102 *noble* coin worth 6s. 8d. (less than Pistol owes, but with the advantage of 'present pay')

106 *sutler* provision-seller. Pistol does not in fact figure in this lucrative role.

114 *quotidian tertian.* This is typical Hostess's confusion; a quotidian ague caused a fit daily, a tertian every third day.

116 *run bad humours on* upset by his displeasure

117 *even* plain truth

119 *corroborate* (strictly, strengthened, but Pistolian for) broken

121 *passes some humours and careers* lets himself go when he feels like it. To 'pass the career' in horsemanship was to do a short gallop at full stretch.

II.2.4-5 *As if allegiance in their bosoms sat,* | *Crownèd with faith and constant loyalty* as if fealty ruled their natures under the crown of faith and loyalty

18 *in head* as an armed force

34 *quittance* due recompense

40 *Enlarge* set at liberty

43 *his more advice* his thinking better of it

44 *security* confidence

53 *orisons* pleas

54 *on distemper* from a disordered condition (the 'temper' being the proper balance of the disposition)

61 *late commissioners* persons lately appointed to the commission to act for the King during his absence. This handing out of supposed 'commissions' does not occur in the sources.

79 *quick* alive

85 *English monsters.* The conspirators' treachery is the more 'monstrous' in that they are *English*; 'monsters' (monstrosities) were commonly shown as exotic marvels.

87 *appertinents* things appertaining

90 *practices* plots

99 *practised on* plotted against

107 *so grossly in a natural cause* so glaringly for their natural ends

108 *That admiration did not whoop at them* that they caused no outcry of surprise

109 *proportion* natural order

110 *Wonder to wait on* astonishment to accompany

112 *so preposterously* in a manner so inverting the natural order

114 *suggest* instigate

115 *botch and bungle up damnation* clumsily disguise the damnable deeds they incite to

118 *tempered thee* wrought thee to his will

122 *his lion gait* his devil's stride (an echo of 1 Peter 5.8 – 'your adversary the devil, as a roaring lion, walketh about seeking whom he may devour'.)

123 *vasty* wide and waste (the two senses are combined)
    Tartar Tartarus (the hell of classical mythology)

126 *jealousy* suspicion

134 *complement* the qualities which make the complete man

137 *bolted* sifted, refined

151–65 *Our purposes God justly hath discovered . . . pardon, sovereign.* The plotters receive their sentences in a manner which strengthens the nation's unity under God.

155–7 *For me, the gold of France did not seduce . . . what I intended.* Holinshed attributes the plotters' treachery to bribes received from the French King but says further that Cambridge's motive was basically to seat on the throne the legitimate claimant Edmund Mortimer, Earl of March (the Mortimer of *1 Henry IV* and *1 Henry VI*), who was expected to die and be succeeded by Cambridge's heirs as next in line.

169 *earnest* part-payment in advance

175 *tender* tend, watch over

181 *dear* dire

183 *like* equally

184 *lucky* fortunate

188 *rub* impediment

191 *expedition* speedy motion

192 *signs* banners

II.3.3 *earn* yearn, grieve

9 *Arthur's* Abraham's (compare Luke 16.22 – 'the beggar died, and was carried by the angels into Abraham's bosom'). The Hostess merges the biblical heaven with

the Arthurian Isle of Avalon, whither her knightly patron has gone to join the company of the Round Table.

11   *a finer end* as fine an end as can be imagined (and certainly finer than going to hell)

    an as if

    christom newly christened (and so in perfect innocence). The Hostess amalgamates 'christen' and 'chrisom', a chrisom child being one dying within a month of birth, during which time it wore the white chrisom cloth put on it at its christening. Bunyan's Mr Badman is reported to have 'died like a lamb, or, as they call it, like a chrisom-child'.

13   *turning o'th'tide.* There is an ancient and widespread belief that a man at the point of death will die as the flood tide turns to the ebb.

13–17   *for after I saw him fumble with the sheets . . . fields.* Many writers from classical antiquity onwards list similar details as signs of approaching death. Dover Wilson cites Thomas Lupton, *A Thousand Notable Things* (1578), Book IX – 'If the forehead of the sick wax red, and his nose wax sharp, if he pull straws or the clothes of his bed, these are most certain tokens of death.'

16–17   *'a babbled of green fields.* This reading, originated by Theobald in his edition of 1733, for the Folio's 'a Table of greene fields' is perhaps the most famous of Shakespeare emendations. The Quarto reads 'talk of floures'.

25   *as cold as any stone.* 'Such is the end of Falstaff, from whom Shakespeare had promised us in his epilogue to *Henry IV* that we should receive more merriment. . . . But whether he could contrive no train of adventures suitable to his character, or could match him with no companions likely to quicken his humour, or could open no new vein of pleasantry, and was afraid to continue the same strain lest it should not find the same reception, he has here for ever discarded him, and made

haste to dispatch him, perhaps for the same reason for which Addison killed Sir Roger, that no other hand might attempt to exhibit him. Let meaner authors learn from this example, that it is dangerous to sell the bear which is yet not hunted; to promise to the public what they have not written' (Johnson).

26   *of* against. Falstaff is making his 'finer end' by ruing his excesses.

35   *rheumatic.* This is a Quicklyism for lunatic, delirious; in *2 Henry IV* she calls Falstaff and Doll 'as rheumatic as two dry toasts' (II.4.54–5), though the 'rheumatic humour' was in fact cold and damp.

35–6   *Whore of Babylon* the Church of Rome (in Protestant interpretation of the scarlet woman of Revelation 17. 3–9, 'great Babylon, the mother of whoredom and abominations of the earth', drunken with the blood of the martyrs, and riding a seven-headed beast symbolizing seven mountains on which she sits). This no doubt put 'rheumatic' into the Hostess's mind, Rome being pronounced 'Room'.

41   *riches.* There is word-play on the normal sense and on 'rich' as red(-faced, -nosed); compare Lodge, *A Looking Glasse for London* – 'you and I have been tossing many a good cup of ale, your nose is grown very rich.'

42   *shog* be off

46   *Let senses rule* keep your wits about you
      Pitch and pay pay as you go, cash down, no credit (a proverbial phrase)

48   *wafer-cakes* (flimsy as) thin pastry

49   *Holdfast is the only dog.* This echoes the proverb, 'Brag is a good dog, but Holdfast is a better.'

50   *Caveto* beware

54   *And that's but unwholesome food.* Compare Andrew Boorde, *Dyetary of Helth* (1542) – 'The blood of all beasts and fowls is not praised, for it is hard of digestion.'

58   *housewifery* careful housekeeping

59   *Farewell! Adieu!* This is the last we see of the Eastcheap company in its familiar haunts.

II.4   (stage direction) *Britaine* Brittany, Bretagne. Shakespeare's spelling indicates the required pronunciation (in line 4, for instance).

7   *line* strengthen

10   *gulf* whirlpool (compare IV.3.82)

13   *fatal and neglected* fatally underrated

25   *Whitsun morris-dance.* Morris-dances were held at Whitsuntide or on 1 May as spring festivities, by performers with blackened faces and bell-hung costumes. The name refers to their supposed Moorish origin, though the characters presented persons in the Robin Hood and other medieval stories.

28   *humorous* capricious

34   *modest in exception* reasonable in raising objections

36   *forespent* formerly indulged

37   *Brutus.* Lucius Junius Brutus feigned stupidity (*brutus* = stupid) as a safeguard while planning to expel the tyrannous Tarquinius Superbus, last King of Rome; he became one of the first consuls, in 509 B.C.

40   *delicate* fine (in quality) and sensitive

45   *So the proportions of defence are filled* thus the necessary defensive forces are fully provided

46   *of a weak and niggardly projection* if planned too scantily

50   *fleshed* inured to carnage

54   *Crécy battle.* Of Henry's campaign Holinshed writes, 'At length the King approached the river Seine, and ... came ... where his great-grandfather King Edward the Third a little before had stricken the battle of Crécy.' Crécy was fought in 1346.

57   *mountain sire.* 'Mountain' may be an error by attraction from 'mountain standing'. If correct, it presumably means 'of more than human stature'.

on mountain standing. Compare I.2.108, note.

69 *Turn head* stand at bay (a hunting term)

77–95 *He wills you, in the name of God Almighty ... true challenger.* Exeter is to be taken as voicing not a propagandist manifesto but a God-approved claim.

83 *ordinance of times* time-honoured usage

85 *sinister* illegitimate (associated with the 'bar sinister' of irregular descent)
   awkward perverse

90 *overlook* look over

99 *fierce* (two syllables)

100 *Jove.* The Greek Zeus, Roman Jupiter or Jove, was lord of the heavens, ruler of gods and men. His weapon was the thunderbolt.

101 *requiring* demanding

102 *in the bowels of the Lord.* The phrase originates in Philippians 1.8, but here echoes Holinshed – '[Henry] exhorted the French King in the bowels of Jesu Christ, to render him that which was his own, whereby effusion of Christian blood might be avoided.'

107 *privèd* bereaved

124 *womby vaultages* hollow recesses

126 *second accent* echo
   ordinance ordnance, cannon

131 *Paris balls* tennis-balls (so called because the game came to England from the French capital)

132 *Louvre.* The spelling 'Louer' (that is, Lover) in the Quarto and Folio suggests a pronunciation quibbling on 'mistress court' in line 133.

136 *greener* less mature

140 (stage direction) *Flourish.* This is to mark the King's rising.

III. *Chorus*

1 *imagined wing* wing of imagination

5 *brave* gaily decked

6   *the young Phoebus fanning* fluttering against the early-morning sun

12   *bottoms* hulls

17   *Harfleur* (accented on the first syllable throughout; spelt 'Harflew(e)' in the Folio)

18   *Grapple your minds to sternage of this navy* let your thoughts seize the sterns of these ships (and be drawn to France)

32   *likes* pleases

33   *linstock* ignited stick (the staff holding the gunner's lighted match)

     (stage direction) *chambers* small cannon (for giving salutes, or for theatre use)

III.1.7   *conjure*. Almost all editions follow Rowe's 'summon' (for the Folio's 'commune'), but, as the new Arden edition argues, 'conjure' is graphically closer and quite as appropriate.

8   *hard-favoured* hard-featured

10   *portage* port-holes, embrasures

12   *gallèd* fretted (by the sea)

13   *jutty his confounded base* beetle over its ruined base

18   *fet* fetched, derived

     of war-proof tested in war

21   *argument* further opposition

27   *mettle of your pasture* quality of your nurture

31   *slips* leashes (for restraining dogs before releasing them)

III.2.3   *Pray thee, Corporal, stay*. It is amusing to have Nym's antiheroics immediately after Henry's valiant rant, but too much should not be made of them as ironic deflation: cowardly camp-followers out for loot are part of war but are not authorities on its values. The play demands heroism even though it admits the reasonable case against heroics which the soldiers present in IV.1.

4   *case* set

5   *humour of it* way it's going

       very plainsong simple truth (tune unadorned by harmonies)

6   *humours* bad humours, rages

21   *cullions* rascals

22   *mould* mortal clay

25   *bawcock* fine fellow (French, '*beau coq*')

26   *These be good humours!* This is a fine way to carry on!

26–7   *wins bad humours* makes everyone angry

29   *swashers* blusterers, swashbucklers

31   *antics* buffoons

35   *breaks words* (1) bandies words (not blows); (2) breaks his word

36–7   *men of few words are the best men.* 'Few words are best' was proverbial.

42   *purchase* booty

46   *carry coals* (1) do any dirty work; (2) put up with insults (a proverbial phrase)

50   *pocketing up of wrongs.* This quibbles on the usual sense, 'putting up with insults'.

53   *cast it up.* This is a quibble.

58   *disciplines of the war* military science

60–61   *is digt himself four yard under the countermines.* Fluellen presumably means to say 'has dug himself countermines four yards under (our mines)'.

62   *plow up all, if there is not better directions.* The Folio is inconsistent in its indications of dialect ('plow', 'better'), which the actor will doubtless regularize.

70–71   *the true disciplines of the wars ... the Roman disciplines.* For apparent echoes of Thomas Digges's *An Arithmeticall Militare Treatise, named Stratioticos* see the Introduction, p. 18.

71   (stage direction) *Enter Captain Macmorris and Captain Jamy.* The addition of the Irishman and the Scot to the Englishman and the Welshman symbolizes the wide provenance of forces under Henry's command.

75   *expedition* readiness (in argument)

81   *Good-e'en* good evening (but used any time after noon)

84   *pioneers* miners

100   *quit* requite, answer

118   *Of my nation?* Macmorris may be so inflammable that he catches fire before he even understands what is being said, or he may think that Fluellen is accusing the Irish of being present only in small numbers.

III.3.1-43   *How yet resolves the Governor ... be thus destroyed?* The modern reader is not likely to applaud what looks like Henry's unholy relish in so ruthlessly depicting war's horrors and then blaming the proposed victims for provoking them. But the play takes him to be in the right and his foes to be in the wrong, his army is in peril, and as commander he must shake his opponents' nerve; having done so he shows mercy. The apparent sadism is only Shakespeare's vividness in description.

4   *proud of destruction* elated with the prospect of death

24   *bootless* vainly

31   *O'erblows* blows away

      contagious. Pestilence was supposed to drop from the clouds – here the pestilence of hysterical cruelty dropping from the clouds of war.

40-41 *as did the wives of Jewry ... slaughtermen.* Matthew 2.16-18 – 'Then Herod ... sent forth, and slew all the children that were in Bethlehem.... In Rama was there a voice heard, lamentation, weeping, and great mourning.'

43   *guilty in defence* guilty because defending yourselves in a wrongful cause

54   *Use mercy to them all.* Shakespeare diverges markedly from Holinshed, who relates that even after the surrender 'the town [was] sacked, to the great gain of the Englishmen.'

55   *sickness growing.* 'The number of his people was much

minished by the flix [flux] and other fevers' (Holinshed).

58   *addressed* prepared

III.4.1–58   The French text in this edition has been regularized, but
not fully corrected, in many details. The Folio version
is, however, sufficiently comprehensible to suggest that
the original script was tolerably accurate.

14   *nailès*. The Folio spelling 'Nayles' throughout (save
for line 41, 'Maylees') suggests disyllabic pronunciation.

47   *count* (pronounced, more or less, 'coont', as 'gown' was,
more or less, 'goon')

49–50   *mots de son mauvais . . . impudique.* Katherine associates
the words with the vulgar French '*foutre*' (coition;
compare '*figo*' at III.6.56, note) and '*con*' (female
organ).

III.5.2   *withal* with

5   *sprays* (bastard) offshoots

6   *luxury* lust

9   *overlook their grafters* look down on those from whom
they were transplanted

11   *Mort Dieu! Ma vie!* The Quarto reads '*Mordeu ma
via*' and the Folio '*Mort du ma vie*', which many editors
render as '*Mort de ma vie*'. At IV.5.3 the Quarto has
'*Mor du ma vie*' and the Folio '*Mor Dieu ma vie*'.
'*Vie*' here is a disyllable.

13   *slobbery* sloppy

14   *nook-shotten* 'having many sharp turns or angles'
(Wright, *English Dialect Dictionary*), angular, crooked
(with the figurative implication of 'angular', 'perverse',
in temper as well as shape)

15   *batailles* (a trisyllable)

17   *as in despite* as if despising them

18–20   *Can sodden water . . . heat?* Can their cold blood be so warmed up by their barley-brew (ale), the stewed-up liquor of the malt-and-water mash they give their weary horses?

18   *sodden* boiled

19   *drench* drink

       sur-reined over-ridden. (For an *Edward III* echo, see III.7.148 below, 'out of beef', note.)

23   *roping* hanging rope-like

26   *Lest poor we.* The first Folio reads 'Poor we', which is defective; the second Folio reads 'Poor we may', which mends the metre but is unauthoritative and a jolt in sense. The proposed reading maintains the train of thought ('Let us not hang ... Lest ... ').

29   *bred out* exhausted by breeding

33   *lavoltas* dances with high capers

       corantos dances with quick running steps

34–5   *grace ... heels ... lofty runaways.* Quibbles abound; the sense is, 'The only thing that distinguishes us is our agility (in dancing, or in fleeing), and we are lofty (high-born, or high-leaping) performers in running (corantos, or away from danger)'.

40–45   *Charles Delabreth, High Constable ... and Charolois.* These names occur in Holinshed's list of the French lords captured or slain at Agincourt, save for Berri and Charolois, who take part in the council of war but not in the battle. Holinshed spells Burgundy 'Burgognie' (Folio 'Burgonie'), Faulconbridge 'Fauconberge' (earlier 'Fauconbridge'), and Foix 'Fois' (Folio 'Loys'); Lestrake (Holinshed) becomes 'Lestrale' in the Folio, which most editors follow.

60   *for achievement* as his sole accomplishment, instead of victory

64   *Prince Dauphin, you shall stay with us in Rouen.* Shakespeare here follows Holinshed, who reports that the French King forbade the Dauphin to fight. In III.7, IV.2, and IV.5, however, the Dauphin is taking part, as he evidently was also in the *Henry V* play mentioned by

Nashe (see the Introduction, p. 8) and in the episode Shakespeare had referred to when Henry 'made the Dauphin and the French to stoop' (*3 Henry VI*, I.1.108). The idea may have originated in a later remark of Holinshed's, that the French mob who pillaged the English camp would have been punished 'if the Dauphin had longer lived'.

III.6.1–2   *the bridge*. The keeping of the bridge over the River Ternoise was essential for the English march to Calais. Holinshed records that Henry, 'doubting [fearing] lest if the same bridge should be broken it would be greatly to his hindrance, appointed certain captains, with their bands, to go thither with all speed before him, and to take possession thereof, and to keep it, till his coming thither. Those that were sent, finding the Frenchmen busy to break down the bridge, assailed them so vigorously that they discomfited them, and took and slew them; and so the bridge was preserved.'

6   *magnanimous* great-souled (the literal sense)

12   *aunchient lieutenant*. Compare II.1.36, note.

25   *buxom* sturdy

26–8   *And giddy Fortune's furious fickle wheel ... restless stone*. Pistol mixes up two traditional emblems of Fortune, as the power turning the wheel on which men rise and fall, and as the blindfold figure balancing upon the rolling stone of change and chance.

37   *moral* allegorical figure

38   *Fortune is Bardolph's foe, and frowns on him*. This echoes the familiar tag, 'Fortune's my foe', and the ballad line, 'Fortune, my foe! Why dost thou frown on me?'

39   *pax* little picture of the Crucifixion, kissed by communicants at Mass. Holinshed's word is 'pix', the box for the consecrated wafers at communion.

41   *Let gallows gape for dog*. Animals were sometimes

195

hanged for misdemeanours; compare the phrase, 'Hangdog look', and Dekker's *Honest Whore*, Part One – 'Now you look like an old he-cat, going to the gallows' (II.1.131–2).

42   *let not hemp his windpipe suffocate.* Holinshed relates that 'a soldier took a pix out of a church, for which he was apprehended, and the King not once removed till the box was restored, and the offender strangled.' In the play Henry does not thus personally insist on his old companion's execution, but the impersonal way in which he receives the news in line 104 marks the gulf which separates his old from his new life.

56   *figo* fig. The phrase has lost its original coarseness, by which it meant the rude gesture, supposedly Spanish in origin (compare line 58), of thrusting the thumb between the clenched fingers or into the mouth.

66–79   *'tis a gull, a fool, a rogue ... marvellously mistook.* Satire on the tricks of bogus soldiers is common in Elizabethan literature.

71   *sconce* fort, earthwork

82   *find a hole in his coat* find a weak spot in him (a proverbial phrase)

84   *speak with him* tell him my news

99–101   *his face ... fire.* Shakespeare may be recalling Chaucer's Summoner, with his 'fire-reed' face blotched with 'whelkes white' and 'knobbes sitting on his chekes'.

99   *bubukles* sores, tumours. Fluellen combines '*bubo*' (Latin, abscess) and '*charbucle*' (a variant of carbuncle).

100   *whelks* pimples

104–10   *We would have all such offenders so cut off ... soonest winner.* Commentators unwilling to allow Henry any motives but those of cold expediency cite this speech as evincing mere calculating policy, but Shakespeare is unreservedly adopting Holinshed's tribute to the English army as observing strict discipline before Agincourt, even in difficult straits – 'Yet in this great necessity the poor people of the country were not spoiled, nor anything taken of them without payment, nor any outrage or offence done.'

110 (stage direction) *Tucket* (a preliminary trumpet signal) *Montjoy*. Like 'Garter' in Britain, this is the title of the chief herald of France, not a personal name.

111 *You know me by my habit*. This is a terse, discourteous opening, which Henry answers in the same vein.
habit herald's tabard

118 *Advantage* the restraint which awaits a favourable opportunity

120 *bruise an injury* (1) squeeze out an abscess; (2) hit back at the cause of our harm

123 *admire our sufferance* be astonished to find that our patience was not caused by weakness

138-45 *tell thy King I do not seek him now ... so many French*. In Holinshed, Henry replies, 'Mine intent is to do as it pleaseth God. I will not seek your master at this time; but if he or his seek me, I will meet with them, God willing. ... And yet wish I not any of you so unadvised as to be the occasion that I dye your tawny ground with your red blood' (compare lines 158-60). He does not, however, admit his army's plight, as he so frankly does here.

140 *impeachment* impediment (French, 'empêchement')
sooth truth

III.7 (stage direction) *Dauphin*. For the Dauphin's presence at Agincourt, contrary to the chronicles, see III.5.64, note.

12 *but on four pasterns* merely on natural hooves. The pastern is the part of the foot between the fetlock and hoof.

13 *as if his entrails were hairs* as if he were a tennis-ball (stuffed, as tennis-balls were, with hair)

14 *Pegasus, chez les narines de feu* Pegasus (the winged horse of classical fable), with fiery nostrils. Some

editors correct Shakespeare's *chez* to the more orthodox *avec*.

17   *the pipe of Hermes*. Hermes, or Mercury, invented the musical pipe and with it charmed asleep the many-eyed monster Argus.

18   *nutmeg* dull brown. Horses' colours were thought to reflect their temperaments. 'A good horse cannot be of a bad colour' was proverbial.

20   *Perseus*. A son of Zeus; his winged sandals bore him through the air to destroy the Gorgon, Medusa.
     air and fire. Compare Prologue 1, note; also *Antony and Cleopatra*, V.2.287–8 – 'I am fire and air; my other elements | I give to baser life.'

23   *all other jades you may call beasts* all other horses are poor specimens, merely animals

26   *palfreys* saddle-horses ('for ordinary riding, esp. for ladies' [*Oxford English Dictionary*], as distinguished from war-horses). The Dauphin errs in nomenclature, unless Shakespeare is implying effeminacy in him, which the context by no means suggests.

30–31   *from the rising of the lark to the lodging of the lamb*. 'To go to bed with the lamb and rise with the lark' was proverbial.

34   *argument* theme for discourse

38–40   *I once writ a sonnet ... mistress*. The idea may come from *Edward III*, where Edward orders a poem of surpassing praise, and, when the poet asks about the intended recipient, replies, 'Thinkest thou I did bid thee praise a horse?' (I.2.92).

43   *bears* carries her riders

44   *prescript* prescribed

47   *shrewdly* sharply (with a quibble on 'shrewishly')

49   *bridled*. There is a quibble on the bridle worn by a horse and the bridle or gag used to quiet a shrew.

51   *kern* light-armed Irish soldier
     French hose wide breeches

52   *strait strossers* tight trousers (the skin of the bare legs)

57   *jade* (1) low-grade horse, hack; (2) trollop

59   *own hair* (that is, as distinct from human mistresses decked out with false hair; compare *The Merchant of Venice*, III.2. 92–5 – 'So are those crispèd snaky golden locks, | Which make such wanton gambols with the wind | Upon supposèd fairness, often known | To be the dowry of a second head.')

62–3   *Le chien . . . bourbier.* 2 Peter 2.22 – 'The dog is turned to his own vomit again, and the sow that was washed to her wallowing in the mire.' The sentence was proverbial, and Shakespeare had already made powerful use of it in *2 Henry IV* (I.3.97–9) when the Archbishop calls the populace 'thou common dog', and continues, '[thou] didst . . . disgorge | Thy glutton bosom of the royal Richard; | And now thou wouldst eat thy dead vomit up'.

71   *a many* a lot

79–80   *faced out of my way* (1) put out of countenance; (2) driven off by (enemy) faces

82   *go to hazard* play dice; *hazard* was so called because of its tricky rules. Compare Holinshed – 'The [French] soldiers the night before had played [that is, played for] the Englishmen at dice.'

89   *he will eat all he kills* (a proverbial tag)

92   *tread out* (1) dance away; (2) tread into extinction

108   *hooded* concealed (like a hawk under the hood that subdues it)

109   *bate.* This is a quibble: (1) flutter its wings for action (referring to a hawk); (2) dwindle (referring to the Dauphin's valour).

121   *overshot* (1) outshot, outdone; (2) mistaken

130   *mope* go blundering about

131   *knowledge* familiar bearings

132   *apprehension* (1) understanding; (2) sense of fear

138   *mastiffs.* English mastiffs were famous for bull- and bear-baiting.

143   *sympathize with* resemble

148   *shrewdly* severely
        out of beef. This seems to echo *Edward III* (III.3.
        159–62) when the King of France says of the English
        soldiers, 'but scant them of their chines of beef, |
        ... | And presently they are as resty stiff | As 'twere
        a many over-ridden jades' (compare 'sur-reined jades'
        at III.5.19, above).

IV. *Chorus*

9   *battle* army
        umbered shadowed
12   *accomplishing* putting the finishing touches to
17   *secure* carefree
25   *gesture sad* grave demeanour
26   *Investing* enveloping
39   *overbears attaint* conquers any blemish (of weariness)
45   *mean and gentle* humble and high-born
46   *as may unworthiness define* as far as our unworthy
        efforts may present it
49–53   *we shall much disgrace ... their mockeries be.* Stage-
        battles were often satirized; compare Sidney's *An
        Apologie for Poetrie* – 'Two armies fly in represented
        with four swords and bucklers, and then what hard
        heart will not receive it for a pitched field?' Jonson is
        equally derisive in the prologue to *Every Man In His
        Humour* about 'three rusty swords' set to fight the Wars
        of the Roses.

IV.1   This admirable scene shows the 'little touch of Harry
        in the night' in relationship with the various ranks
        which form the army, the King's brothers, generals,
        camp-followers, captains, and common soldiers.
7   *husbandry* management
10   *dress us* prepare ourselves. Holinshed reports that
        though the English were 'hungry, weary, sore travelled,
        and vexed with many cold diseases', yet they took holy

communion and made confession; compare lines 172–80, below.

23   *With casted slough* like a snake after it has cast its dead skin (before which it is torpid)

34   *God-a-mercy* I thank thee (strictly, 'God have mercy', but confused with 'gramercy' ['graunt mercy', that is, great thanks])

39   *gentleman of a company* non-commissioned officer

40   *Trail'st thou the puissant pike?* That is, are you in the infantry? (The pike was carried by holding it below the point, trailing the butt along the ground.)

44   *bawcock* fine fellow (French, '*beau coq*'); compare III.2.25.

45   *imp* scion, son. Pistol calls the King 'most royal imp of fame' in *2 Henry IV*, V.5.43.

48   *lovely bully* splendid fellow

55   *Saint Davy's day* 1 March (the Welsh national day, when Welshmen wear their national emblem to mark the supposed anniversary of their victory over the Saxons on that date in A.D. 540).

60   *figo.* Compare III.6.56, note.

65   *fewer.* The Folio reads 'fewer', the Quarto 'lewer' ('lower' in the third Quarto). Since Gower has spoken only two words, and later promises to 'speak lower', many editors read 'lower' here. But Fluellen's reproof is against 'tiddle-taddle' and 'pibble-pabble', and the comedy is in his loquacious warning to the taciturn Gower to speak less.

66   *admiration* cause of astonishment

67   *prerogatifes* due rights

82   *out of fashion* (1) out of the expected form or shape; (2) unconventional in manner

93–4   *A good old commander . . . gentleman.* The various ranks on the English side know and trust each other.

99–107   *I think the King is but a man . . . as ours are.* In a sense the King is quibbling in equating the reactions of 'the King' to his own as supposedly those of an ordinary man; yet what he says is in fact true – the King is a human being, though with the extra weight of responsibility.

101   *element* sky

104   *affections are higher mounted* feelings soar higher

105   *stoop* descend (the falconry word for the hawk's swoop on its prey)

113   *at all adventures* whatever might come of it

114   *my conscience* (1) what I honestly believe; (2) what I actually know (a slight quibble)

123–4   *his cause being just.* The moral bearing of this discussion, and the validity of the King's case, depend on the justice of his cause; this assertion is not a mere official gloss but a fundamental tenet of the play.

133   *the latter day* the Day of Judgement

138   *charitably* in Christian charity

141–2   *proportion of subjection* due relation of subject to ruler

143–54   *So, if a son . . . services.* This argument has been thought sophistical on the grounds that Williams's hypothesis is that the King's cause may not be good, whereas Henry's answer is concerned only with the soldiers' possible misdemeanours. But by all the hypotheses of the play Henry's cause is righteous. If his soldiers die in sin, therefore, the sin must result from their own wrongdoings, not from their fighting wrongfully. For Dr Johnson's comment, see the Introduction, p. 48. As in the address to Scroop, Henry presses his arguments so long as to suggest that he enjoys rhetorical virtuosity, but what he actually says is perfectly valid.

148–9   *irreconciled* unabsolved

155–6   *arbitrement of* settlement by

164   *beadle* officer of the law (a minor functionary who whipped offenders)

169   *unprovided* unprepared (for death)

175   *death is to him advantage.* This echoes Philippians I.21 in the Genevan and Bishops' Bible versions – 'Christ is to me life, and death is to me advantage.'

181–2   *'Tis certain ... the King is not to answer it.* Williams assents because he is convinced, not because he is browbeaten.

183   *I do not desire he should answer for me* I do not want him to have to answer for me (that is, I hope I shan't be killed)

192   *You pay him then!* Well, you *are* going to pay him out, aren't you!

193   *elder-gun* pop-gun (made from a hollow elder stick)

198   *round* blunt

210   *take* give

218–19   *lay twenty French crowns* (1) bet twenty écus (about 6s. each); (2) venture twenty French heads

220–21   *but it is no English treason to cut French crowns.* For an Englishman to clip bits off English coins, or English skulls, would be treasonable, but for him to do so to the French is not so at all.

223–77   *Upon the King! ... best advantages.* Johnson has a characteristic note – 'There is something very striking and solemn in this soliloquy.... Something like this, on less occasions, every breast has felt. Reflection and seriousness rush upon the mind upon the separation of a gay company, and especially after forced and unwilling merriment.' All the same, there is something of the oratorical display in its *parti pris* – or perhaps, more humanly, a touch of petulance suggesting tense nerves.

224   *careful* anxious

229   *wringing* aches and pains

238   *thy soul of adoration* the real nature of the adoration offered thee

246   *Thinks thou* (a frequent second-person singular form for verbs ending in a dental or guttural consonant)

247   *blown from adulation* inflated by the wind of flattery

253   *balm ... ball* oil of consecration ... orb of sovereignty (given to the monarch at coronation)

256   *farcèd* stuffed up

266   *Phoebus* (the sun-god)

267   *Elysium* (the place of ideal happiness – in classical mythology, the abode of the virtuous dead)

268   *Hyperion* (the father of the sun-god – often taken for the sun-god himself)

270   *profitable labour*. The King is rather forcing his argument; the labour of the 'wretched slave' is hardly to be called 'profitable'.

273   *fore-hand* superiority

274   *member of the country's peace* participant in the peace the country enjoys under proper rule. 'The King's [or, God's] peace' was a legal term for 'peaceful recognition of the authority, . . . and acceptance of the protection, of a king or lord' (*Oxford English Dictionary*).

277   *advantages* (1) benefits from (if 'peasant' is the subject); or (2) benefits (if 'hours' is the subject – with the frequent plural noun and singular verb)

278   *jealous of* anxious about

285–98   *Not today, O Lord . . . Imploring pardon.* At this crisis of the war Henry admits the moral problem underlying his reign – whether God will visit upon him the consequences of Richard II's deposition and murder by Henry IV, or whether his own succession is religiously validated by the justice of his rule.

294   *Two chantries.* Henry founded the religious houses of Bethlehem at Sheen and of Sion at Twickenham, on opposite sides of the Thames, but there seems no evidence that this was done to expiate Richard's fate.

295   *still* continually

IV.2.3–4   *Via! Les eaux et la terre! . . . Ciel, cousin Orleans!* In the Folio these speeches read, '*Via les ewes & terre.*' – '*Rien puis le air & feu.*' – '*Cein, Cousin Orleance.*' The sense is, probably, 'Away! [over] water and land!' – 'Nothing more? Not air and fire?' – '[Yes,] Heaven itself!'

9   *dout* put out

superfluous courage blood (identified with valour) of which our horses have more than they need

16   *shales* shells, outer cases

19   *curtle-axe* cutlass

26   *squares* formations (in square form)

27   *hilding* good-for-nothing

29   *speculation* onlooking

33   *tucket sonance* trumpet flourish (as signal for military or stage action)

34   *dare the field* (1) defy the foe; (2) daze the prey (a fowling term, 'to dare' being to dazzle or fascinate birds so that they can be captured)

37   *carrions* corpses for birds to scavenge. A parallel notion to that here and in lines 49–50 occurs in *Edward III* (IV.5.49–51) – 'these ravens for the carcasses | Of those poor English that are marked to die | Hover about.' (Compare 'If we are marked to die …', IV.3.20, below.)

39   *curtains* banners

40   *passing* more than

42   *beaver* visor

43–4   *candlesticks, | With torch-staves in their hand.* Candlesticks were sometimes made in the form of horsemen, the candle being the lance held upright; in *The White Devil* (III.1.69–70), Webster writes, 'he showed like a pewter candlestick, fashioned like a man in armour, holding a tilting-staff in his hand.'

45   *Lob* droop

47   *gimmaled* jointed (of twin parts). The Folio spelling is 'Iymold'. 'Gymould mayle' occurs in *Edward III* (I.2.29).

49   *their executors* the disposers of their remains

49–50   *the knavish crows, | Fly o'er them all.* See line 37, above, note.

52–3   *To demonstrate the life of such a battle | In life so lifeless as it shows itself* to set forth what such an army is like in such a lifeless state as it is in

58   *guidon* pennant (the commander's sign). Many editions, following the Folio, read 'guard: on', but the detail clearly derives from Holinshed, who writes, 'The Duke of Brabant, when his standard was not come, caused a banner to be taken from a trumpet [compare line 59] and fastened to a spear, the which he commanded to be borne before him instead of his standard.'

59   *trumpet* trumpeter

IV.3.3-4   *three-score thousand ... five to one.* This would make the English army 12,000, though in line 76 it is 5,000; Shakespeare neglects details which in performance will go unnoticed. Holinshed numbers the French at 60,000 but makes the proportion six to one.

6   *God bye you* God be with you (Folio, 'God buy' you.'). Various forms of the phrase include 'God be wi' you', 'God buy ye', and 'Goodbye'.

7-10   *If we no more meet till we meet in heaven ... adieu!* This seems to foreshadow *Julius Caesar*, V.1.114-18 – 'whether we shall meet again I know not. | Therefore our everlasting farewell take. . . . | If we do meet again, why, we shall smile. | If not, why then this parting was well made.'

16-18   *O that we now had here ... no work today.* In Holinshed this speech is given merely to 'one of the host', and Westmorland is not at Agincourt. Shakespeare, however, makes him one of the main supporters of the Bolingbroke line and a leader in the battle.

18   *work* fighting (as often in Shakespeare)

22   *The fewer men, the greater share of honour.* 'The more danger, the more honour' was proverbial. In *Edward III* the King refuses to send a single man to reinforce the Black Prince, who is in mortal peril, so as not to diminish his glory (III.5.40).

28-9   *But if it be a sin to covet honour ... soul alive.* This recalls Hotspur's greed for honour in *1 Henry IV*, but whereas Hotspur wished, rantingly, 'to wear | Without corrival all her dignities' (I.3.206–7), Henry speaks in a comradely way which encourages emulation.

40   *the Feast of Crispian.* 25 October is the day of Saints Crispinus and Crispianus (compare line 57), who fled from Rome under Diocletian's oppression but were martyred in A.D. 287.

48   *And say, 'These wounds I had on Crispin's day.'* This line occurs in the Quarto only but sounds authentic.

49   *yet* yet even should the time come when

50   *with advantages* with additions (a humorous touch typical of the comradely warmth so abundant in this speech)

51   *our names.* As also in line 60, Henry seems to speak primarily to and for his leaders; yet the spirit of his address goes far beyond the leaders only – if it is *their* names which will be remembered, it is the common soldiers who, with a sense of fellowship, will celebrate the remembrance.

61–3   *he today that sheds his blood with me ... his condition.* The 'happy few', who in line 60 seem to be Henry's immediate entourage, are here extended to cover all who shed or endanger their blood with him, and therefore to embrace all in his small force.

69   *bravely* handsomely (since, Holinshed remarks, the French 'made a great show', in contrast to the sombre English)

70   *expedience* celerity

80   *compound* come to terms

91   *achieve* (1) gain; (2) kill, finish off

93–4   *The man that once did sell the lion's skin ... hunting him.* The idea is proverbial, deriving from Aesop's fable of the hunter who sold a bear's skin before he had killed the animal; in the fable he himself escaped death, but only narrowly. (Compare II.3.25, note.)

104   *abounding.* There is a quibble-suggestion of 're-bounding'.

105   *crasing* shattering. Many editors amend to 'grazing', but both Quarto and Folio agree on 'crasing', and no change is needed.

107   *in relapse of mortality* by a deadly rebound

111   *painful* toilsome

117   *or they will* even if they have to

119   *turn them out of service* demobilize them by removing their liveries. A servant or soldier wore his master's liveried coat, which was stripped off when he left. There is a semi-quibble on the two kinds of service.

122   *gentle* noble

123–5   *They shall have none, I swear, but these my joints . . . yield them little.* Holinshed reports that, when the French herald asked what ransom he would give, Henry replied 'that his dead carcass should rather be a prize to the Frenchmen than that his living body should pay any ransom'.

131   *vaward* vanguard. Henry 'appointed a vaward, of the which he made captain Edward Duke of York, who of an haughty courage had desired that office' (Holinshed).

IV.4   (stage direction) *Excursions* sorties

2–3   *Je pense que vous . . . qualité.* The Folio's French in this scene has been regularized but not completely corrected. Verbs and pronouns in the second person vacillate between singular and plural forms.

4   *Calitie . . . me.* The Folio reads, 'Qualtitie calmie custure me.' 'Qualtitie' is doubtless meant as a parrot-echo of '*qualité*' (Folio, '*qualitee*'), but misspelt in printing. By sound-association it prompts Pistol to an Irish refrain ('*Cailin ōg a' stor*' [= 'Maiden, my treasure']) of an Elizabethan song, given in Clement Robinson's *Handefull of Pleasant Delites* (1584).

8   *Perpend* ponder. Shakespeare uses the word five times, always with speakers who are mock-solemn – Touchstone in *As You Like It*, the Clown in *Twelfth Night* –

or pompous-pretentious – Pistol here, Falstaff in *The Merry Wives of Windsor*, and Polonius in *Hamlet*.

9   *fox* sword. The maker's mark, a wolf, on fine steel swords was mistaken for a fox.

11   *Egregious* extraordinary

13   *moy*. This, now spelt 'moi', rhymes in sixteenth-century usage with other words in '-oy' – for example, with 'destroy' in *Richard II* (V.3.119–20). Compare 'le Roy', at IV.1.49.

14   *Moy*. Pistol takes this to be a coin; the word occurs in French and English for a measure of quantity (about a bushel).

15   *rim* midriff, diaphragm

18   *bras* (pronounced 'brass' in French of the time)

20   *luxurious* lascivious
     mountain goat savage lecher (the goat being a symbol of lustfulness)

22   *pardonne-moy*. The Folio's '*perdonne moy*' is probably meant to be pronounced as the second person singular, phonetically very close to Pistol's 'a ton of (o') moys'.

29   *fer* (a meaningless echo-word)
     firk trounce
     ferret worry (as a ferret worries its prey)

63   *As I suck blood*. The characteristic ejaculation which at II.3.53, among Pistol's cronies, was merely predatory is here meant to terrify the enemy.
     I will some mercy show. Pistol is breaking military law. Thomas Digges's *Stratioticos* (1579) declares, 'Every soldier shall present such prisoners as are taken to their captain immediately at their return to the camp, and none shall either kill them or license them to depart' (pages 278–9).

69–70 *roaring devil . . . wooden dagger*. This refers to what was apparently a popular morality-play incident. The Clown in *Twelfth Night* sings of 'the old Vice . . . | Who with dagger of lath . . . | Cries, "Ah, ha!" to the Devil', and who offers to 'Pare [his] nails' (IV.2.120–26).

Samuel Harsnet's *Declaration of Popish Impostures* (1603) refers to 'the old church-plays, when the nimble Vice would skip up nimbly like a jackanapes into the Devil's neck, and ride the Devil a course, and belabour him with his wooden dagger, till he made him roar' (pages 114–15).

73–5   *The French might have a good prey . . . boys.* This hints at the massacre to follow (IV.7.1–4); Falstaff's page is to follow his dead master.

IV.5.3   *Mort Dieu! Ma vie!* Compare III.5.11, note.

7   *perdurable* (accented on the first syllable)

11   *in honour! Once.* The Folio reads 'in once', a word evidently having dropped out. The Quarto's version of line 23 is 'Lets dye with honour, our shame doth last too long', and this probably supplies the omission. Other suggestions are 'in harness' and 'in arms'.

23   *Let life be short, else shame will be too long.* 'Better die with honour than live with shame' was proverbial.

IV.6.8   *Larding* enriching (with the liquor of his blood)

9   *owing* owning

11   *haggled* hacked

21   *raught* reached

28   *pretty* comely (without the present 'dainty' sense)

31   *my mother* my softer feelings

33–4   *compound | With mistful eyes* allow my eyes to become misty

35–8   *But hark! what new alarum is this same? . . . Give the word through.* Elegiac sentiment turns suddenly to brutal reality.

37   *Then every soldier kill his prisoners!* Had Shakespeare explained this savage order as Holinshed does, that is, as a grievous but necessary measure to save the small English army from disaster under renewed attack,

hampered as it was by hordes of prisoners, Henry would have been spared some hostile criticisms from commentators, but he seems unaware that any exoneration is needed. The following comments from Fluellen and Gower are no help; Gower thinks the massacre justified because the King's tents have been plundered, and Fluellen's outburst turns it to comedy, as does a piece of apparent stage business preserved in the Quarto where, after Henry's order, Pistol (present but hitherto speechless) ends the scene with his tag line, 'Couple gorge'.

IV.7.31, 42   *figures* parallels

42–51   *As Alexander killed his friend Cleitus ... Monmouth.* Inflamed with wine after a banquet, Alexander quarrelled with his friend and commander Cleitus in 328 B.C. and killed him. That this incident should be used as a (ludicrously fallacious) parallel to Henry's dismissal of Falstaff is curious. The apparent purpose is to poke fun at Fluellen's illogic, but in this reminder of Falstaff's fate some critics detect an implicit criticism by Shakespeare of Henry's ruthlessness. Yet the tone is too light to carry such an implication; as with the French prisoners, comedy enters not to attract attention to but to divert it from the King's harshness (necessary in both cases, and specifically approved by Fluellen and Gower). Falstaff is so sunk in the past that Fluellen cannot even recall his name.

46   *great-belly doublet.* The doublet had a stuffed 'belly' or lower part. Considered as a real person Falstaff would hardly have needed padding, but Shakespeare's mind goes back to the actor who performed the part.

54   *trumpet* trumpeter

59   *skirr* scurry

67   *fined* pledged

77   *Fret* struggle

78   *Yerk* kick, strike

83   *peer* appear

97   *garden where leeks did grow.* It is not clear whether
      Fluellen refers to the battle of A.D. 540 (compare IV.1.
      55, note) or to Crécy; the episode he cites has not been
      traced. Shakespeare may have gathered a tradition
      from Welshmen in London, as he seems to have done
      for details of Glendower's character in *1 Henry IV*.

98   *Monmouth caps* round brimless caps (originally made at
      Monmouth)

99–101 *and I do believe ... day.* Dover Wilson cites Francis
      Osborne, *Works* (8th edition, 1682, page 610), as
      evidence of distinguished support for Fluellen – 'Nor
      did he [the Earl of Essex] fail to wear a leek on St
      David's Day, but besides would upon all occasions
      vindicate the Welsh inhabitants and own them for
      his countrymen, as Queen Elizabeth usually was wont,
      upon the first of March.'

105   *Welsh plood.* Henry's great-grandmother was Welsh,
      and he himself born at Monmouth.

133   *sort* rank
      from the answer of his degree exempt from answering
      one of his station

134–5 *as good ... as the devil is.* The idea was traditional, the
      devil being of the highest rank among angels; compare
      King Lear, III.4.139 – 'The prince of darkness is a
      gentleman.'

138   *Jack-sauce* saucy knave

149–54 *Here, Fluellen, wear thou this favour ... dost me love.*
      Henry's jest involves straightfaced lying, but not more
      so than many a leg-pull, soldierly or other, and he at
      once ensures that no harm shall follow (lines 165–77).
      Fluellen's gratification is very funny (lines 155–9).

168   *haply* perhaps

IV.8.1   *I warrant it is to knight you, Captain.* The comradely tone between the soldier and his captain is characteristic of the English army, whereas the French are widely divided into nobles, peasants, and mercenaries.

16   *lie in thy throat.* A lie in the throat was one uttered deliberately and inexcusably; a lie in the teeth was a degree less grave and objectionable.

36   *avouchment* assurance

46–56   *All offences ... pardon me.* The honest rightness of Williams's answers is admirable, a further sign of the manliness existing between all ranks in the King's army and evinced when Henry rewards him and takes care to reconcile him to Fluellen.

75–99   *Charles Duke of Orleans, nephew to the King ... Vaudemont and Lestrake.* This transcribes Holinshed nearly word for word.

103   *Kikely* (spelt thus in Holinshed; '*Ketly*' in the Folio)

105   *five-and-twenty.* Holinshed gives this figure 'as some do report', though he also records 'other writers of greater credit' as reckoning 'above five or six hundred' English dead. Modern historians estimate about 7,000 French dead and 400–500 English, a discrepancy striking enough. By uncritically accepting an absurd figure, Shakespeare, contrary to the realism he had shown in *Henry IV*, seems to capitulate to the 'miraculous' view of Henry.

108   *even* equal

122   *Non Nobis ... Te Deum.* These are the opening words of Psalm 115 (part of 113 in the Vulgate), 'Give praise not unto us, O God', and of the canticle *Te Deum laudamus*, 'We praise Thee, O God'.

V. *Chorus*

3–4   *th' excuse | Of time.* Between Agincourt (1415) and the Treaty of Troyes five years elapsed; compare lines 38–41, note.

10   *Pales* fences (as with palings)

12   *whiffler* attendant (whose job it is to clear the way)

21   *full trophy, signal, and ostent* every token, sign, and
          display of honour

23   *working-house* place of industry

25-8   *The Mayor and all his brethren in best sort ... Caesar
          in.* 'The mayor of London, and the aldermen, apparelled
          in orient grained scarlet, and four hundred commoners
          clad in beautiful murrey [cloth of mulberry colour],
          well mounted, and trimly horsed, with rich collars, and
          great chains, met the king on Blackheath, rejoicing at
          his return' (Holinshed).

25   *in best sort* of the highest station

29   *lower but loving likelihood* like probability, less exalted
          but eagerly desired

30-32   *the General of our gracious Empress ... on his sword.*
          For Essex's expedition to suppress Tyrone, see the
          Introduction, page 7. Begun early in 1599, the play
          reflects the vigorous military preparations and confi-
          dence which launched the enterprise.

38-41   *The Emperor's coming ... France.* The Emperor Sigis-
          mund came to England to negotiate on behalf of France
          in May, 1416; further English invasions of France took
          place in 1416-19; and the Treaty of Troyes was signed
          in 1420. The play recognizes no appreciable interval
          between the events of IV.8 and those of V.1 (Dr
          Johnson indeed thought that V.1 should be the last
          scene of Act IV).

43   *remembering* reminding

V.1.5   *scauld* scurvy
    18   *bedlam* lunatic
          Troyan (often, like Corinthian, Ephesian, Greek,
          etc., used for a boon companion, but here, in effect,
          knave)
    19   *Parca's fatal web* the web of life (spun and cut by the
          three Parcae or Fates)

214

27   *Cadwallader* (a famous seventh-century Welsh warrior)

34   *mountain-squire* squire of the barren Welsh hills

35   *squire of low degree* (an allusion to the title of a medieval romance)

37   *astonished* stupefied

40   *green* fresh
       coxcomb fool's head

52   *broken* wounded (not 'fractured')

55   *groat* fourpenny piece

60   *earnest* first instalment (as a pledge that a bargain will be fulfilled)

67–9   *an ancient tradition . . . valour.* Compare IV.1.55, note.

70–71   *gleeking and galling* mocking and jeering

76   *housewife* hussy, jade (pronounced 'hussif')

77   *Doll.* Both the Quarto and the Folio read 'Doll', but, since Doll Tearsheet was Falstaff's woman and Nell Quickly Pistol's, many editors change to 'Nell'. Some argue that Falstaff originally appeared in *Henry V* (as promised in the epilogue to *2 Henry IV*) and that his part was later transferred to Pistol, 'Doll' remaining unchanged through an oversight though it should have been altered to 'Nell'. The theory is unlikely, and 'Doll' is probably a mere slip, arising from the similarity of the two women's positions and names. Apart from many difficulties in envisaging Falstaff in France, this speech and the action preceding it are very appropriate to Pistol, very inappropriate to Falstaff.
       spital hospital

78   *malady of France* venereal disease

79   *rendezvous* refuge

83–5   *To England will I steal . . . Gallia wars.* 'The comic scenes of *The History of Henry the Fourth* and *Fifth* are now at an end, and all the comic personages are now dismissed. Falstaff and Mrs Quickly are dead; Nym and Bardolph are hanged; Gadshill was lost immediately after the robbery; Poins and Peto have vanished since, one knows not how; and Pistol is now beaten into obscurity. I believe every reader regrets their departure' (Johnson).

V.2.17 *The fatal balls of murdering basilisks.* Basilisks were: (1) fabulous reptiles (hatched by a serpent from a cockatrice's egg) which killed by projecting a venomous influence from their eye-balls; (2) large cannon (originally marked with the device of a basilisk).

27 *bar* tribunal

31 *congreeted* greeted each other

33 *rub* hindrance

40 *it* its (the old genitive form)

42 *even-pleached* evenly layered, plaited

44 *fallow leas* unsown arable land

45 *The darnel, hemlock, and rank fumitory.* These are weeds particularly liable to grow on cultivated land; in *King Lear* they are included among 'the idle weeds that grow | In our sustaining corn' (IV.4.3–6).

46 *coulter* blade in front of the ploughshare

51 *teems* abounds

52 *kecksies* (plants with) dry hollow innutrient stems

61 *diffused* disordered

63 *reduce into our former favour* restore to the favourable aspect we used to show

65 *let* hindrance

68 *would* would have

77 *cursitory* cursory

79 *presently* immediately

82 *accept and peremptory answer* decision and definitive reply

90 *consign* sign jointly

94 *When articles too nicely urged be stood on* when items are insisted upon too particularly

96 *capital* principal. The marriage was in fact the first article of the Treaty of Troyes; compare lines 97, 326.

121   *is the better Englishwoman* qualifies as a good Englishwoman (in preferring plain dealing)

124   *such a plain king.* Johnson expressed surprise that
'Shakespeare now gives the King nearly such a character as he made him formerly ridicule in Percy' (*1
Henry IV*), but, as the nineteenth-century editor S. W.
Singer rejoined, 'Shakespeare only meant to character-
ize English downright sincerity; and surely the previous
habits of Henry ... do not make us expect great re-
finement or polish in him upon this occasion, especially
as fine speeches would be lost upon the Princess from
her imperfect comprehension of his language.'

134   *measure* (skill in) metre

135   *I have no strength in measure* I am no good at dancing

136–41   *If I could win ... never off.* Among other praises of
Henry, Holinshed writes: 'In wrestling, leaping, and
running, no man [was] well able to compare with him.'
As Prince Hal, when fully armed for war Henry 'vaulted
with such ease into his seat' that he seemed the angelic
rider of a fiery Pegasus, to 'witch the world with noble
horsemanship' (*1 Henry IV*, IV.1.107–10).

141   *jackanapes* monkey

142   *greenly* like a green, callow, youth

146   *not worth sunburning* one that the sun could not make
worse. A sunburnt face was thought unbecoming;
compare *Troilus and Cressida* – 'The Grecian dames
are sunburnt and not worth | The splinter of a lance'
(I.3.282–3).

148   *be thy cook* serve me up to your taste

149–51   *If thou canst love me for this ... thee too.* This cheerful
mockery of romantic extravagance finds a close parallel
in Rosalind's common-sense to Orlando, in *As You
Like It* (IV.1.83–94).

152   *uncoined* (1) unalloyed, genuine; (2) not put into circu-
lation

155–6   *rhyme themselves into ladies' favours.* Henry deriding
rhyming wooers recalls Benedick admitting that he 'was

not born under a rhyming planet' (*Much Ado About Nothing*, V.2.36), Berowne claiming that, being 'honest', he would never 'write a thing in rhyme' (*Love's Labour's Lost*, IV.3.177), and Hotspur ridiculing Glendower's 'mincing poetry' (*1 Henry IV*, III.1.134).

158   *but a ballad*. Ballads were often mere doggerel, and scorned as such.

180-82   *Je – quand sur le possession ... mienne*. The Quarto suggests a lively stage adaptation of this; see the Collation on pages 232-3.

181   *Saint Denis*. Henry appeals to the patron saint of France.

189   *truly-falsely* true-heartedly but incorrectly

202   *scambling* fighting

206   *Constantinople*. The city did not fall to the Turks until 1453, thirty-one years after Henry died, but its recovery was thereafter a project which haunted Christian leaders. The 'boy' whom Henry foresees winning it was in fact the incompetent Henry VI under whom England suffered the Wars of the Roses.

214-15   *mon très cher et devin déesse*. Henry's French is, as Katherine says, '*fausse*'.

222   *untempering* unsoftening

228   *ill layer-up* wrinkler (like a 'wet cloak ill laid up', *2 Henry IV*, V.1.82)

230   *thou shalt wear me, if thou wear me* you will find me suiting you, if you take me

240-41   *broken music*. This quibbles on the technical term for music arranged for wind and string instruments.

265   *nice* punctilious, finicky

267   *list* limits

268   *places* (high) rank

289   *make a circle* (that is, as if for magical rites; with a bawdy quibble also)

290   *blind* (1) sightless (like blind Cupid); (2) oblivious of all else

303   *summered* nurtured (as cattle are in summer pastures)

303-4   *Bartholomew-tide* 24 August (when the flies supposedly feel the late summer's warmth and grow sluggish)

307   *This moral ties me over* this reflection means I must wait

315   *perspectively* as if in a perspective (an optical device which showed different images when viewed from different angles)

320–21   *so the maiden cities . . . her.* As lover, Henry insists on Katherine for his wife; but as King, standing for his country's rights, he demands all that is due to his crown.

328   *subscribèd* signed in agreement

330   *matter of grant* conferment of lands or titles

332–3   *très cher . . . Praeclarissimus.* The discrepancy in meaning between the French and the Latin words ('most beloved . . . most renowned') arises since 'praeclarissimus' is a misprint in Shakespeare's sources for 'praecharissimus' (that is, 'praecarissimus', 'most beloved').

342   *pale* white (the chalk cliffs)

354   *spousal* married union

355   *ill office* malevolent interference

357   *paction* compact (Folio, 'Pation')

358   *incorporate* united (as marriage makes man and wife one flesh)

363–4   *My Lord of Burgundy, we'll take your oath, | And all the peers'.* In *The Famous Victories of Henry the Fifth* Burgundy and the Dauphin take their oaths on the stage; see also the Introduction, page 8, for Nashe's reference to a similar incident.

366   (stage direction) *Sennet* trumpet signal

Epilogue

2   *Our bending author.* Compare *Hamlet* – 'For us, and for our tragedy, | Here stooping to your clemency, | We beg your hearing patiently' (III.2.144–5). Possibly Shakespeare himself was the Chorus and here spoke in his own person.

5   *Small time.* Henry died at thirty-five, having reigned nine years (1413–22).

AN ACCOUNT OF THE TEXT

THE earliest text, that of 1600, is a 'bad' Quarto, that is, one derived from Shakespeare's manuscript only by an irregular process resulting in much corruption. Second and third Quartos followed in 1602 and 1619 (misdated 1608); each is a reprint of the first, with even less authority. The first Folio edition, of 1623, provides the text on which all later reprints have been based. It was set up from Shakespeare's manuscript, though clearer, better punctuated, and freer from irregularities than several other texts so derived; Shakespeare may have worked with more care than usual.

The evidence for this authenticity is presented by John Dover Wilson in the New Cambridge edition. It consists of apparent Shakespearian spellings transmitted into the text (such as 'vp-peer'd' for 'up'ard' [II.3.24], 'Deules' and 'Deule' for 'devils' and 'devil' [II.3.30, 33], 'Moth' for 'mote' [IV.1.174], and 'vawting' for 'vaulting' [V.2.137]), misprints resulting from Shakespeare's kind of script (for instance, 'name' for 'mare' [II.1.22], 'Straying' for 'Straining' [III.1.32], 'Leuitie' for 'lenitie' [III.6.109], and 'nam'd' for 'name' [IV. Chorus. 16]). There are variations in the designating of characters, to be expected from an author in the process of composition; the Hostess, for instance, appears as '*Quickly*', '*Hostesse*', and '*Woman*'; Fluellen is sometimes '*Welch*'; '*King*' stands for Henry and for Charles of France – in V.2 there is a mixture of '*King*', '*France*', '*England*', and '*French King*', which needs editorial regularization. Characters may be introduced in stage directions and then given nothing to do in the scene; conversely, others may play a part without having been introduced. There are also stage directions which sound like authorial notes rather than exact instructions (for example, '*Enter two Bishops*' [I.2.6]; '*Enter the King and all his Traine before the Gates*' [III.3.0]; '*Drum and Colours. Enter the King and his poore*

Souldiers' [III.6.84]; '*Enter the French Power, and the English Lords*' [V.2.276]). The Folio text, then, is the indisputable authority.

The Quarto text is much shorter, some 1620 lines as against some 3380. It omits many passages, three complete scenes (I.1; III.1; and IV.2), and the prologue, choruses, and epilogue. The surviving verse approximates roughly to that of the Folio, though the sense is often garbled and the metre irregular; at times it is no more than paraphrase. The prose scenes fare still worse; printed in irregular lines capitalized as if verse, they give a scrappy rendering of the corresponding parts of the original, sometimes conveying no more than the gist of the Folio version. The Quarto does, however, furnish some apparently authentic readings lost in the Folio, including two whole lines (II.1.101 and IV.3.48), and it preserves the verse form of Pistol's speeches, nearly all of which the Folio gives as prose (see Collations, pages 225–6). It also includes several oaths, over and above those which appear in the Folio (see Collations, page 233). Since the 'copy' for several plays was to varying extents expurgated before the Folio was printed, some of these oaths may have been cut from the authentic text. Nine of them, out of the total of fifteen, come from Fluellen, and this may be significant of a cutting down of his exuberance. Unfortunately, so corrupt is the Quarto text that one cannot tell whether Shakespeare or the unauthorized compiler put them into Fluellen's mouth. Some, at least, are probably genuine expressions of his Welsh fieriness, but which are which cannot be ascertained. (Any expurgation to which *Henry V* may have been subjected was clearly incomplete; many oaths remain, particularly – though not solely – those that are serious and reverent.)

The brevity of the Quarto doubtless owes something to the forgetfulness of those compiling it. The text seems to be a reported one, written down from recitation probably by disloyal actors (the proper course was for the performing company to sell an authentic text to a publisher of its choice, when it judged such a sale advisable). Scholars have tried to assess the degrees of accuracy in various parts of the Quarto so as to ascertain which actors may have been involved, but the discussion has proved inconclusive. The Quarto's deficiencies probably result also from heavy cutting of the original text to produce a shortened version for a provincial tour – in any case, the full text would need some pruning before it could be staged, though not nearly as much as it gets in the Quarto. This condensation saves eleven acting parts and much acting time. The phrasal changes are botchings to compensate for imperfect memory, and auditory errors resulting from a reporter's mishearings (for example, 'the function' for 'defunction' [I.2.58], 'Inger' for 'Lingare' [I.2.74], 'Foraging' for 'Forage in' [I.2.110], 'England' for 'inland' [I.2.142], 'a thing' for 'a sin' [II.4.74], 'shout' for 'suit' [III.6.76], 'partition' for 'perdition' [III.6.95], and 'de la Brute' for 'Delabreth' [IV.8.91]).

When a reading in the Quarto agrees with that in the Folio this agreement is strong evidence for correctness, since it has survived the hazards of abbreviation, recollection, and reporting. Now and then the Quarto offers a better reading than the Folio, but its authority is of the slightest, and the Folio reading must prevail unless clearly erroneous.

COLLATIONS

The following lists are selective, not comprehensive. They include the more noteworthy variants but omit many minor changes which are insignificant in the determination of the true reading, changes such as obvious misprints, trifling omissions, small variations in word order, and grammatical details not affecting the sense. Only the more interesting of editorial regularizations of the French passages have been recorded; to collate in full would have meant citing nearly every word. Variants between the first Quarto and first Folio texts, which are very numerous indeed since the Quarto is so irregular, have been noted only when the Quarto variant has been accepted, either in the present or in several earlier editions, or when it is unusually interesting; the interest may lie in its offering a possibly correct alternative to the accepted reading, or in its revealing compositorial vagaries or other operations in textual transmission (auditory errors, verbal alternatives, and the like).

When a reading in the text exceeds a word or two, only its opening and closing words are quoted for identification, but the whole passage is to be taken as representing the variant version. Q1, Q2, and Q 3 mean the first, second, and third Quarto editions (1600, 1602, 1619); F1, F2, F3, and F4 mean the first, second, third, and fourth Folio editions (1623, 1632, 1663–4, 1685). 'J. Dover Wilson, 1947' and 'J. H. Walter, 1954' mean the New Cambridge and new Arden editions respectively, by those editors.

I

ACCEPTED Q1 READINGS

(a) *Variants*

The following readings in the present text derive from Q1, not from F1. Each represents the Q1 form in modernized spelling; if, though derived from Q1, it differs interestingly the actual Q1 form follows, in brackets. Each Q1 reading is followed by the F1 variant, unmodernized and unbracketed. Later interesting variants, if any, come last, in brackets.

I.2. 183 True:] *not in* F1
     209 several] *not in* F1
     213 End] And
II.1. 22 mare] name
      26 NYM] *not in* F1
           How now, mine host Pistol?] (*Nim.* How do you
           my Hoste? Q1) *In* F1 *this is a continuation of
           Bardolph's speech at line 25.*
      69 thee defy] defie thee
     101 NYM I shall have ... betting?] *not in* F1
     112 came] come

II.2. 147   Henry] *Thomas*
    176   you have] you (you three F2)
II.3. 15   fingers' ends] fingers end
III.6. 30   her] his
    109   lenity] Leuitie
IV.1. 35   *Qui va là?*] (Ke ve la? Q1) *Che vous la?*
    301   friends] friend /
IV.3.13–14   And yet I do thee wrong ... valour.] Q1 *locates this correctly, though making Clarence the speaker of lines 12–14 and garbling the text.* F1 *makes this a continuation of Bedford's speech at line 11.*
    48   And say, 'These wounds ... day.'] *not in* F1
IV.5. 11   Let's die in honour] (Lets dye with honour Q1) Let vs dye in (Let us die instant) (Let's die in harness) (Let's die in arms)
    15   Whilst by a] (Why least by a Q1) Whilst a base
V.1. 85   swear] swore

(b) *Metrical Speeches*

The following metrical speeches (from Pistol) appear in Q1 as verse (though sometimes so erratically that the verse form may be accidental), and in F1 as prose. Editors follow Q1 in presenting them as verse, though basing the text on F1. It is not clear in Q1 and F1 whether several one-line speeches are meant as verse or prose. They are given as verse in this edition if they sound histrionic. Metrical speeches which are not in Q1 and which F1 gives as prose are listed on pages 228–9.

II.1.27–9   Base tike, call'st thou me host? ... lodgers.
    43–50   'Solus', egregious dog? ... follow.
    68–76   'Couple a gorge!' ... enough.
    102–8   A noble shalt thou have ... hand.
II.3.44–53   Come, let's away ... blood to suck!
III.6.20–21   Captain, I thee beseech ... well.
    24–8   Bardolph, a soldier firm ... stone–
    38–48   Fortune is Bardolph's foe ... requite.
IV.1.37–8   Discuss unto me ... popular?

IV.1. 44–8   The King's a bawcock . . . name?
IV.4. 47–8   Tell him my fury . . . take.
    63–4   As I suck blood . . . me!
V.1.18–20   Ha, art thou bedlam . . . leek.
    76–83   Doth Fortune play the housewife . . . steal;

2

ACCEPTED READINGS LATER THAN F1

(a) *Variants*

The following readings in the present text (given first) originate in editions later than F1; if proposed by a modern editor, they are identified in brackets. The F1 variant comes next, unmodernized and unbracketed. Other interesting variants, whether earlier than F1 or later, come last, in brackets; the sources are given of such of them as originate in the Quartos or the later Folios, or in modern scholarly editions.

  I.2. 94   imbare] imbarre (imbace Q1 : embrace Q3 : imbar F3)
    163   her] their (your Q1)
  208–9   Come to one mark . . . town,] *one line in* F1, *with* 'several' *omitted*
 II.1. 34   drawn] hewne (here)
    76–7   enough. | Go to!] enough to go to.
    79   you, Hostess] your Hostesse
 II.2. 87   him] *not in* F1
    114   All] And
    139   mark the] make thee
    159   I] *not in* F1
 II.3. 16   'a babbled] a Table
 II.4. 107   privèd] (J. H. Walter, 1954); priuy (pining Q1)
III. Chorus
    4   Hampton] Douer
    6   fanning] fayning

III.1.   7   conjure] (J. H. Walter, 1954); commune (summon)
         17   noblest] Noblish (noble)
         24   men] me
         32   Straining] Straying
III.2. 114   hear] heard
III.3.   32   heady] headly (deadly)
         35   Defile] Desire
         54   all. For . . . uncle,] all for vs, deare Vnckle.
III.4.7-13   KATHERINE De hand. Et les doigts?
              ALICE Les doigts? Ma foi, j'oublie les doigts,
              mais je me souviendrai. Les doigts? Je pense
              qu'ils sont appelés de fingres; oui, de fingres.
              KATHERINE La main, de hand; les doigts, de
              fingres. Je pense que je suis le bon écolier; j'ai
              gagné deux mots d'anglais vitement. Comment
              appelez-vous les ongles?] F1 *gives to Alice* 'Et
              les doigts?' (*line 7*), *to Katherine* 'Les doigts?
              Ma foi, j'oublie' *down to* 'oui, de fingres' (*lines
              8–10*), *to Alice* 'La main, de hand' *down to* 'le
              bon écolier' (*lines 11–12*), *and to Katherine the re-
              mainder.*
         38   N'avez-vous pas déjà] *N'aue vos y desia*
III.5.   11   *Mort Dieu! Ma vie!*] *Mort du ma vie* (Mordeu ma
              via [at line *5*] Q1, mor du [at line *11*] Q1)
         26   Lest poor we] (This edition); Poore we (Poore we
              may F2)
         46   Knights] Kings
III.7.   12   pasterns] postures
         63   *et la truie*] *est la leuye*
IV. Chorus
         16   name] nam'd
         27   Presenteth] Presented
IV.1.   92   Thomas] *John*
        174   mote] Moth
     226-30   We must bear all . . . enjoy!] *six lines in* F1,
              ending 'beare all. | . . . Greatnesse, | . . . sence |
              . . . wringing. | . . . neglect, | . . . enioy?'

IV.1. 238 What is thy soul of adoration?] What? is thy Soule of Odoration?

    284 if] of (lest); or (J. Dover Wilson, 1947)

  284-5 numbers | Pluck] numbers: | Pluck

  293-5 Toward heaven, to pardon blood ... do,] *four lines in* F1, *ending* 'blood: | ... Chauntries, | ... still | ... doe:'

IV.2. 9 dout] doubt

    58 guidon. To the field! | I will] Guard: on | To the field, I will

IV.4. 4 *Calitie*] (This edition); Qualtitie (Quality F4)
             Calen o] calmie

    15 Or] for

    35 *à cette heure*] asture

  51-2 *l'avez promis*] layt a promets

    55 *remerciments*] remercious
             suis tombé] intombe

    65 *Suivez*] Saaue

IV.6. 34 mistful] mixtfull

IV.7. 76 their] with (the)

   123 'a live] aliue

V. Chorus

    10 with wives] Wiues

V.2. 12 England] Ireland

    50 all] withall

  54-5 as ... wildness,] all ... wildnesse.

    77 cursitory] (J. Dover Wilson, 1947); curselarie (cursenary Q1: cursorary Q3)

    93 Haply] Happily

 186-7 *que vous parlez, il est meilleur*] *ques vous parleis, il & melieus*

   317 never] *not in* F1

   326 then] *not in* F1

(b) *Metrical Speeches*

The following speeches (mostly from Pistol) have been arranged as verse by editors, though they are given as prose in

F1. There is either nothing or very little in Q1 to correspond to them. Metrical speeches given as verse in Q1 but as prose in F1 are listed on pages 225-6.

II.1.64-5	Give me thy fist . . . tall.
118-19	Nym, thou hast spoke . . . corroborate.
II.3. 3-6	No, for my manly heart . . . therefor.
III.2.6-10	The plainsong is most just . . . fame.
14-19	If wishes would prevail . . . bough.
22-5	Be merciful, great Duke . . . chuck!
IV.1.54-5	Tell him I'll knock his leek . . . day.
IV.4. 4-5	*Calitie! Calen o . . . Discuss.*
7-11	O Signieur Dew . . . ransom.
14-16	Moy shall not serve . . . blood!
19-21	Brass, cur? . . . brass?
23-5	Say'st thou me so . . . name.
37-9	*Owy, cuppele gorge, permafoy . . . sword.*

(c) *Act- and Scene-Divisions*

Q1 has no Act- and scene-divisions at all. F1 has 'Actus Primus. Scœna Prima' before I.1 but marks no later scenes. It puts 'Actus Secundus' before III. Chorus, 'Actus Tertius' before IV. Chorus, 'Actus Quartus' before IV.7, and 'Actus Quintus' before V. Chorus. Editors have amended the Act-divisions and inserted scene-numbers as in the present text.

(d) *Stage Directions*

The wording of the stage directions in this text follows as closely as practicable that in F1. Amendments and additions have been made only when necessary to clarify the action or to assimilate the entry and exit directions to it. The following stage directions, introduced by editors, differ sufficiently from those of F1 to qualify for recording; added *Exits* and *Exeunts*, when self-evident, are not listed, nor are characters' names when these merely regularize entry and exit directions. The reading in the present text is given first, that of F1 second.

I.2.	6	*Enter the Archbishop . . . Ely*] *Enter two Bishops.*
	222	*Exeunt some attendants*] Not in F1

II.1.	33	*Nym draws his sword] Not in* F1
	42	*He sheathes his sword] Not in* F1
	59	*They both draw] Not in* F1
	62	*He draws] Not in* F1
	63	*Pistol and Nym sheathe their swords] Not in* F1
	97	*He sheathes his sword] Not in* F1
	108	*Nym sheathes his sword] Not in* F1
II.2.	181	*Exeunt Cambridge, Scroop, and Grey, guarded] Exit.*
II.3.	56	*He kisses her] Not in* F1
II.4.	67	*Exeunt Messenger and certain lords] Not in* F1
III.2.	21	*He drives them forward] Not in* F1
	27	*Exeunt all but the Boy] Exit.*
	53	*Enter Fluellen, Gower following] Enter Gower.*
III.3.	0	*Some citizens ... walls.] Not in* F1.
IV.1.	222	*Exeunt Soldiers] Exit Souldiers. [after line 217]*
IV.8.	73	*He gives him a paper] Not in* F1
	101	*The Herald gives him another paper] Not in* F1
V.1.	33–4	*He strikes him again] Not in* F1
V.2.	271–2	*He kisses her] Not in* F1
	276	*Enter the French King ... Lords] Enter the French Power, and the English Lords.*

3

REJECTED VARIANTS

The following list contains some of the more interesting and important variants (whether earlier or later than F1) and proposed emendations not accepted in the present text. The reading of this edition is (unless otherwise identified) that of F1, modernized; it is followed by the rejected variants, unmodernized. The sources are given of such variants as originate in the Quartos or later Folios or in modern scholarly editions. When no source is given, the reading is one proposed by an earlier editor which has not gained general acceptance. Only a small selection of the very numerous Q1 variants is offered.

I.1. 49 wonder] wand'rer
I.2. 72 find] fine Q1
      99 man] sonne Q1
     112 pride] power Q1
     142 Our inland] your *England* Q1
     165 sumless] shiplesse Q1
     166 ELY] *Lord* Q1: WESTMORLAND
     173 'tame] spoyle Q1: tear taint
     175 crushed] curst Q1: crude
     199 kneading] lading Q1
     208 Come] flye Q1
     234 waxen] paper Q1
     244 is] are Q1
     255 spirit] study Q1
II. Chorus
      20 But see, thy fault France hath in thee found out, |
          A nest] But see thy fault! France hath in thee found
          out | A nest
      31 we'll] well
      32 distance, force] distance while we force
II.1. 49 take] talke Q1
     49–50 Pistol's cock is up, | And flashing fire will follow]
          Pistolls flashing firy cock is vp Q1
      80 face] nose Q1
     111 that's] (that F1) theres Q1
II.2. 118 tempered] tempted
II.3. 14 play with] talk of Q1
      24 knees,] knees, and they were as cold as any stone
          Q1
      39 hell] hell fire Q1
      50 *Caveto*] cophetua Q1
      59 Adieu!] adieu. | *Pist.* Keepe fast thy buggle boe.
          Q1
II.4. 57 his mountain] his mounting   his mighty
III.5. 15 Where] whence Q1
      54 captive chariot] chariot, captive (J. Dover Wilson,
          1947)

231

III.6.   59   FLUELLEN Very good.] *Flew*. That is very well. |
Pist. I say the fig within thy bowels and thy durty
maw. | *Exit Pistoll*. | *Fle*. Captain *Gour*, cannot
you hear it lighten & thunder? Q1

        76   suit] shout Q1

III.7.   14   *chez*] *qui a   avec*

IV.1.   65   fewer] lewer Q1: lower Q3

IV.3.   44   shall see] outliues ⎫ *These* Q1 *variants occur in the*
            and live] and sees ⎭ *corresponding line*, 41.

     105   crasing] grazing

  128–9 thou wilt once more come again for a ransom]
thou'lt once more come again for ransom

IV.4.   64   Follow me] Follow me cur Q1

IV.5.   14   base pander] bace leno Q1

      16   contaminated] contamuracke Q1

      18   our lives] our liues | Vnto these English, or else
die with fame Q1

IV.6.   15   He cries] And cryde Q1
my] deare Q1

   37–8 kill his prisoners! | Give the word through.] kill
his prisoner. | *Pist*. Couple gorge. Q1

IV.8.79–111 KING HENRY This note doth tell ... Thine!]
Q1 *gives this passage as a continuation of Exeter's
speech but prefixes 'Exe.' also to* ''Tis wonderful'
in line 111. Q3 *continues lines 79–99 to Exeter*
('This note doth tell ... Lestrake') *and then gives
lines 100–101 to the King* ('Here was a royal fellowship ... dead?'), *lines 102–5 to Exeter* ('Edward the
Duke of York ... five and twenty'), *and lines 105–11
to the King* ('O God, Thy arm was here! ...
Thine!').

    123 enclosed] enterred Q1

V.1.   77   Doll] Nell (*See Commentary*.)

V.2.180–82 *Je – quand sur le possession ... mienne*.] Let me see,
Saint *Dennis* be my speed. | Quan *France* et mon.
| *Kate*. Dat is, when *France* is yours. | *Harry*. Et
vous ettes amoy. | *Kate*. And I am to you. |

Harry. Douck *France* ettes a vous: | *Kate.* Den *France* sall be mine. | *Harry.* Et Ie suyues a vous. | *Kate.* And you will be to me. Q1 (*See Commentary.*)

222 untempering] untempting

252 *d'une – notre Seigneur – indigne*] (*d'une nostre Seigneur indignie* F1) d'une vostre indigne d'une de votre seigneurie indigne

4

OATHS

The following list shows the oaths that occur in Q1 but not in F1; the F1 reading, which is that also of the present text, is given first, modernized. On this difference between the two texts, see 'An Account of the Text', p. 222. A few more oaths occur in parts of Q1 to which nothing in F1 corresponds.

II.1.	28	Now by this hand] Now by gads lugges
II.3.	7	Would I were with him] God be with him
	40	Well] Well, God be with him
III.2.	3	Pray thee] Before God
	20	Up to the breach] Godes plud vp to the breaches
III.6.	3	I assure you, there is] By Iesus thers
	13	in my very conscience] by Iesus
	62	I'll assure you] By Iesus
	102	but his nose] But god be praised, now his nose
IV.1.	76	If the enemy] Godes sollud [*sic*], if the enemy
	88–9	I think we shall never see] God knowes whether we shall see
	192	You pay him then] Mas youle pay him then
IV.7.	1	Kill the poys] Godes plud kil the boyes
	66	How now, what means] Gods will what meanes
IV.8.	62	By this day and this light] By Iesus
V.1.	38	I say] by *I*esu

V.2. 272 You have witchcraft] Before God *Kate*, you have witchcraft

5

STAGE DIRECTIONS IN QI AND FI

The following are the more interesting of the stage-direction variants between QI and FI. The QI directions are given first.

I.2.   0 QI, *Enter King* Henry, Exeter, 2. *Bishops*, Clarence, *and other Attendants.*] FI, *Enter the King, Humfrey, Bedford, Clarence, Warwick, Westmerland, and Exeter.* [*after line 6*] *Enter two Bishops.*

II.1. 23 QI, *Enter* Pistoll *and Hostes Quickly, his wife.*] FI, *Enter Pistoll, & Quickly.*

II.2.   0 QI, *Enter Exeter and Gloster.*] FI, *Enter Exeter, Bedford, & Westmerland.*

    11 QI, *Enter the King and three Lords.*] FI, *Sound Trumpets. Enter the King, Scroope, Cambridge, and Gray.*

II.4.   0 QI, *Enter King of* France, Bourbon, Dolphin, *and others.*] FI, *Flourish. Enter the French King, the Dolphin, the Dukes of Berry and Britaine.*

III.2. 21 QI, *Enter* Flewellen *aud* [sic] *beates them in.*] FI, *Enter Fluellen.*

    27 QI [*after line 53*], *Exit* Nim, Bardolfe, Pistoll, *and the Boy.*] FI [*after line 27*], *Exit.*

III.3.   0 QI, *Enter the King and his Lords alarum.*] FI, *Enter the King and all his Traine before the Gates.*

III.4.   0 QI, *Enter* Katherine, Allice.] FI, *Enter Katherine and an old Gentlewoman.*

III.5.   0 QI, *Enter King of* France Lord Constable, *the* Dolphin, *and* Burbon.] FI, *Enter the King of France, the Dolphin, the Constable of France, and others.*

III.6.   0 QI, *Enter Gower.*] FI, *Enter Captaines, English and Welch, Gower and Fluellen.*

  84 QI, *Fnter* [sic] *King*, Clarence, Gloster *and others.*]

F1, *Drum and Colours. Enter the King and his poore Souldiers.*

III.7. 0 Q1, *Enter* Burbon, Constable, Orleance, Gebon.] F1, *Enter the Constable of France, the Lord Ramburs, Orleance, Dolphin, with others.*

IV.1. 34 Q1, *Enter the King disguised, to him* Pistoll.] F1, *[at line 1] Enter the King, Bedford, and Gloucester. [at line 34] Enter Pistoll.*

       83 Q1, *Enter three Souldiers.*] F1, *Enter three Souldiers, Iohn Bates, Alexander Court, and Michael Williams.*

IV.3. 0 Q1, *Enter* Clarence, Gloster, Exeter, and Salisburie.] F1, *Enter Gloucester, Bedford, Exeter, Erpingham with all his Hoast: Salisbury, and Westmerland.*

       78 Q1, *Enter the Herald from the French.*] F1, *Tucket. Enter Montioy.*

IV.4. 0 Q1, *Enter Pistoll, the French man, and the Boy.*] F1, *Alarum. Excursions. Enter Pistoll, French Souldier, Boy.*

IV.5. 0 Q1, *Enter the foure French Lords.*] F1, *Enter Constable, Orleance, Burbon, Dolphin, and Ramburs.*

IV.6. 0 Q1, *Enter the King and his Nobles,* Pistoll.] F1, *Alarum. Enter the King and his trayne, with Prisoners.*

IV.7. 52 Q1, *Enter King and the Lords.*] F1, *Alarum. Enter King Harry and Burbon with prisoners. Flourish.*

V.2. 0 Q1, *Enter at one doore, the King of* England *and his Lords. And at the other doore, the King of* France, *Queene* Katherine, *the Duke of* Burbon, *and others.*] F1, *Enter at one doore, King Henry, Exeter, Bedford, Warwicke, and other Lords. At another, Queene Isabel, the King, the Duke of Bourgongne, and other French.*

       98 Q1, *Exit King and the Lords. Manet,* Hrry [*sic*], Katherine, *and the Gentlewoman.*] F1, *Exeunt omnes. Manet King and Katherine.*

       276 Q1, *Enter the King of France, and the Lordes.*] F1, *Enter the French Power, and the English Lords.*

GENEALOGICAL TABLES

TABLE I. *Henry V and the Throne of France*

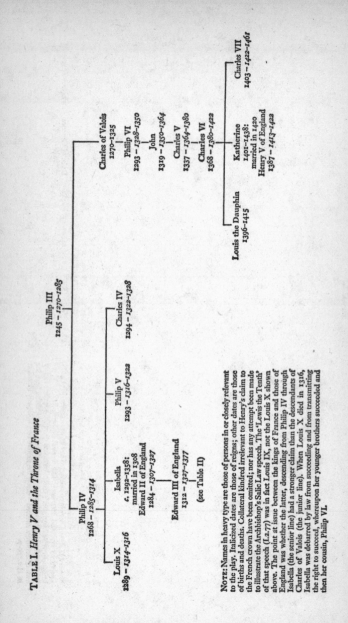

Philip III
1245 – 1270–1285

Philip IV
1268 – 1285–1314

Charles of Valois
1270–1325

Louis X
1289 – 1314–1316

Philip V
1293 – 1316–1322

Charles IV
1294 – 1322–1328

Isabella
c. 1292–1358:
married in 1308
Edward II of England
1284 – 1307–1327

Philip VI
1293 – 1328–1350

John
1319 – 1350–1364

Charles V
1337 – 1364–1380

Edward III of England
1312 – 1327–1377
(see Table II)

Charles VI
1368 – 1380–1422

Charles VII
1403 – 1422–1461

Louis the Dauphin
1396–1415

Katherine
1401–1438:
married in 1420
Henry V of England
1387 – 1413–1422

NOTE: Names in heavy type are those of persons in or closely relevant to the play. Italicized dates are those of reigns; other dates are those of births and deaths. Collateral kindred irrelevant to Henry's claim to the French crown have been omitted; nor has any attempt been made to illustrate the Archbishop's Salic Law speech. The 'Lewis the Tenth' of that speech (I.2.77) was in fact Louis IX, not the Louis X shown above. The point at issue between the kings of France and those of England was whether the latter, descending from Philip IV through Isabella (the senior line) had a stronger claim than the descendants of Charles of Valois (the junior line). When Louis X died in 1316, Isabella was debarred by law from succeeding and from transmitting the right to succeed, whereupon her younger brothers succeeded and then her cousin, Philip VI.

Table II. *Claimants to the Throne of England*

	1	2	3	4	5	6	7
				Edward III *1312 – 1327–1377*			

**Edward,
the Black Prince**
1330–1376 — (1)

**William
of Hatfield:**
died in infancy — (2)

**Lionel,
Duke of Clarence**
1338–1368 — (3)

**John of Gaunt,
Duke of Lancaster**
1340–1399 — (4)

**Edmund Langley,
Duke of York**
1341–1402 — (5)

**Thomas,
Duke of Gloucester**
1355–1397:
murdered, probably
by Richard II's order — (6)

**William
of Windsor:**
died in infancy — (7)

Richard II
1367 – 1377–1399 – 1400

Philippa
1355 – *c.* 1380:
married in 1368
Edmund Mortimer,
Earl of March
1351–1381

**Roger Mortimer,
Earl of March**
1374–1398

Henry IV
1367 – 1399–1413

**Richard,
Earl of Cambridge**
13??–1415:
executed for
conspiracy

**Edmund Mortimer,
Earl of March**
1391–1425:
declared heir pre-
sumptive to Richard II
in 1398

Anne,
1388 – *c.* 1413 ·······

Henry V
1387 – 1413–1422

**Richard,
Duke of York**
1411–1460

Henry VI
1421 – 1422–1461 – 1471:
deposed 1461, restored
1470, again deposed 1471,
and murdered

Edward IV
1442 – 1461–1483

**George,
Duke of Clarence**
1449–1478

Richard III
1452 – 1483–1485

NOTE: Names in heavy type are those of persons in or closely relevant to the play. Italicized dates are those of reigns; other dates are those of births and deaths. Collateral kindred irrelevant to claims under lines 3, 4, and 5 have been omitted. The contest arose from the fact that Richard II should have been succeeded not by the Lancastrian Henry IV but by Edmund Mortimer. The Yorkist Richard, Earl of Cambridge, married Mortimer's sister Anne and conspired against Henry V to seat the childless Mortimer on the throne and thereafter have his own descendants succeed – this is the motive very obliquely hinted at in II.2.155-7.

NEW PENGUIN SHAKESPEARE

General Editor: T. J. B. Spencer